Solstice

Ruth Aylett
Greg Michaelson

Stairwell Books //

Published by Stairwell Books
161 Lowther Street
York, YO31 7LZ

www.stairwellbooks.co.uk
@stairwellbooks

Paperback ISBN: 978-1-917334-12-9
eBook ISBN: 978-1-917334-19-8

Chapter 1 - Helen

Wednesday June 8th – La Trinité sur mer, France

I'm on the Bridge, not the usual spot for a ship's engineer, because I'm trying to run diagnostics on the navigation console. According to the first mate, it put up an error code, though I've already checked its logs without finding any funnies. All electronics, this ship. It has the latest Integrated Bridge System controlling just about everything with touchscreens, and navigation is via something that looks more like a game controller than the usual helm. Private yachts aren't a lot like the cruise ships I've worked and the *Midsummer Queen* drips technology as well as money. At least we're moored, though out in the bay rather than in La Trinité's harbour.

What's mithering me is the sound of loud voices not too far away – well, one loud voice. That'll be Cal. It usually is. I give the first mate a 'not again' look, and he gives me a 'just get on with it' look back.

I say 'first mate' – left to me he'd be 'Boris' since he's as Russian a gowk as they come. But everyone, even the Captain, calls him by his actual name, Yuri Petrovich, as if he was some kind of big wheel, which first mates usually are not. Mebbe he's a relative of the Russian owner, who knows? Another oddity to add to the list for this gig.

Anyway, Boris-the-bloody-misogynist fits him better, since he's made it clear more than once that a woman Electronics Officer – that's me of course – makes as much sense to him as a cat with two heads. Not for the first time, I'm glad of my height, which is a couple of inches more than his. Suck it up, man.

The loud voice stuff has stopped, and then the door to the Bridge opens and it's Captain Tucker, looking as blindingly male-model as always, which must be another private yacht thing. Immaculate white uniform setting off his dark, dark skin; broad shoulders; moves like a dancer; enough charisma to knock you out at fifty paces. I mentally slap my wrist for gushing like that, but I just can't help it.

Must have been him Cal was going on at, and yes, not for the first time. Cal's feet would not touch the ground on any other ship I've sailed in – straight into the brig. But Cal is Mr Ross' man, and Mr Ross has chartered the yacht, so it's a stand-off. Since I am a Mr Ross hire too, if only for this trip, I have more to do with Cal than I want.

'Ah, Helen,' says the Captain.

I try not to wince. First-naming, yet another thing I haven't come across before on my ships. I'd much rather he said 'McIver', like every other Captain I've served under. Or if we must be on familiar terms, my usual work handle is 'Hulkie', on account of my size and height.

I give him a formal 'Yes Sir' and he looks slightly hurt. I can't help feeling bad – somehow you don't like to disappoint him.

'I wonder if you'd do me a favour,' he says next. 'We have to pick up Mr Ross' PA, from La Trinité, and I wondered whether you'd take the tender over to fetch them.'

I know about the pick-up of course, it's why we are off the French coast. Brittany and La Trinité sur Mer is not exactly on our route across the Atlantic from St Vincent, given our destination is the Hebrides. But it's a real gob smack to be asked to go fetch the guy myself. That's not what an Electronics Officer does, it's what a Deckie does. There again, Cal is the acting Deckie on this trip. I bet that's what the loud voices were about. Still, you don't do favours for a Captain, you execute commands, however nicely phrased and however unwelcome.

'Aye aye Sir,' I say, trying not to sound as fashed as I feel.

'Thanks Helen,' he says, giving me his terrific smile. Which is a bit like being caught in headlights. 'You're a star. I won't forget it. Yuri Petrovich will sort out the arrangements. By the way, about your request for shore leave at the weekend for a family event – Mr Ross wants to talk to you about it tomorrow. We'll do a video call at ten.'

Then I'll get to meet Mr Ross at last – this gig was all set up through an agency. And with a bit of luck Mr Ross will tell me I can't go to the christening. Quick work by cousin Malcolm's daughter, she only married just over a year back. Mebbe she's more of a Catholic than I thought. But big family events are not my thing, though I had to ask about going to get Mam off my back about it.

Still, once I'm in the tender and bouncing fast over to the port, I start to feel better. What with Boris and Cal, not to mention the ship

2

being too small for the Captain's charisma, and that list of oddities, the ten days across the Atlantic have been a bit on the stressy side. It's good to have some time to myself, with the June sun glittering on the water, a cloudless blue Breton sky, and just a light westerly to keep the temperature down.

Must be nearly fifteen years since I was in La Trinité. It's not on the usual cruise circuits, it does large sailing yachts. They have these competitions in the spring and lots of big names turn out for them. When I was still prenticing at Nissan and trying out sea-faring stuff, I spent my annual leave one May on a trimaran in the ArMen Race as volunteer crew. Not sure I was really an asset. I'd been out sailing at weekends with one of Dad's Nissan friends on a tiny yacht, which gave me some idea of what to do, but our team was well down the placings in the end.

Or did I? That was Hulkie before the Incident. Did that happen to the me that's here and now? That fog again, that not-knowing. As if I had dementia. I do the mental shrug I've developed and focus on spray and sun. And anyway, as I get close to the port, I can see some of the yachts from this year's race – a few weeks back – are still in town. Lovely vessels.

Once I've tied up, I stroll along the quay looking for the bar where I'm due to meet this guy: Le Tréh. Sounds very Breton, rather than French. I soon see it, only a few tens of metres away, painted a rather sober grey with some umbrellas out the front and people enjoying a glass in the sunshine. I'm in my dress uniform, dazzling whites, with a *Midsummer Queen* logo on my jacket as well as on the band of my cap. This is to make me easy to recognise. For some reason I couldn't get a description of the PA, who's called Ri-al, two syllables, not 'Real' like it sounded at first. 'Just Rial,' Boris told me, rolling his eyes as if I was gaumless when I asked: 'Is that his first or last name?'

I get to the café and a figure stands up, turns to me.

Ouf.

Rial is, well, nothing like anybody I've ever met. I thought he was a bloke, though I suddenly realise nobody has actually said this. Because mebbe he's a she. Tall, very slender, very pale, hair so blond it's almost white, down to the shoulders. Impossibly bright blue eyes, like the icebergs on an Arctic cruise I worked. Smooth, narrow face, with beautiful regular features. Also dressed in white – a loose fitting shirt and white jeans. OK, could be 'they' really is the best label.

You know those illusion diagrams on the Internet, where you can see a candle or two people in profile, depending how you look at it? I

3

can feel my brain painfully trying to make Rial a man or a woman, just like that. And then I'm aware I've been standing gawping much too long.

'Hi, are you Rial? I'm here from the *Midsummer Queen* and Mr Ross to ferry you over.'

'Hello, Helen McIver. Or would you rather I called you Hulkie?'

Such a musical voice, but from the pitch still could be a man or a woman. And wait a minute, they may have been told my name given I'm the meet-and-greet, but how do they know about Hulkie being my handle? Can't see Boris or the Captain passing that on.

'Hulkie will do fine,' I tell them.

Rial only has a holdall, not all that large, nor especially weighty I decide, as they pass it to me before stepping elegantly into the boat. Which hardly seems to dip, as if Rial is a lot less heavy than they look.

Of course I try to pump them as we bounce back to the *Midsummer Queen*.

'Have you been working for Mr Ross long?'

Rial smiles. I think. It's an ambiguous expression.

'Oh yes, many, many years. More than you can count.' Hmm, sounds like Rial must be older than they look.

'Good boss?'

'Mr Ross is a man of unique gifts.' Well, that wasn't what I asked, so I can draw my own conclusions there. Mebbe it's just as well I'm only hired for this gig.

Bit of a pause. Rial is not a chatty person. Let's try again.

'Did you have time to look around outside La Trinité? The Carnac standing stones are amazing.'

I went there myself, doing the tourist bit after that race – or at least the pre-Incident Hulkie did. Move on, move on, brain.

'Yes,' Rial says. 'I have visited them many times.'

And another pause. I'm pushing a rock uphill here. Well, in for a penny, in for a pound.

'I hope this doesn't sound rude, but what pronoun should I use for you?'

I know from social media that's the polite way to pose the question, but I've never had to do this before.

'They and them please,' Rial says quite firmly.

Oh well, this old Wearside dog can manage new tricks, I'm sure. Just stop dithering, brain. What does it matter which gender Rial is?

'And how about you?' Rial asks me.

'Er yes, she and her are good for me.'

4

Bit of a conversation killer though, and we do the rest of the crossing in silence.

Journal June 8

I feel like a gowk every evening when I write this journal up. Hulkie the writer? For goodness sake, man! Though I used to turn out a decent composition at school I suppose, and I've read that many Sword and Sorcery stories I probably could write one if I had the time. But keeping the stress down is what this journal stuff is really about, as I keep telling myself.

Yes, I did use the *Midsummer Queen*'s excellent Internet connection to search for the ArMen Race of fifteen years back. *Google* is your marra. Though not really this time. It's still called the ArMen race but I can't for sure remember the name of the trimaran and of course it doesn't list crews. So there's no proof the Hulkie of here-and-now was in it.

Isn't that what usually happens when I let it get to me and try to check something? Not enough information. I thought my Seafarer's Service Book would be easy, but guess what, with all those gigs over more than ten years I can't be sure whether the entries I think might be different for here-and-now Hulkie are just me not remembering right.

It all makes my brain hurt. Because *before* the Incident, me and the Hulkie who lived in this timeline, another sort of *me*, led separate lives, each in our own timeline. Well, rather similar lives it turns out, with similar parents and a similar Wilf. Then *bang*, three witchy women zap the whole timeline I'm living in, along with all the people living in it (brain hurts some more). Except me and cousin Malcolm, who because we helped them out, got whacked over to *this* timeline. And what happened to the Hulkie who was already here? Is she me? Am I her? Are we a sort of merger? Is me-ness to do with what I remember?

Wilf's cat is still the only thing I am sure about. The Wilf before the Incident certainly did not have a cat. Wilf here-and-now does — and it's a grey tabby, which is even creepier. Still feel the shock of finding out what I thought was a nice grey tabby cat pre-Incident was actually a witchy-woman little helper and not a cat at all! Of course I bit my tongue hard about this Wilf's animal, and didn't comment, but seems like he's had it since it was a kitten.

The green stone sitting on the bedside table is the only other concrete evidence my brain isn't making the whole Incident up. And cousin Malcolm was no help at all when I tried to talk to him a while back, he just shrugged and said 'it is what it is'. But he's such a stick-in-the-mud as a ranger on Rannoch Moor that any number of timeline Malcolms would be just the same.

I shouldn't have let the cat set me off but it did, and now it's like an itch I can't scratch. I keep wondering whether there was anything important here-and-now Wilf told the other Hulkie that I won't know about until I put both feet in it. Though he does seem the same as pre-Incident Wilf, and it was going well until we had the falling out and I buggered off on this gig to let the dust settle.

Let's just do the mental shrug or I'll be worrying all night and not sleeping. Change the subject.

What a piece of work that Rial is. Gan canny with them, Hulkie! The Captain and Boris must have met them before, perhaps when the hire was set up. When we came aboard they both welcomed Rial but there was a tense feel about it, almost as if they were both a little bit scared of them. Great, just what I need, another stressy element.

As for Cal – he positively cowered. I don't know what Rial has on him but his usual bite-you-in-the-ankle aggression was totally gone. Now that could be a positive.

Just hit another weird thing on this ship. I was off earlier checking the engine diagnostics with Velho, our engineer, given we sail tomorrow, and I could hear music coming from somewhere. Not the sort of thing you get off someone's Spotify play-list either. Eerie somehow, and in the air. Velho just shrugged when I asked him about it, but he's that talkative he could join the Trappists. I couldn't work out where it was coming from, though I went up on the main deck and then had a little walkabout. By the time I got back here it seemed to have stopped. Did Rial have a flute in that holdall?

Time to turn in with some ebook Swords and Sorcery. Still can't get used to not taking watches when we are moored, but the all-singing all-dancing electronics are supposed to set off an alarm if anything bad happens. And the permanent crew all seem happy with that too. Private yachts, hmm.

Chapter 2 - Malcolm

Wednesday June 8th – Rannoch Moor

It was a warm, bright day: the sun high over Rannoch Moor. I'd just finished making the soup when the phone rang. I turned down the heat and found the mobile.

'Hi dad!' said Alison. 'Sorry, but we're going to be a bit late.'

'Is everything all right?' I said.

'Och yes,' said Alison. 'Everything's fine. I just picked up a hitchhiker. She was soaking wet.'

'Is it raining?' I said. 'It's lovely here.'

'Same here,' said Alison.

'Where are you?' I said, puzzled.

'Tyndrum,' said Alison. 'Just down the road. Can she come for lunch, please?'

Alison always had a soft spot for strays. Quite unlike her mother. Not that I was a stray.

'Of course!' I said. 'How's the bairn?'

'Gurgling away, bless him,' said Alison. 'He's taken a shine to Miran.'

'Miran?' I said. 'That's unusual. Where's she from? And how did she get so wet?'

'Can't talk now,' said Alison. See you soon!'

And ended the call.

I set the table for three, and got the highchair out of the cupboard. Then I tapped 'Miran' into the app on my mobile. Slavic. Peace. Or world.

I suspect that I look up names more often than most people. We get some strange ones in the visitors' book at work. I'm pretty sure I'd never come across Miran, but my memory's not as good as it was *before*.

There was a frantic noise from my bedroom. The cat had caught a vole, and trapped it in a corner. I took the glass off my bedside cabinet, popped it over the trembling vole, slid a magazine underneath the glass, opened the window, and shook the vole free.

The cat looked at me with marked disdain, and leapt through the window in hot pursuit.

I put the glass back on the bedside cabinet, next to the green stone. Well, the stone is really white marble, suffused with green serpentine. Absently, I picked it up, but it just felt like a stone. *Before*, it had thrummed and glowed in the presence of strangeness.

I heard Alison's car scrunching across the gravel. I put the stone down, and went outside to greet her.

Alison pulled up and got out of the car. Giving me a quick but firm hug, she opened the tailgate, and extracted the buggy from a mound of baby gear.

From the back of the car, a bedraggled young woman slowly emerged, clutching my grandson. She seemed about the same age as Alison, though much slighter. Not that Alison's big. Well, not compared to my cousin Helen. The young woman looked like she'd stepped out of a theatrical costumier. She was wearing a plain grey dress with a waistcoat over a loose white shirt. The waistcoat was finely embroidered.

'This is Miran,' said Alison, taking the baby from her. 'And this is my dad, Malcolm.'

'Nice to meet you!' I said, extending my right hand, in approved visitor greeting mode.

'Don't be so British, dad!' said Alison, strapping the bairn into the buggy.

Miran smiled, but said nothing.

'You really are wet!' I said. 'Come on in, and we'll find you a towel.'

'I left some clothes, didn't I,' said Alison, grabbing a bulging cool bag. 'Climbing clobber. It should fit.'

'Still in the spare room,' I said. 'Clean and folded. And towels are in the linen cupboard.'

'Thanks, dad!' said Alison. 'Come on.'

And she pushed the buggy into the house.

While Alison took Miran through to the spare room, I lifted the bairn into the highchair.

The bairn. He's really called Christopher. Or Chris. Or Topher. But mostly the bairn, until they settle on something.

I do so like the bairn. Well, of course! But he's not one of those whingy babies that get agitated if they're more than a foot away from a parent. The bairn really seems to know me. He likes sitting on my lap while I tell him profundities about geology. He's very fond of round stones. Picking them up and holding them up to his face. Though no longer trying to get them into his mouth.

The bairn particularly likes the Neolithic arrowhead that hangs from a thong round my neck. I never take it off. It's not so much for good luck as protection. I'm certainly not superstitious. But what happened *before* might happen again.

I'd found the arrowhead in the quarry in Creag na Cailleach, where the Wiccans celebrated the equinox. I'd given one to Helen and one to Polly. I'd also given one to Alison, or I thought I had. The arrowhead seemed to ward off forgetting, when things changed.

Alison came back into the kitchen, and sat down next to the bairn.

'I thought I'd leave her to it,' said Alison, waggling her fingers at her delighted son. 'I hope he's behaving himself.'

'Of course!' I said. 'So, what's her story?'

'I can't make sense of it,' said Alison. 'She speaks perfectly good English. In some ways it's too good. But it's as if she doesn't quite have the words to explain what's happened to her.'

'Where did you find her?' I asked.

'I'd pulled off the road at the *Tartan Trading Post*,' said Alison, 'to give the bairn a top up, when I saw her in the bus shelter. She looked lost. I asked if I could help. She was very vague. She said she was trying to get to some island, to find her boyfriend, but she isn't at all clear about where. I couldn't just leave her there. And I thought you'd be able to help. You know the area backwards, and you've got loads of maps.'

'I'll see what I can do,' I said. 'But why was she soaking wet?'

'I did try to her ask her,' said Alison, 'but she pointed back west along the A85, and I think she said she'd come out of the mountain, which sounds a bit bonkers.'

Out of the mountain? *Before*, I'd have dismissed this out of hand.

'I know,' I said. 'Cruachan. The hydro scheme. They're extending it.'

'Surely there's really tight security,' said Alison. 'She must be confused.'

'Who knows,' I said. 'Anyway, we should eat. Does the bairn need anything?'

'We could try him on some baby food,' said Alison. 'I'll give him another feed, just before we go.'

As Alison fossicked in the bag, Miran appeared from the spare room. She looked like the waif from a Charlie Chaplin film, in a jersey and jeans that were a couple of sizes too big.

'Have a seat,' I said. 'You must be famished.'

The smiling bairn leant over towards Miran as she approached the table. Miran glanced questioningly at Alison, who nodded approvingly. I felt a brief pang of jealousy as Miran picked up the bairn and sat him on her lap. The bairn crooned and grasped at her neck. To my amazement, Miran reached under her shirt's high collar, and drew out a Neolithic arrowhead on a leather thong.

'Here,' she said softly, drawing the thong over her head. 'Is this what you want?'

'Gosh!' said Alison, unscrewing a jar of grey gloop. 'That's just like yours, dad. He does seem to like them.'

'He does, doesn't he,' I said. 'Do you still have one?'

'I don't think I've ever had one,' said Alison, spooning gloop into the fledgling's mouth.

'But I gave you one,' I said, 'at the wedding. I certainly meant to give you one.'

'Are you sure?' said Alison. 'Maybe it got lost amongst all the other presents. I do hope not. I'll have a look when I'm home. That was a pretty crazy day, you know.'

'That was a pretty crazy week,' I said. 'Come on, let's eat.'

Over lunch, Alison and I bantered away. Miran sat quietly, focused on the baby. I made a couple of attempts to ask her about herself, but I gave up when Alison gently shook her head at me.

I do so like Alison. Well of course! So quick to pick up on other people. So good at putting them at their ease. Quite unlike her mother. Not that I was ever uneasy.

'That was grand!' said Alison, pushing back her chair. 'I'd better give his lordship a quick feed. Come on, pass him over.'

'Do use the sitting room, if you'd like some privacy,' I said.

'Don't be silly!' said Alison. 'But the sofa would be nice.'

'I'll tidy up first,' I said.

'I can do that,' said Miran, handing the bairn to his mother.

'Come on,' said Alison. 'We need to talk about the christening.'

The christening. As if the wedding hadn't been bad enough. But that was *before*.

'I hope I don't have a starring role this time,' I said, as Alison and the bairn settled down on the sofa.

'Och no,' said Alison. 'Just moral support. You know I can't much be bothered with all this churchy stuff, but Grant's family's keen. So's mum.'

'Is she definitely coming?' I said.

'I think so,' said Alison. 'She's had the flights booked for ages.'

'Is she bringing anyone?' I said.

'That I don't know,' said Alison. 'How about you? Is Polly coming?'

'I'd like her to,' I said. 'But things have been a bit lumpy.'

'That's a shame,' said Alison, swapping the bairn from one side to the other. 'She's very welcome, of course. I hope you can both work things through.'

'So do I,' I said. 'I think we're serious about each other. But maybe it's all a bit soon.'

'Too soon for what?' said Alison. 'You and mum have been separated for years.'

'We've been apart for years,' I said.

'Same difference,' said Alison.

'Bringing Polly to the christening feels like a statement,' I said. 'Besides, I've no idea how your mum would react.'

'Everyone was well behaved at the wedding,' said Alison. 'And I'm sure this'll be less stressful.'

'Is Helen coming?' I said.

I wasn't sure I was ready for Helen. We'd parted in strained circumstances, and I'd barely heard from her since. Not that either of us had made the effort.

Still, Helen would likely be one of the few from my side of the family, even though they hailed from Lewis, which was little more than a ferry away to the north of the Uists.

'We hope so,' said Alison. 'We've invited her, and Wilf. But she said she'll be working, and she's not sure if she'll be able to make it. Here, you take him.'

Alison passed me the bairn, and buttoned up her shirt.

'We best get going,' said Alison, standing up, 'if we're going to miss the traffic. I'll take Miran back to Glasgow with me. She can stay with us until she gets herself sorted out.'

'Are you quite sure?' I said. 'You barely know her.'

'Och yes,' said Alison. 'She gets on really well with Chris.'

'Won't Grant mind?' I said.

'Och no,' said Alison. 'He's a real softy.'

11

But there was no sign of Miran in the kitchen.

'I wonder where's she's got to,' said Alison, as I strapped the drowsy bairn into the buggy. 'Maybe she's outside. I'll take a look.'

Alison picked up her bag, and pushed the buggy back to the car.

There was a sudden scream from the rear of the house. Anxiously, I hurried through to the bedroom. Miran was standing stock still beside the bedside cabinet.

'It called to me!' cried Miran. 'It called to me!'

On the bedside cabinet, the stone pulsed green. I hurriedly picked it up and put it in my pocket.

'How can they already know I'm here?' said Miran, as I ushered her outside. 'If they come looking, please don't tell them. Please don't tell.'

'It's all right,' I said. 'It's all right. You're safe with us.'

'Come on!' called Alison through the open driver's window. 'Let's get going.'

Miran got into the back of the car, next to the baby seat.

'Cheers dad!' called Alison, driving off. 'I've put her clothes in the washing machine. We'll sort something out. Thanks for lunch! See you on Friday!'

'What about the maps?' I called back.

But I was too late.

I was drying up the crockery when Glynis let herself in. Glynis is my neighbour. I think she's one of the few people who know what happened *before*, like Helen.

'How's your daughter?' said Glynis. 'And your grandson?'

'Both doing away, thanks,' I said.

'Her companion's troubled, isn't she,' said Glynis. 'I think someone's after her.'

I've almost given up asking Glynis how she knows things she can't. Almost.

'How can you possibly know that?' I asked. 'I don't suppose the polis are after her.'

Glynis's husband Dougie is the local policeman. Some people think that's how Glynis always knows what's going on. But I know better.

'I saw them,' said Glynis. 'This morning,'

'Who did you see?' I said.

'They were on the embankment,' said Glynis. 'Shimmering. They turned to face me and smiled. As I went towards them, they melted away.'

Before, I'd have thought Glynis entirely fanciful.

12

'What did they look like?' I said.

'They were tall and thin and pale,' said Glynis. 'They had long white hair, and were dressed in white. Like a wraith. Except their eyes were a piercing blue.'

'Sounds more like a hippy,' I said. 'Have you seen them before?'

'No,' said Glynis. 'But spectral beings are almost invariably bad news. You should tell your daughter's companion to take care. Anyway, do you fancy a cuppa?'

I rolled the green stone round my fingers.

'Yes please,' I said. 'That'd be nice.'

Chapter 3 - Helen

Thursday June 9th - La Trinité sur mer, France

8am on the dot, and Velho and I are starting up the gas turbines. Gas turbines! The first time I've been on a ship with water-jet engines. They make us astonishingly fast. More than 50 knots if we want! Though the downside is they slurp up the fuel. We refuelled back in the Azores, but we'll be nearly empty by the time we get to Stornoway.

With that speed, we'll be past Finisterre in an hour or so, and we should hit our next stop by evening. Castletownbere, over on Ireland's west coast. A new port for me.

At least I think so.

'Any idea why we're not going up the Irish Sea, man?' I ask Velho once we're done. 'Must be quicker, surely?' Also with less swell, and lower fuel budget. We could have stopped at Waterford, which I have been to and liked. That trip is on my current Seafarer's Book, which means here-and-now Hulkie also did.

Velho gives me a long look, the way he does when he is deciding whether to say something. There's a reason why Finns have that rep for not being chatty people.

'I think you'd have to ask Yuri Petrovich,' he says finally. 'I just make sure we get wherever we're going.'

He could have said 'because it's more complicated' – more traffic, and the waters belong to England, Ireland, Wales, Scotland and the Isle of Man, as I well know. But this just reinforces my feeling that the permanent crew have been told not to answer any questions from me about this trip. Of course we won't get local customs inspection while we stay in international waters the other side of Ireland, and Castletownbere isn't a big league Irish port. Hmm.

Well, now we're underway, I can leave Velho to keep an eye on the turbines while I take myself up to the Bridge. If Boris has any more error-codes I want to see them as they happen.

I'm hardly out of the engine room on my way up there, when I'm ambushed by Cal. Looks like he's been waiting for me. Uh-oh.

'Hulkie. Can I have a word?'

Well, that's unusual, you don't usually get a choice. What's he after?

'Sure, man. How can I help?' Best customer service manner.

'You meet with Mr Ross this morning?'

'That's right. I put in for shore-leave. There's a family event at the weekend I've been asked to attend.'

'So not to check up on me?'

'Cal, it's not always about you.' Oops, that wasn't customer service voice speaking. Deep breath. 'And anyway, I don't go on about fellow crew members to off-ship people. To be blunt, in your shoes I'd worry a good deal more about the Captain's opinion.'

'Oh, Captain Coconut, brown outside, white inside. Que cabrón. Black Bermudans need someone to look down on and Caribs are it.'

Didn't know Cal was a Carib, though come to think about it, I have heard him muttering about 'my island' when he's been off on one. Still, his family name is Bane as far as I know, which suits him, but isn't very Caribbean sounding.

'Look Cal, I'm sorry you and the Captain don't get on, but be realistic man, he is the guy in charge. What's the point in rubbing him up the wrong way all the time? Anyway, I'm off to the Bridge to check the navigation console for Yuri Petrovich again, and take my word for it, I won't be talking about you to Mr Ross.'

Cal grimaces as I mention Boris and looks as if he is about to say something, but I'm off before he gets it out. Walking away is how most of my dealings with Cal finish.

As I get to the Bridge the Captain comes out.

'Helen, ten sharp in my cabin for the call with Mr Ross please.' But his dazzling smile makes it seem like a request. 'Oh, and Rial will be joining us for the meeting.'

Just what I need. Rial wasn't at breakfast, which suited me fine. My brain is still doing the man/woman switching, and it's tiring. But there's Rial now, out on the main deck, watching the ocean. Looking that pale you'd almost think the sun was shining through them. No, not really, that's just sun in my eyes.

On the bridge Boris is fiddling with the autopilot. Once we get out of coastal waters the *Midsummer Queen* largely sails herself.

'Hi, Yuri Petrovich. Just following up on yesterday's nav system error. How's it looking?' Up to now I've done well at using his full name the way I'm supposed to. Let's hope I don't slip-up at some point and call him Boris to his face. He'd love me even more then.

'Well, you think you solve something yesterday, McIver, then you think again. You change something without checking? Because lots more errors today.'

Boris points at the screen for the autopilot course visualisation and I blink. There should be a nice neat white line mapping out our course all the way to Castletownbere. Instead of which there is a growing fan that fades into nothing after about 100km, according to the scale along the bottom. As if the autopilot is just not sure.

'I changed nothing, Yuri Petrovich. I'll check the logs again, man, but unless they have more information than yesterday, we're looking at a hardware problem and component by component fault analysis. We need to be in port for that.'

That isn't of course what Boris wants to hear. He says something in Russian which from his face is probably quite rude, but there's no percentage in rising to it. Then:

'Helpful like usual, McIver. Lucky I am well-qualified navigator.'

'We all have full confidence in you, Yuri Petrovich.' I can play this game too.

Well, I start fault-tracing as far as you can while underway, and I am still at it when we get to 9.55 and I need to go present myself at the captain's cabin. And all the while I am doing this, I am aware not only of Boris and his contempt, but also that Rial, out on the main deck, is now staring into the Bridge with those iceberg eyes.

The Captain's cabin is not the flashiest on-board – that would be one of the passenger suites. But it is larger than mine. And if we weren't on a skeleton crew, I'd be sharing. The Captain's is big enough to house a shiny desk with several family photos on it – a wife and two small children by the look of it. Also a large wall monitor facing three chairs. The *Midsummer Queen*'s comms are as state-of-the-art as everything else — the satellite link means passengers can stream video even out in mid-ocean. I've watched a few films on my laptop in the evenings.

'Do sit here, Helen,' the captain says, with one of those glorious smiles, indicating the chair at one end. 'And Rial, here please,' he says, pointing at the other end, politely, but without a smile. He sits down between us. I'd have liked to sit next to Rial just to see their reactions, but so it goes.

P ROSS PEYROUX CONNECTING TO AUDIO - appears on the screen with a blank box. Then it clears and Mr Ross appears. My first sight of my current employer.

Brown face, lots of white hair: he has a full head of it and an impressive beard. Both neatly trimmed and groomed. Though he's not as elderly as all that, his face is hardly lined. Looks Italian rather than French, in spite of his name. That tailored jacket in a fashionable shade of mint green is very Italian. Beaky Roman nose, olive skin, dark eyes. Very sharp and on-the-ball you'd say. Gan canny, Hulkie! He's no gowk.

'Hello, Captain Tucker, good to see you again. And my Rial.' A slight accent in that confident voice, though not an obviously Italian one. 'You must be Helen McIver – good to meet you too.'

'Thank you for giving us some of your valuable time Mr Ross,' the Captain says, very deferentially. 'Before we chat about the sailing plan for the next week, Helen here wanted to ask a favour.'

'Ask away, Helen,' Ross says, turning those dark eyes on me. Even over the Internet there's a feeling of force that makes me nervous. And I'm not a nervous person.

'Thank you, Mr Ross. My parents have asked me if I can attend a family christening this weekend in the Hebrides, on South Uist, since we'll be in the area. It's my cousin's grandchild, and they wanted me to see if I could take a couple of days of shore leave. But it's alright if that's not terribly convenient, I know it's short notice.'

'A fortuitous request. As it happens, I was about to discuss with your Captain delaying your arrival at Stornoway – the refuelling facility is booked out until next week it seems. Captain, how do you feel about a stop-over at South Uist?'

Well, that didn't actually sound like a real question.

'I can certainly look into it, Mr Ross, though it is short notice to book a mooring and I'll have to see what is available at that end of the islands. But Helen has become a valued crew member, so if it can be done, I've no objection. And there's no fuel penalty, it is on our route.' Oh dear, he's a bit too nice under the circs, looks like I really might have to go.

'There is a mooring at Lochmaddy, North Uist, Captain. I think you will find it has space and Hulkie can use one of the leisure bikes on board to travel down to South Uist, it's no distance.'

17

Wow – that is Rial speaking! How did they suddenly become an expert on travel in the Hebrides? Plus what are they doing using my informal handle in a formal meeting? How embarrassing. Do I dare take that up with them later?

'Thank you, my Rial,' says Mr Ross in a warm tone, with no hint of know-your-place or sarcasm. 'I can take it then you think this will have no negative impact on our plans?'

'On the contrary, I think it may even advantage them, Sir,' says Rial.

Now what does that mean? Cheaper mooring than hanging around at Stornoway, or what?

'Useful information, thank you Rial,' says the Captain, very politely. 'Then I agree Helen can go to the event.'

Oh joy.

Me Mam is a telephone person and there's not going to be a signal until we're very close to Ireland. And to be honest, phone calls with Mam can be a bit of a trial, hard to get a word in edgeways sometimes. Luckily Dad does the Internet – he is in some network of guys rebuilding old sports cars. He has an MG in pieces in his garage. So, in the afternoon, after more futile tinkering with the autopilot systems, I get started on an email to tell him the news about the christening, and ask when they will arrive.

But before I can send it, there's a 'ping' for an incoming, and it's from Dad, headed *Christening!* When I open it, it isn't a relay of Mam putting on a bit of extra pressure like I expected. It's about my brother Donnie, down in London, and his wife Louise. They are expecting their second – which had been good news, since it takes the pressure off me on the grandchildren front. But this isn't good news.

Louise has gone into labour at 32 weeks, Dad says, and they are dashing down to London to support Donnie and help with young Lily, who's not quite three herself. That means no christening for them. I'm really sorry for Donnie and Louise, but it all feels a bit fishy somehow. That's because they missed the wedding of Malcolm's daughter as well – both versions, before and after the Incident. That was down to Dad's hernia op. But, hey, that's a rabbit hole and I tell myself not to be paranoid. Anyway, I send my message, adding in all best wishes for Donnie, Louise and the bairn, and almost at once there is a relieved reply saying how it's a weight off their mind and of course they will keep me posted.

To be honest it's a weight off my mind as well. One reason I didn't want to go was because I knew Mam would go on about Wilf, and how nice he is, and how I should settle down, and how it's a shame and so on and so on. Hey, come to think about it, I'll get a chance to collar cousin Malcolm, who's the only person I can talk to about the Incident.

I keep my eyes peeled for Rial but there's no sign of them all afternoon: must be holed up in their cabin, or mebbe with the Captain. They seem to have a lot more authority than I thought on this trip. Perhaps I should let the meeting etiquette thing go.

We arrive at Castletownbere after six, and I help Vehlo power down the turbines and run the final diagnostics. We get moored, though again well out in the harbour, not up at a quay. Then we all go to eat.

Of course, being a private yacht, we have a fancy chef, not just a ship's cook. And of course he's French. As up his own arse as every other French colleague I have worked with but knows his stuff – I'll have to watch my weight on this trip.

He's far too grand to actually dish out the scran, and as we're on a skeleton crew, our Steward Elena has to do it – usually she'd have a couple of assistants I'm sure. She's actually Eirini, and that's what the Captain calls her, but like me she prefers her handle on board and uses the one Greek women's name most people can get right. It's a bit close to 'Helen' of course. The Captain's first-naming thing is a pain.

As the two women on board we chat quite a bit and when she has distributed the *saumon en papillote* she plumps down next to me.

'You doing shore leave tonight, Hulkie?'

I haven't actually been ashore in the evening since the Azores, but I'm inclined to give this one a miss even if the Captain allows it. After all, I have two whole days of shore leave coming up. Plus Castetownbere doesn't look like a must-see. Vehlo rarely goes ashore and he's been teaching me backgammon. I tell her I'll stay put.

'But you come, Eirini,' says Boris, who is opposite us. That wasn't a question.

'Of course, Yuri Petrovitch,' Elena replies. Hmm, she doesn't sound happy

Journal June 9

Speechless. No words. Can't write. Can't breathe.

OK, some time just passed then. I've heard of panic attacks but never had one. Until now anyway. Starting to come to. Breathe Hulkie, breathe.

I have to write it up, it's evidence.

OK, here goes.

Maybe an hour ago I was reading my Sword and Sorcery, already in bed. I heard that music again. Not from any particular direction, just somehow in the air.

And this is the point. My green stone started to glow! It came alive again! Like before the Incident. I had to pick it up.

And the music stopped after a while, I don't know, ten minutes? But the stone is still glowing! I can feel it has done that binding thing again. Like before the Incident. I have to be close to it or I feel terrible.

Why didn't I drop it over the side when I still could?

I thought I'd hung onto it because that and Wilf's cat were the only concrete evidence the Incident ever happened. Well, also the little arrowhead pendant Malcolm gave me, that I wear round my neck. But what if that wasn't why? What if it still had some hold over me, even though I thought it was dead?

It looks like it's only a green stone, but I know it's either magic or high-tech, or even sort-of alive, like a parasite in my mind. Anyway, a witchy woman thing. I curse the day I picked it up from the body of their little helper. And cousin Malcolm has one too, though in his dense way, he just never understood how mine made me like a druggie, addicted to it, couldn't be parted from it.

What do I do now?

Did someone out there know my plan, the one I have never talked about? To go back to the Calanais stones on Lewis and look for the old woman I met there before the Incident. The one who seemed to know what was going to happen. To ask her how to stop having two pasts, the one from before the Incident and the one belonging to here-and-now Hulkie.

I'm sure the music comes from Rial. They know more than they should. I'm going to have to tackle them, this is about a bit more than meeting etiquette. Come on Hulkie, you can do it. Somehow.

All this, and I have to go to the bloody christening. Well, I'm defo going to have some words with Malcolm. Mebbe this time he'll be more helpful. I wonder if his stone has come alive too?

Chapter 4 - Malcolm

Thursday June 9th – Rannoch Moor

I was awakened by a persistent beeping from the bathroom. The washing machine. Miran's clothes.

I got up and emptied the washing machine. The waistcoat had all but disintegrated. I laid it out on the towel Miran had used. Maybe the seamstress in Fort William could rescue it. In the bottom of the drum was a scattering of tiny pearls. I scooped them up and put them in the soap dish.

After breakfast, I pocketed the green stone, just in case. I was perplexed by why it had reacted to Miran. I'd checked it before I went to bed, but there was no response. And it was still dormant now.

Then, just as I did each workday, I drove along the track out of Achallader, turned right onto the A82, and followed the road north over the moor.

When I arrived at the Visitor Centre, by the side of Loch Ba, there was a brand-new Humvee parked outside. I knew it was brand-new. I'd seen it in the 4x4 dealership in Fort William, just last weekend, when I went for spares for my Land Rover. Someone's got lots of dosh.

The Humvee driver's window rolled down, and a mid-Atlantic accent called:

'Are you Malcolm Nicholson, the Ranger?'

'That'll be me,' I said. 'How can I help you?'

The driver's door opened, and a petite woman, dressed in a charcoal grey suit and too much makeup, clambered out.

To be frank, I think that almost any makeup is too much. Bernie, Alison's mother, always had to 'put on her face' before she left the house. I'd tell her that her real face was entirely fine with me. And she'd tell me that I'd no clue what it was like being a corporate woman. Fair enough, I suppose. But too much makeup's like a mask. And that makes me wary.

Not wary enough.

'I'm Lucinda Lopez,' said the woman, offering me a business card.

I took the card and quickly scanned it. *Quantum Solutions*. I'd heard they were going to take over the abandoned *Fundamental Forces* plant, up on the moor beyond the Menzies Stone. What on earth did they want with me?

'Welcome to Rannoch Moor, Dr Lopez,' I said, putting the card in my breast pocket. 'How can I help you?'

'You Brits are all so formal,' said my visitor. 'Call me Lucy. May I call you Malcolm?'

'Of course,' I said. 'How can I help you, Lucy?'

Lucy looked the Visitor Centre up and down.

'It's seen better days,' said Lucy.

'That it has,' I said.

Two spartan stories of breeze block, the Visitor Centre was once a Second World War early warning post. It must have been harrowing, standing on the roof with binoculars, counting the bombers heading for the Clyde, knowing all you could do was phone ahead. Still, it's less draughty than the old Nissen hut of *before*.

'Maybe we can help,' said Lucy. 'Might we go inside, please, Malcolm?'

Why would an American high-tech company want to help *Rural Resources*?

'Do come in,' I said. 'Would you like some tea?'

'Coffee please, Malcolm,' said Lucy. 'Decaffeinated if you've got it. Black, no sugar.'

I unlocked the front door and turned on the lights. While Lucy browsed the posters, I filled the kettle in the scullery and plugged it in. Then I found two clean mugs, a tea bag and a sachet of decaff.

'Fascinating place!' said Lucy, scrutinising a wall chart. 'So much geology!'

'You're interested in geology?' I said. 'So am I.'

What a fool I am.

'That's such a coincidence, Malcolm,' said Lucy. 'I used to be a materials scientist, specialising in silicates. My doctorate is on novel semiconductors.'

'You've come to the right place,' I said. 'We're surrounded by fifty-seven varieties of silicate.'

Lucy double-took. Then she laughed.

'Heinz!' she said. 'You are funny, Malcolm. That was before my present role. Now, where's that coffee?'

We sat opposite each other at the specimen table. It's a good thing I always clear it away after each coach load. Visitors really like handling bones and stones and feathers. And that gives me something to talk about.

'Why is *Quantum Solutions* interested in us?' I said, cupping the mug in my hands.

'Didn't your head office tell you I was coming?' said Lucy, gingerly sniffing her coffee.

'Glasgow?' I said. 'But *Rural Resource* is decentralised. We're Central Highland region, based in Fort William. We really don't have much to do with head office.'

'That's a shame, Malcolm,' said Lucy. 'Let me bring you up to speed. You must know that we're here to invest in a really exciting project. We think quantum computing is the future.'

'I heard something about a breakthrough on the news,' I said.

'That's right, Malcolm,' said Lucy. 'It's all hush hush right now, but I can tell you that we think we can push up accuracy from 75% to over 95%. That's got huge implications for QC deployment.'

'Sounds very promising,' I said. 'But why come here?'

'That's a good question, Malcolm,' said Lucy. 'There are two reasons. One is that the granite bedrock gives superb shielding. And the other is that the old *Fundamental Forces* plant already has solid foundations and three-phase power provision. That really reduces our costs.'

'What's this got to do with me?' I said.

'Well, Malcolm,' said Lucy. 'We're worried that the initial stages might be disruptive. We want to give something back.'

'Why would it be disruptive?' I said. 'Surely you'll get access out of Rannoch Station. That's far further east.'

'That's true, Malcolm,' said Lucy. 'But it's much easier for us to run power from here.'

'But there are already power lines,' I said.

'Those pylons are truly unsightly,' said Lucy. 'And they lose a lot of power in transmission. We think we can do better.'

'You want to replace the power lines?' I said. 'That sounds great!'

'It's not that simple, Malcolm,' said Lucy. 'We've an option on the output from the Cruachan development. We want to bring power across the moor, along room temperature superconductor cables. They're almost 100% efficient.'

'What's not to like?' I said.

'I'm pleased you're so positive, Malcolm,' said Lucy. 'In return we'd like to look at futures for your Visitor Centre. We could start with a makeover. Perhaps refurnish the museum upstairs. Longer term, we could help replace the whole building with something more sustainable and ecologically friendly.'

Really? And how does she know about the museum?

'What do you want from me?' I said.

'We were hoping for your endorsement, Malcom,' said Lucy. 'That would help a lot with the planning process.'

'But I can't speak for *Rural Resource*,' I said hastily.

'I'm sure they'd take your opinion seriously,' said Lucy.

'What exactly would we be endorsing?' I said.

'We'd need to run the cables through the moor,' said Lucy.

'Cut and cover?' I said. 'As long as disturbance is minimised, that shouldn't be a problem.'

'We'd need to put in a sealed road,' said Lucy.

Bloody hell!

'A sealed road?' I said, incredulous. 'What's wrong with the track? Your Humvee wouldn't notice the difference.'

'As I said, Malcolm,' said Lucy, 'it's not that simple. The cables are experimental. We're going to need maintenance access to them day and night. The best way is to run them in a culvert alongside a sealed road.'

'There's no way you'll get permission!' I said.

'You'd be surprised,' said Lucy. 'A road would open up access to the moor. Not just for wealthy tourists ticking off their bucket lists. There's a lot of interest in high places.'

Enough already.

'I'll pass on your message to my manager,' I said, standing up. 'I'm sure you'll hear from them.'

'Thank you, Malcolm,' said Lucy, putting down her untouched mug. 'I'll need to get going. I've a busy day. My next stop is our *Quantum*

Solutions facility. I've enjoyed our little chat. As a gesture of good will, we'll send you a proper coffee maker. Have a nice day.'

Feeling shaken, I phoned Fort William. The call went straight to voicemail. I left a brief message asking them to get back to me. Then I phoned Henry Craig.

Henry is our local rabble rouser. But that's unfair. Henry's heart is always in the right place. If there's a good cause, he's on it. But if there's a bad cause, Henry probably started it.

My relationship with Henry is complicated. After we first met, at a Glencoe conservation round-table, he kept trying to rope me into his schemes. Opposing cruise ships. Yes! Reintroducing bears. Hmmm... But as a *Rural Resource* employee, I'm not supposed to be publicly involved in anything even vaguely to do with the Central Highlands. Of course, what I do privately is my own business, and I'm not above the occasional leak. Megan, Henry's long-suffering wife, might say 'the occasional gossip' would be more accurate.

Thinking about it, though, Henry hasn't been visible for quite a while. He's not even involved with the opposition to the Cruachan expansion. Before, he'd have been lying down in front of the bulldozers.

Megan picked up the phone.

'Malcolm!' she said. 'How nice!'

'Hello Megan,' I said. 'How's the brood?'

Megan and Henry have five children. Three was more than enough for me, even if only one wants anything to do with me.

'Bouncing off the walls,' said Megan. 'Are you looking for Henry?'

'I am,' I said. 'Is he around?'

'For sure,' said Megan, 'but before I hand you over, how are you?'

'Mostly well,' I said.

'How mostly is mostly?' said Megan.

'You know how it is,' I said. 'Things aren't the same.'

'Indeed,' said Megan. 'But you'll get used to it. I always do.'

Always?

'And Henry?' I said.

'Oblivious,' said Megan. 'He always is.'

Always?

'Does he not remember anything?' I said.

'No,' said Megan. 'He never does. Anyway, you can ask him yourself. Hang on...'

Buzzing noises.

'Malcolm!' said Henry. 'What a surprise! You've caught me at a bad time. The studio are breathing down my neck.'

Henry's best seller *Preacher Man* was being made into a film. Set in the Hebrides after Bonnie Prince Charlie was exiled, it involves an itinerant preacher, who travels the islands, salving souls and breaking hearts. And solving the odd crime or two along the way. Polly was involved with the publicity, which was one reason we didn't see as much of each other. One reason.

'I thought you'd finished the script ages ago,' I said.

'I did too,' said Henry. 'But they keep wanting changes. Anyway, what can I do you for.'

'Do you know anything about *Quantum Solutions*?' I said. 'It seems they want to put a road across the moor.'

The line went quiet.

'Henry?' I said. 'Are you still there?'

'Sorry,' said Henry. 'I was just thinking.'

'Sounds right up your street,' I said, 'if you'll pardon the pun.'

'It's an appalling idea,' said Henry. 'In other circumstances, I'd be right on it. But I really am tied up right now.'

'Isn't there someone you could drop a word to?' I said. 'You know I can't do anything myself.'

'I'm totally out of touch with all that,' said Henry.

'That doesn't sound like you,' I said. 'Has something happened?'

'Nothing cosmic,' said Henry. 'After *Fundamental Forces* went bust, I realised I was spending too much time on campaigns that never came to anything. So I decided to focus a bit more on writing. And my family.'

'Aye well,' I said. 'Maybe I could send an anonymous letter to the press.'

But I knew I'd never write it.

'Look,' said Henry. 'I'd better crack on. Good luck with the letter. I'll hand you back to Megan.'

'Thanks anyway,' I said. 'Catch you soon.'

Buzzing noises.

'Well?' said Megan. 'Did you ask him?'

'Not in so many words,' I said. 'But he really has changed.'

Megan laughed.

'He's still the same old Henry,' she said. 'On the inside, at any rate.'

'I do hope so,' I said. 'I suppose you'd know. But I'd best give you some peace.'

'It's always nice to hear from you,' said Megan. 'I was saying that to Polly, just the other day.'

Oh!

'You're in touch with Polly?' I said. 'I hadn't realised that you knew each other.'

'Maybe not *before*,' said Megan. 'But we do now. Anyway, don't be a stranger!'

And put the phone down.

As I hadn't made myself any sandwiches, I went up the road to the *Altnafeadh Hotel* for lunch. Dougie ate there, day in, day out. Maybe he'd know more about *Quantum Solution*'s plans.

But there was no sign of Dougie's Battenburg in the car park. Jeannie the waitress thought he was off to Tulliallan for a briefing. That didn't bode well. Dougie's beat was usually quiet. There must be something brewing.

The rest of the day went slowly, apart from a brief pit stop by around twenty ageing German motorcyclists, who wouldn't sign the visitor book and used up almost all the toilet paper. I could just imagine them powering their BMWs down *Quantum Solution*'s new road.

That evening, back at my cottage, I fed the ravenous beast, and made myself an omelette. As I settled down on the sofa to watch the evening news, Lucy Lopez's card rose up out of my shirt pocket. I had another look at the card:

Quantum Solutions, a subsidiary of Peyroux Holdings

Peyroux Holdings. That was a familiar name. Of course. Polly. I rescued my tablet from under the cat, and moused up *Preacher Man* on *IMDB*. Sure enough, my memory was right:

Preacher Man ... produced by Great Alien Plum, a subsidiary of Peyroux Holdings.

Peyroux Holdings. Was Henry really a reformed character? Or had he been nobbled?

Maybe I should phone Polly? I needed to ask her about the christening. And I could mention *Peyroux Holdings* in passing.

In passing. No. Not right now. There was too much to say, and I feared the likely outcome. Cursing my cowardice, I lay down on the sofa and turned up the sound.

Chapter 5 - Helen

Fri June 10th - Castletownbere, Ireland

My day starts much too early with a crash against my cabin door. It jolts me out of some nightmare: at least my heart is racing and for a moment I think I'm going into a panic attack like last night. But I am not a panicking person. I'm NOT a panicking person. Whatever the bad news of the stone coming to life, there *has* to be a way of dealing with it. Though the stone is in the pocket of my nightwear, the only way I could relax enough to get to sleep at all.

I take two slow, deep breaths and then leap out of bed. Now I can hear a voice outside my door. And I think I know whose that is. I open the door. Yes, it's Cal of course. But at 4.30am? At least, being June, it's already light, though a bit chilly for night gear.

'Cal, what are you doing, man?' I begin, keeping my voice down. No point in waking the whole ship up.

'Walking the spirit paths,' he slurs, and rocks unsteadily on his feet. I grab him before he can crash into me.

'Steady now, steady. What's up man?'

Is he blootered? He doesn't smell of alcohol. But his eyes. Hmm, pupils very dilated, he's on something for sure.

'El gillipolas, he stole my island. He stole me.'

'What? Who stole what?'

'My mother's island. *My* island.' Then he says something I can't quite make out, like 'O-be-ya-oman' island – is that the name of the island or what?

'OK, OK Cal. We can't do anything about that right now, come back to your cabin. You need to lie down, man, you're not very steady, are you?'

Good thing we're moored, or he'd be right over. Though as he's pretty scrawny and I'm a good head taller than him, I guess I can hoick him up again if I have to. But better not to have to.

'Cal the steady ready slave. Stole my island. Stole me. Prisoned her.'

Not at all the time and place to blather. I get my arm under his shoulder and lug him along to his cabin. Luckily he doesn't resist though he does start a tuneless song of some kind: 'Miran is my darling, eyes like jewels... Sin ti, no puedo vivir, Miran Miran...'. If that's his girlfriend, I think she'll need some gumption. '...Oh Miran Miran Miran where have you gone, oh lost lost Miran, eyes like jewels...' Could be she doesn't have the gumption then.

'Shush Cal, we don't want to wake people up.'

Phew. I get him into the cabin, hoist him onto the bed and pull his legs up onto it. He tries to sit up, and I push him back down again, as gently as I can.

'No Cal, it's still night-time. Time to sleep. You must be tired. Sleep now Cal.' Treating him like Donnie's little one, last time I visited. His eyes start closing. Then they open wide again.

'Don't tell Rial, don't tell Rial. Don't tell Ross. Please please don't tell them.' He grabs my hand. 'Don't tell them please please please.'

'No worries Cal, I won't tell them. This is just you and me.'

'You can help me, you have the power to help me.'

Goodness knows what that means. Time I got back to my own cabin for sure.

'It's all OK, man. Time to sleep.'

He relaxes and his eyes close again. I wait for five minutes to be sure he's asleep and then leave him to it.

I exit the cabin wondering where he got whatever he's on as I couldn't see anything like a supply in there. In his pockets perhaps – he wasn't in night clothes.

I jump as another cabin door further down the corridor suddenly opens and Elena comes out, looking very fetching in a silky nightdress that puts my T-shirt and tartan night trousers to shame. Oops, that isn't her cabin either.

She sees me of course and looks alarmed.

'Good night', I say quickly – though it's hardly that anymore – and dive into my own cabin. I guess Boris has her on a string, he's the kind of man who would. Not my problem.

The day grinds on in that slow way it always does when you haven't had enough kip. I hide in the engine room with Vehlo for a few hours during the morning while he gens me up some more on gas turbines. Engines are about the only things that get him into a more human chattiness. I really do not want to see Cal if I can avoid it; I am not sure I can cope with Rial when I'm this knackered, nor Elena either under the circs.

Our chef – 'Monsieur' is what he answers to, pretentious git – puts out a small buffet for the middle of the day. That way we can grab some scran and get on with whatever we are doing. I nip in when the lounge looks empty, hoping for some of his tasty vol-au-vents and some salade niçoise. Yes, he really does know his stuff.

I am just about to exit with a loaded plate for a quiet lunch in my cabin, when Elena appears. Damn.

'Oh Hulkie, I was hoping to catch you.'

'Just off to eat, things to do in my cabin, mebbe later, man,' I say hurriedly and edge towards the door.

'I was surprised to see you so early today,' she says before I can get away.

'Well yes, man,' I say. 'Cal was a bit under the weather in the night.' I am the skeleton crew member with a med certificate, which means it is down to me if anyone is sick or injured.

'You won't mention it to the Captain?' she says. 'That you saw me?'

'Elena, it's none of my business what crew do in their own time. And I'm no blabber.'

My own bet is the Captain knows anyway.

'Oh,' she suddenly says, staring at my front.

I look down and see the little stone arrowhead pendant that cousin Malcolm gave me is not tucked under my top, as it should be. That's what happens when you are knackered.

'Are you a daughter of Hecate?' she asks in a peculiar tone.

'A what?'

'The pendant, they have it, a sort of a badge.'

The old woman at the Calanais, before the Incident, told me the pendant meant you were a witch. Of course, I am no such thing, though cousin Malcolm knows a bunch of women who say they are Wiccans, which is apparently the proper name for them. Mebbe they have them in Greece too.

'No, not at all,' I say. 'This was a present from my cousin.' I tuck it back under my top.

'Well of course you could not say,' Elena says. 'But they have powers. They can help people in difficult situations.'

Right on cue her 'difficult situation' turns up, as Boris walks in. I hope he didn't hear any of that. I glare at Boris, can't help it, and Elena jumps and blushes.

'You two woman, making a little conspiracy eh?' he says in a not-very-joking tone.

'Of course not, Yuri Petrovich,' I say. 'I'm told women crew can chat to each other, no law against it, is there?'

And I'm out the door before the conversation can get any worse. Leaving Elena to deal with whatever comes next. Not my problem.

Though later it turns out it is. Mid-afternoon I'm out on the main deck, from where I can see the southern end of the Hebrides, the island of Barra. We're churning along pretty fast and should certainly reach North Uist by 6, or thereabouts.

And then Cal finds me. He looks the worse for wear, with great big bags under his eyes. Not very surprising.

'Hulkie, the Captain wants to see you. On the Bridge. You won't tell him about last night, will you?'

Oh, not again.

'Look Cal, another crew member saw me out of my cabin after I got you back into yours. If anyone asks, I plan to tell them you banged on my door because you were feeling poorly and needed a painkiller. Just stick to that story if anyone asks you. But that's all. Got it?'

I bite my tongue before I can ask him what the hell he took and where he found it. I plan to look up 'spirit paths' later anyway.

'Bueno, vale, voy. I guess.' He doesn't sound nearly as grateful as he should.

When I get to the Bridge, of course Boris is there as well as the Captain.

'Ah, Helen,' says the Captain, less radiantly than usual. 'I just wanted a quick chat as there was a bit of vandalism on board last night and I wondered if you could cast any light on it?'

Cal might have mentioned that! What did he get up to?

'I'm afraid I have no idea, Captain. I got Cal some painkillers in the night as he was feeling a bit under the weather and then made sure he was comfortable in bed after he took them, but otherwise I was in my cabin all night and heard nothing at all. I hope the damage wasn't serious?'

Boris glares at me. He'll have had it out of Elena that she saw me in the corridor and would just love to pin something on me.

'That bitch-son, he takes more than painkillers,' Boris growls at me.

'Not that I've noticed, but I'll take your word for it, Yuri Petrovich,' I say very politely. 'As I'm standing in for your Doctor, all I can do is treat what I see.'

'I think we should avoid groundless accusations, shouldn't we, Yuri Petrovich?' the Captain says. 'Thanks for dropping by Helen.'

Off I go trying not to look smug or make a face at Boris. My guess is if they grill Cal he'll just be rude to them. Or so I hope.

But I do wonder what exactly got vandalised. Neither of them seemed keen to tell me that.

It's nearly six when we get to Lochmaddy. I've never been there before – at least I don't think I have. The harbour is scenic in that bleak sort of way you get in most of these islands, in among treeless hills. Which look very fetching in the early evening sunlight. There'd be good hill-walking here, though I'm unlikely to get the chance.

As a port it's neither big nor bustling. Just one pier for the ferry and an L-shaped boardwalk with some small boats, apparently a 'Marina'. Right. There are three tiny yachts and a set of open boats with outboards tied up along it. We moor out in the loch and I help Velho power down the turbines.

And after we've eaten, Boris and Elena go ashore again. They turn up ready to embark on the tender already kitted out in life jackets. A little odd, since we have a supply on the tender. To my surprise Rial turns up too, though without a life jacket. I haven't seen them all day and they weren't at our meal, but they materialise while I'm helping to get the tender organised. I can see Boris is annoyed, but also - as I saw when Rial arrived - he is scared too. He doesn't say anything. Then Rial gives me a good long look, which isn't a pleasant experience.

'We need a chat, Hulkie,' they say. 'But I'll catch you tomorrow before you leave.' That's not good news at all.

'Sure, man,' I say, in what I hope is a light tone.

And organising the tender is another thing Cal should be doing, but even if he were willing – hah! – you could probably trust him to mess it up.

Journal June 10

Remind me never to work on a private yacht again. This gig was a bad idea, even if it gives me the chance to sneak off to Lewis without making a big deal about it. It's not my style, but I am tempted to go down with 'food poisoning' at the christening and slide out of the whole thing.

Pretty clear there's a stash of something illegal on this ship and that's what Cal got his paws on. Not cocaine, though, even though we've come from the Caribbean. I've seen plenty of coke heads and they don't behave like Cal did. But it could spell big trouble for me. If we get a customs search, and they find whatever it is, I'll be questioned about what I know. That's nothing at all for certain: but just being on the ship will do my rep no good at all. On the other hand, breaking my contract would look even worse. Really, I should report my suspicions to the nearest customs authority, but then the shit hits the fan and some of it hits me. As if I didn't have enough problems right now.

I looked up Cal's 'walking the spirit path'. Like I thought, it turns up in a set of weird Caribbean religions. I've heard of voodoo of course, but apparently the islands the British got have one called 'obeah'. Bingo! That's what Cal was on about, the bit I couldn't work out. 'Obeah woman', not the name of an island. Bet there's some psychedelic thing people take to go into trances. Not that he was in a trance exactly, but still. And what was that stuff about 'his island', not to mention his mother? An Obeah woman? That would make *her* some kind of witch!

As for 'chatting' to Rial tomorrow, I'm not looking forward to that. Do I dare tackle them about the music and the stone? Certainly not in front of other crew. Have to see how it goes.

And another email from Dad: Louise has delivered a tiny boy. They've called him Michael. Sounds like there is no major problem, but of course he's in an incubator and will have to stay in the high-support baby unit for weeks yet. They are stopping down there for now. Could be worse, I guess. I'll wait for the dust to settle before I try to visit.

But my shitty day finished with yet more stress. Wilf. I said we'd chat every week on a Friday while I was away. That was also a task for today.

Our falling out a month back still replays in my head. I was sounding off about the christening and how little I like events like that, when he said 'Oh but you seemed to get on OK at your cousin's wedding'. Like a gowk I went 'How do you know, you weren't there?' My major blunder. I just forgot the wedding happened twice for me, once before and once after the Incident. But not for here-and-now him. And he *was* there the second time. Then he was sore put-out because inviting him to the wedding was like a big step for us both. And I bit back, and so we fell out.

Today was another round of polite tiptoeing, which is all we've managed since then. I can't face telling him about all the complications here, and certainly not about the stone coming to life, and then's what's left to say? He sounded frustrated more than cross. 'Hulkie, your life can't be quite as flat as that,' he says, 'tell me something at least'. But I couldn't. At this rate we're heading for a split.

Thank goodness I'm off the ship for a while from tomorrow.

Chapter 6 - Malcolm

Friday June 10th – Rannoch Moor

I was folding my suit into my backpack when the phone rang.
Polly. Aye well.

'Polly!' I said. 'How nice! I was just thinking of you. How are you doing?'

'It's all a bit of guddle,' said Polly. 'How's yersel?'

'Much as,' I said. 'Look, are you coming to the christening?'

'That's why I'm phoning,' said Polly. 'I just don't think it's feasible. I'm so sorry.'

Phew.

'That is a shame,' I said. 'It would be much easier to handle the hordes if you were there.'

'That's sweet of you to say so,' said Polly, 'but I'd got the vibe you'd likely be relieved.'

'Why would you say that?' I said.

'Do you want me to come?' said Polly.

'Only if you want to,' I said.

'I'm asking if **you** want me to come,' said Polly.

'Of course I do!' I said.

'Are you sure?' said Polly. 'I suppose I could move things round.'

'Not if you don't want to,' I said.

'You don't want me to come, do you,' said Polly. 'I wish you'd just say so.'

'Look,' I said. 'I do find it awkward being with you when Bernie's around.'

'The wedding was fine,' said Polly, 'wasn't it?'

'The wedding was weird,' I said. 'Both of them.'

'I meant the one I was at,' said Polly. 'And why's the christening on South Uist, of all places?'

'I told you,' I said. 'That's where Grant's family's from. I don't think Alison's too bothered. And I imagine Bernie's pleased.'

'At some point, you've got to stand up to her,' said Polly.

'Is that an ultimatum?' I said.

Polly laughed.

'Not yet,' she said. 'All right, I won't rearrange things.'

Phew.

'If you're sure,' I said.

'I'm sure,' said Polly. 'But we really do need to talk things through.'

'Of course,' I said. 'Look, are you free the next weekend? I could come to you?'

'I've actually got to go to Jura,' said Polly. 'Location scouting.'

'Location scouting?' I said. 'I thought you were doing everything with green screen and CGI.'

'Bloody Henry Craig,' said Polly. 'He says he wants authenticity. There's nothing authentic about that barrel of haggis droppings he calls a script. We were all ready to go, and he suddenly turned up with another rewrite.'

Here goes nothing.

'Suppose I came to Jura?' I said.

'Oh Malcolm!' said Polly. 'That'd be grand! Are you sure?'

'Oh yes,' I said. 'Quite sure.'

'I'll get right on it,' said Polly.

'Before you go,' I said. 'I'd like to ask you something. Have you ever come across a materials scientist called Lucy Lopez?'

'That cow!' said Polly. 'You want to keep well away from her!'

Blimey!

'You know her?' I said.

'She got the job I was supposed to get,' said Polly. 'At *Quantum Solutions*. That would have made life much easier. Our life.'

'What do you mean "supposed to get"?' I said.

'I told you,' said Polly. 'You don't pay any attention, do you. We were paired in the group selection stages. Nasty piece of work. Took every chance to shmooze the panel. At the final interview, they said that they decided my skills weren't quite the right fit. That's when they offered me the publicity post with *Great Alien Plum*. I could hardly say no.'

'I do pay attention,' I said. 'Honestly. I just didn't remember her name.'

'I believe you,' said Polly. 'Thousands wouldn't. Why do you mention her?'

'She turned up yesterday at the Visitor Centre,' I said.

I explained how Lucy Lopez had tried to butter me up.

'She's bad news,' said Polly. 'Just keep away from her.'

'That's the plan,' I said. 'I don't suppose could you tell me a wee bit about quantum computing, could you? In words of one syllable.'

'You'll be sorry,' said Polly. 'All right. Suppose you've got loads of information, but to find anything you've got to work through it bit by bit.'

'Like a search engine,' I said.

'That's right,' said Polly 'Well, if the information's got regular patterns, you can set things up so you can inspect the whole lot at once and mostly get the right answer.'

'Mostly?' I said.

'I'm coming to that,' said Polly. 'It's possible to manipulate bundles of atoms such that they're in a sort of suspended animation, representing lots of information all at the same time. When you probe them in the right way, they settle down into representing just one piece of information, mostly the one you want.'

'Mostly?' I said again.

'About 75% of the time,' said Polly. 'It's all based on probabilities. You have to repeat the probe over and over again to be sure you're getting the right answer.'

'That mostly makes sense.' I said. 'You are good! Where does *Quantum Solutions* come in?'

'They've had some sort of breakthrough,' said Polly. 'They claim they've been running the standard experiments and getting closer to 95%.'

'That's what Lucy Lopez said,' I said. 'When did that happen?'

'Must be nearly two years ago,' said Polly. 'Around September, I think.'

Oh. Right.

'Nothing to do with cats in boxes, then?' I said, recalling a confusing television programme.

'Don't try that at home,' said Polly. 'Not unless you want to get scratched. Anyway, I need to crack on.'

'Oh, just one thing more,' I said. 'Do you know anything about *Peyroux Holdings*?'

'Not really,' said Polly. 'They're some sort of shell company.'

'But you went for a *Quantum Solutions* interview, and got a job with *Great Alien Plum*?' I said.

'I told you,' said Polly. 'That was through a specialist recruitment agency. I've no idea what the connection is. I can ask, though. Talk soon! Big hugs!'

'Big hugs!' I said.

And ended the call.

I need to talk with Helen. It sounds like it's all kicking off again.

I finished packing, and checked the christening details. The event itself was on Saturday, in St Mary's Catholic Church in Bornish, on South Uist. I was booked into the *Ormacleit Castle Resort*, just up the road from the church. They'd send a minibus to meet the flight from Glasgow.

Then I checked the flight departure time. Three hours to go before it left. A bit tight, but the roads should be quiet. I went next door to see Glynis, who said she'd be happy to feed the cat for the next few days. Then I stashed my backpack under the tarpaulin in the back of the Land Rover and set off south.

Just down the road, I stopped at the garage at the *Tartan Trading Post* and filled up the tank. Gazing vacantly around, as the litres racked up, I spied a bedraggled young man in the bus shelter opposite the garage. The young man waved at me.

Miran was bedraggled. Was this her missing boyfriend? Or was this the stalker Glynis had seen? Or just some random stranger? Whatever, best not to get involved.

Self-consciously ignoring the young man, I finished refuelling, and was about to pay, when the attendant came out of the booth and crossed the forecourt. The rear offside tyre looked flat. She was right. I drove over to the inflator, fed the slot, and hooked up the tyre. The tyre wouldn't take any pressure. Sighing, I unbolted the spare wheel. The spare was flat, and I'd no more coins of the right denomination. At the booth, I changed a ten-pound note, pumped up the spare, jacked up the car and swapped the wheels. Then I put away the jack and the old wheel, and went back to the booth to pay for the fuel. The machine wouldn't accept my usual card. I found the one I never use, and racked my brains for the PIN.

When I finally got back into the Land Rover, I checked the time again. An hour had gone, just like that. There was no way I'd make the connection. I phoned the airport. There was another flight, but it was already overbooked. No, I couldn't have a refund.

I checked the ferries. It was too late for the sailing from Mallaig to Lochboisdale, but the ferry from Uig to Lochmaddy was just about feasible. But what to do with the Land Rover? The return flight was to Glasgow. I'd have to make my way back to Uig. Or I could just junk the return flight. I phoned the harbour and booked my passage. Then I messaged Alison to tell her I'd be late.

If you've not been there, the road north through the bleakness of Rannoch Moor, to the pinch point Pass of Glencoe, is stunning. But if you drive it almost every day, it's just like any other road – too long and too busy – especially if you're watching the clock. Luckily, the traffic was light, and the sheep kept off the tarmac, so I made good time to Fort William. Thereafter, the run up the Great Glen is a bit too much like a succession of calendar illustrations. Blooming heather. Majestic pines. You'd almost expect a piper in every layby. But from Fort Augustus to the Skye Bridge it's bonny, especially when the rhododendrons are in bloom. Yes, I know you're not supposed to like these non-native symbols of Victorian colonialism, but their garish tones sure make a change from the brown on brown of parched bracken and grass.

Over the bridge, the road winds round the flanks of the Cullins, and drops down into Portree. I was making good time. I decided to take a break.

The *Harbour Café*'s always been a reliable source of scones. I parked on the quay side. I'm not fond of the cream tea, an overrated English fabrication, but you can't beat a warm scone with butter and raspberry jam.

I was sitting at the café window, contemplating another scone, when the back door of the Land Rover opened, and the bedraggled young man from Tyndrum climbed out. He cautiously looked around, spotted me, and, instead of fleeing, came into the café.

Bloody hell! How come I didn't notice he was there?

'Forgive my intrusion,' said the young man, sitting down next to me, 'but is this the island?'

'It's the Isle of Skye,' I said, stunned beyond remonstrance.

'Sky!' said the young man. 'A heavenly name. This must be the place I'm seeking.'

What could I do? Shout at him for cadging a ride? Interrogate him mercilessly? Call the police? Dougie would just have laughed.

And who on earth was he? He seemed nothing like Glenys's supposed wraith. Why was he soaked when it hadn't rained for days? Had he come out of the mountain as well? He's hardly Peer Gynt.

'Who exactly are you?' I said.

'Nando,' said the young man.

'Like the chicken chain?' said the proprietor, proffering Nando the menu. 'What would you like?'

'The same as him, please,' said Nando.

'Coming right up,' said the proprietor.

'And who are you?' said Nando.

'Malcolm,' I said.

'Greetings, Malcolm,' said Nando. 'Thank you for your succour.'

The proprietor placed a plate of fresh scones in front of Nando. I watched him as he wolfed them down, as if he hadn't eaten for days. He was clean shaven with long curly black hair, which came down over the collar of a brown leather jerkin fastened with a buckled belt, like central casting's idea of a fairy tale huntsman.

'Thank you!' said the Nando, pushing himself back from the table. 'Now, where can I find the lord of this island?'

'The Lord of the Isles?' said the proprietor, collecting up the crockery. 'The castle's at Finlaggan. On Islay. You're too far north.'

'I'd best be off then,' said Nando. 'I'll not forget your kindness.'

He stood up and left the café.

'What a strange bloke,' said the proprietor, handing me the bill. 'Good of you to help him. Can you manage cash, please? I can't get a connection.'

I reached into my pocket, and pulled out some notes and the green stone. The green stone pulsed dimly in my palm.

This is bad news.

'That's a nice piece of green marble,' said the proprietor. 'You should have it mounted.'

'It's really white marble,' I said reflexively, handing them a £20 note. 'Calcium carbonate. It's suffused with serpentine. The high iron and magnesium make it green.'

'Whatever,' said the proprietor. 'I'll get your change.'

Outside, I anxiously checked the back of the Land Rover. Under my backpack was a silver coin. I didn't recognise the design, but one side had a king's head and the inscription REX IOCABUS – King James. That could make it over 400 years old. The trouble was it looked like it had been minted yesterday. I pocketed the coin. I'd check it later. There was bound to be an app for that.

It was a relief to leave Portree, and head on north to the ferry at Uig, knowing, or at least hoping, that the young man was off in the opposite direction.

As I drove along Lock Snizort, I came back to what Polly had said about multiple possibilities being in suspension. Quite often, reality feels like that. What if this? What if that? But suppose there really were multiple possibilities, not suspended, but all progressing in parallel. Could things somehow shift between them? Were the green stones somehow caught up in it all? They only seemed to react to the unworldly. But what if ours was the unworldly world?

Enough idle musings; I concentrated on overtaking yet another tractor.

The sailing was delayed by high winds. I messaged Alison to let her know I'd be even later. I didn't mention the young man. He had to be connected with Miran, judging by the stone's reaction.

The crossing was rough, and I was relieved when we finally approached Lochmaddy. Nearing the mole, I spied a large yacht moored offshore. How cousin Helen would have scorned its ostentation.

The ferry docked, and the Land Rover was ushered up the ramp. It was a muggy night so I rolled the window down. As I was turning right off the mole into what passes for the town, I heard a sudden snatch of eerie music. I checked the rear mirror. On the quayside was an uncanny figure, with piercing blue eyes in a very pale face, and long almost-white hair. Anxiously, I fumbled for the green stone.; it was pulsing angrily. Helen was the only person I could talk with about the green stone. But, in lots of ways, Helen was the last person I wanted to see.

The run down to the hotel should have been spectacular, with views west over the machair to the Atlantic, and east to the inner islands and mainland. But I was worn out, and just wanted to lie down.

At reception, I registered and offered my card, but was told everything was pre-paid. Someone's had deep pockets.

I really wasn't in the mood for family bonhomie, but that was why I was there. I asked for directions to the dining room. Luckily, I was told that dinner was ending, but room service was available for another hour, so I went straight upstairs.

In my room, I quickly scanned the menu, chose things I thought wouldn't take too long, and dialled reception. I then settled down on the bed and browsed the hotel brochure.

Apparently, Ormacleit derives from a Viking place name; nearby, there are the remains of settlements. The original castle was built for the Ninth Clanranald chief, Alan Macdonald, at the start of the 18th century. According to local legend, it was burnt to the ground on the very day he was killed at the Battle of Sheriffmuir, in 1715.

It's most striking that the castle roof was green marble. Now, bits can be found all over the grounds. Maybe that'll confuse all these folk that are triggering my stone.

The food arrived quickly. I augmented it from the minibar. Replete, I tried to phone Polly, but her mobile went to voice mail. I left her a brief message, texted Alison to say I'd arrived, got undressed and into bed, and fell straight to sleep.

Chapter 7 - Helen

Saturday June 11th - Lochmaddy, North Uist

When I get up, I still feel that I haven't had enough kip even though the night was minus interruptions this time. More bad dreams. A chaotic jumble of things leading up to the Incident. American physicists who are spies, a cat that isn't really a cat, old women who turn out to be weavers of timelines. And a strong and very unpleasant sense of everything cracking up. Which of course it finally did.

I load my white dress uniform into my backpack, add my washing things and my e-reader. It's around an hour down the islands to St Mary's Catholic Church on South Uist, and the christening is not until 2, which gives me plenty of time. I'll check into the *Ormacleit Castle Resort* first, which is where Dad says they were booked. I can get changed there. It sounds very fancy, but luckily I don't have to pay for it, and neither, come to that, did Dad. Apparently the happy couple are financing the whole party. Goodness knows how much that is costing them. Malcolm-the-granddad is bound to be there too.

Elena is bringing out Monsieur's big platter of pastries as I get to breakfast. Good timing.

Hmm, she looks as if she hasn't had enough kip either.

'No Yuri Petrovich?' I ask. In a neutral tone. I hope.

She gives me a dirty look all the same. 'Yuri Petrovich is ill,' she says.

One too many single malts last night for Boris, I guess.

'He has a stomach bug,' says the Captain helpfully. 'Nothing serious, so don't worry, Helen, I don't think we need medical support.'

Cal laughs in his usual bitter sort of way, but says nothing, and helps himself to more pastries.

'I can help you get the bike out,' Velho says. As we're not at a pier we have to take it across in the tender.

'Why don't I help with the bike while Velho gets the tender set up?' comes a melodic voice from behind me. Yes, it's Rial.

And that is what happens after breakfast.

Rial and I go to what everyone seems to call 'The Playroom' because it holds the ship's toys for its guests. Two jet skis, wet suits and snorkel gear, and two snazzy electric bikes, one with red trim, one with blue. The red one is still plugged into the charger, and is on full charge.

'Ok, I'll take this one,' I say.

'The other one has no charge anyway,' says Rial, though they don't seem to have checked it first.

Then: 'Hulkie, I can see things are difficult for you on this ship.'

Ah, this is the chat Rial promised.

'It's a limited time contract, man,' I say. 'And not my first with some little difficulties.'

'I know you are considering leaving. I think you should resist that thought.'

'What? How do you work that one out?'

'It's my job to know things.'

'Well man, you seem to know a lot of things you shouldn't know.' Oops, that just slipped out.

I can feel a vibration in my pocket and I just know it is my green stone. I'm getting really pissed off by all this stuff, and on impulse I pull it out of my pocket. Yes, it is glowing brightly.

'Then you know about this too, do you man?'

'Of course,' Rial says, far too calmly. 'It speaks to me.'

Christ-on-a-bike.

'So are you one of *them*, the witches?'

'No, I am of a different kind. But I can still help you.'

'Help me how?'

'This is not the time to speak of it,' Rial says, opens the Playroom door, and picks up the front of the bike.

Bastard! I know I'm not going to get anything more out of them. And I know I'll have to come back to the ship to find out what they mean. A different kind of what?

At the stern platform, Velho has the tender neatly docked.

'Captain says blue bike, I think', he comments when he sees we have a red one.

'No charge on it, man,' I tell him, and he shrugs and helps me get the bike into the tender.

This end of the islands makes Lewis look like a glittering metropolis. Lochmaddy is what in other places would make a village, but it is still bigger than anything further south. I start out on a two-lane road, but after a while, somewhere down the east side of North Uist, the road goes single track with passing places.

Luckily there isn't much traffic, though when I'm close to the causeway to South Uist I hear a vehicle behind me and pull over to let a minibus pass. It has *Ormacleit Castle Resort* on its side, presumably some kind of a shuttle. It will have a local driver who is happy to go rather faster than I am on this narrow road. Also it's a while since I was on a bike. Mam was always against motor bikes, so she and Dad helped me get my first Nissan while I was still working there and had the discount.

It's getting on for midday by the time I see what must be the *Ormacleit Castle*. Not a castle as such, at least no tower or battlements, more of a mansion. Very heavily restored I see, as I pull into its car park. With a huge stone and glass extension to the side of the more ancient looking masonry. According to its signage they have golf, kayaking, wind surfing and kite surfing. There is a great view of the sea. There is a strong westerly blowing, the way it often does on these islands, but as this is June and midge season, that's a good thing, keeps the little horrors away.

The car park has quite a few vehicles in it, including the minibus that overtook me way back on the road. And an ancient and rather battered Land Rover that is probably cousin Malcolm's.

By reflex I bring up the lid of the luggage compartment on the back of the bike before I remember everything is in my backpack. Then freeze.

The compartment is not empty. There are some packets in it, covered in clear plastic. I can't see any label. I fish one out carefully. It's some sort of brown powder.

This is bad. This is very bad.

What do I do?

I could hand it in to the local police. But I just know they will arrest me before crawling all over the ship. That would certainly end my contract with a bang. But what about Rial? Not sure I want to be on their wrong side. Nor Boris' either, come to that. And I'd miss the christening as well.

Mebbe I can find a way to dump it all into the hotel dustbins without anyone noticing. I decide to check in, unload my backpack, have a recce and then come back for the packets when I know where the hotel bins are.

The hotel interior is spacious and tartan. The foyer carpet is a green and blue tartan with white and black lines across it and the wall behind the reception desk has a more aggressive tartan with blue, green and red, framing an enormous picture of a woman in a blue dress. A large caption says she is Flora MacDonald. Oh yes, Speed Bonnie Boat and all that.

My room is very swish, up on the second floor, with a sea view. And a tartan carpet. But I don't linger there, just have a pee, dump out my stuff from the backpack, and get back downstairs again.

I emerge from the lift but before I can decide which way to look for the bins – round the back I am guessing – someone calls me.

'Helen! I'm so glad you could come!'

It's Bernie, looking very elegant in a lilac suit. Bernie is cousin Malcolm's wife, well, ex- in fact, though I don't think they have actually divorced. Which makes her the bairn's proud grandmother. But she's been like the big sister I don't have over the years. No way can I ghost her.

'Hi Bernie. How's Paris?'

Here-and-now Bernie works in HR for the big French electricity company EDF, and I haven't seen her since she moved out there.

'I'm really enjoying it. Have we got time for a wee coffee and sandwich just now, so I can tell you about it? It'll be bedlam after the christening and I'll need to circulate and blether with Grant's family.' Grant is the happy father at this event.

Well, I can't tell her no, and that's what we do. I try not to worry about the stuff in the bike. After all, I'm the only person here who knows about it.

We catch up over some tasty salmon and cream cheese bagels, and a large Americano that I really need, given my sleep deficit. Bernie shows off some of the French slang she has picked up, impressively fast given she has only been there a year or so. I keep the chat focused on her, as there's too much I don't want to talk about just now, starting with Wilf.

'And have you met a nice man yet?' I ask her.

I've told her so many times she should move on from Malcolm. It's not the first time for this question.

She goes a little pink.

'Oh, Helen, I just might have done.'

I have to be really careful here. Before the Incident, Bernie-then had a romance with a French guy over in Glasgow, who turned out to be not all he seemed. But none of that happened to Bernie-here-and-now.

'Tell me more!'

'Well, he's called Thierry...'

I try not to jump. That was the name of the guy before the Incident.

'... and he's a psychologist. I met him through work, he's part of the EDF HR support team.'

Good grief, same guy! Or at least, a here-and-now version of the same guy. That is just weird.

I let her tell me more about both Paris and Thierry, and then admire her suit. Of course it's Parisian: very stylish. As soon as we finish the sandwiches and I decently can, I tell her I need to get some luggage from my bike and then change.

'Come and visit me, Helen,' she says as we get up. 'I've a spare bedroom in the flat and I can show you round'. She doesn't mention Wilf. I think she's cute enough to have noticed his name hasn't come up.

'Love to! I'll be in touch!'

Outside I check there's nobody about and nip round the back of the hotel building. There's a delivery yard and some industrial size bins in the corner. Right now the yard is quiet. Just the thing.

I walk back round to the car park and open the bike's luggage slot again. And blink.

It's empty.

I feel around inside it, look at the ground. But how could the packets have fallen out? They have definitely gone. I feel as if I've been punched in the belly for a moment. Deep breaths, deep breaths.

Well, there's nothing I can do about this. If the police descend on the christening party I'll just deny all knowledge. Or mebbe some crew member – like Boris for example – has contacts down here and they have grabbed the packets? I really hope that's it, as then it's not my problem anymore. I shrug and go back inside to change into my white dress uniform. I am not exactly going to be inconspicuous in this crowd.

The actual christening is not all that long. It's the first one I've been to and while I know it involves splashing water on the bairn's head, in fact this happens three times. And of course the bairn is not happy about the first splash, and loudly indignant about getting two more.

Plus some oil rubbed onto his noddle, by which time he's a shade of red and furious.

But there was stuff to get through before that bit, and even more afterwards, when we have a Mass. That I recognise all too well, having already sat – and also kneeled and stood - through one. Twice, in fact, at both versions of the wedding. I remember during the post-Incident wedding when Wilf was there, he muttered to me, at some point, 'Howay, man, this is energetic stuff.'

My mind wanders as I start thinking that he's a good guy, I am fond of him really, and mebbe I should try a bit harder not to push him off.

Then there are lots of photos outside the church, and I have to hang about to be in some of them, though I don't get to actually hold the bairn like cousin Malcolm does. He's more expert than I expected and beams. I've not seen him look that happy before. And the bairn looks cheerier too. I think Alison gave him a feed during the Mass.

At last we get back to the hotel. No sign of any police cars – phew.

Our do is up on the first floor in a conference room with hardly any windows. It involves big self-service queues and then sitting down somewhere at big round tables to eat it. At least the scran's pretty decent. Fish fillets in lemon sauce, lamb stew and pasta veggie option. I really want to talk to Malcolm of course, but he's at a table with Grant and Alison, her brothers, the godparents, and the other grandparents. I try to catch his eye but fail. Is he avoiding me or am I imagining that?

I wander around after a bit and chat to a series of not very interesting people in a mechanical customer-service sort of way. I'm in the crowd round the bar when a slightly freaky young woman comes up, stares at me as if I've grown another head, and backs off into the crowd very fast. Oddly, I feel a vibration from the stone in my pocket. Who was she?

Before I can pursue her, the speeches start. Then christening cake and fizzy wine with toasts. Apparently, the cake is saved from the wedding, some kind of tradition. Lucky it's the kind of fruitcake that would still be edible if dug out of a Pharoah's tomb. And I still can't get anywhere near Malcolm. More pointless chat. The freaky young woman is nowhere to be seen.

Eventually I get tired of the whole thing and go back downstairs into the foyer. There's a bar down here, and a quiet single malt should revive me.

I sit there sipping the malt and staring out at the sea, which is turning silvery-grey, the way it does when the sun goes low in the sky. The white lines are breakers. It must still be blowing out there. I can see a couple of determined evening wind surfers. One tips over as I watch.

A middle-aged couple come into the bar and order 'Two of your great whiskies' in loud American voices. I nearly drop mine. I know those voices. From before the Incident. Breathe, Hulkie, breathe. Am I going to get through today without a fully-fledged panic attack?

They are – or they were – the American physicists I dreamt about last night. The ones who dabbled in spying. Martha and Dean. But none of that happened here-and-now. They can't be the same, or not exactly. I really hope these ones are in Big Finance instead. After Bernie's Thierry shock I have a sudden feeling bad things are closing in on me. Yes, of course I am going to try to hear what they say – and luckily, or not, they sit down not very far away.

For a good ten minutes I learn more about golf handicaps and the effect of a high wind on golf balls than I want to. Then Martha goes:

'Well, honey, one more day and it's back to the treadmill. I sure hope Glasgow's not as black as it's painted.'

'The *Quantum Solutions* guys will have us in the best hotel they have, Martha, they've been all over us. And I looked up the *Fodor's* online – there's Loch Lomond right next door. And Loch Ness isn't much further – we can go hunt the monster.' That's Dean then.

'I have some concerns about those *Quantum Solutions* guys. A seminar is all very well, but seems like a lot of take and not a lot of give. They claim a 95% accuracy on quantum collapse but their paper is way short on detail.'

'We both know about commercial secrecy though.' Dean again.

'Sure thing, but we also know the math says, in principle, that level of accuracy's not just good for calculations. Chain it up with an AI system and you could get pretty reliable what's next predictions. That's a big worry. That's what our friends in the Company want to know about. If that gets sold to the wrong people...'

Dean looks round at this point and I quickly look out of the window again.

'Martha, let's save this sort of discussion for somewhere a little less public,' he says, lowering his voice to what he must think is a level I can't pick up.

'OK, OK, honey, don't go all paranoid on me.'

They revert to chat about the next day's golf and their onward travel. Then they leave for their room. I get myself another single malt. I really need one.

And ten minutes later, guess what? Malcolm wanders into the bar. On his own. I leap to my feet.

'Malcolm! Good to see you, man. Let me get you a drink.'

Malcolm doesn't look very happy to see me. But he can hardly walk out again, can he?

'Oh, Helen. Hello. I don't think I need a drink after all that fizz.'

'You've got a point. How about I get us some coffees?'

I've cornered him.

The barman takes the order. 'Someone will bring them from the kitchen, I don't have a machine here.'

We sit down.

'What a bonny bairn,' I say, trying to get off to a good start.

'Yes, isn't he,' says Malcolm with a big smile. 'We get on really well.'

And we're off on family chat. He relaxes a bit.

The coffees arrive with a young man in the hotel's tartan get-up. He's a bit clumsy, as if he's not quite with it, and drops one of the teaspoons onto the table as he lifts the cups off his tray.

'Thanks,' I say, taking my cup from him before he can drop that.

We both sip our coffees for a while as I consider how to broach the whole thing about the Incident, my stone coming back to life, and my Lewis plan. He has to know about it.

'Malcolm,' I begin. 'Those green stones we had. Have you still got yours? Does ever glow like it used to before?'

But as I say that, and before he can reply, I suddenly hear – oh bloody hell – that creepy music from the ship. I look round expecting Rial to have materialised, but don't see them.

'Can you hear that?' I say, about as alarmed as I could be.

'That weird music?' Malcolm says. 'Where's it coming from? It's just like when I came off the ferry and saw that ghostly figure.' He looks pretty alarmed too.

'Ghostly figure?'

But before he can reply, all of a sudden I start feeling really off. As if I've had a lot more than two single malts. I have to get back to my room. Chucking up in the bar is not on.

And I leave. Very fast.

Chapter 8 - Malcolm

Saturday June 11th – Ormacleit Hotel, South Uist

At around 8am, I was roused from solid sleep by banging on the door. 'Dad! Dad! Come and have breakfast!'

Alison. Ever the dutiful daughter.

I quickly showered and dressed, and found my way to the dining room. The whole family was assembled. Well, that's an exaggeration. My parents weren't there. To be blunt, my mum's a fundamentalist Protestant who won't countenance Catholicism. Not that she's anything against Catholics, mind, unless they happen to be my wife. She wouldn't come to Alison's wedding. I didn't ask if she was invited to the christening.

Beaming, Bernie beckoned me across to her table. I hadn't seen her for over a year. She was tanned, and had lost weight. France clearly suited her. As we exchanged a chaste matrimonial kiss, she whispered that she'd something to tell me, but it could wait.

It certainly could.

I sat down opposite my sons, Richard and Neil, who at last had the grace to acknowledge my existence. They'd taken their mother's part when she'd announced that, if I wanted to live on Rannoch Moor instead of in Bearsden, that was just fine with her. Yes, I was really hard to be around. I was traumatised and claustrophobic. So would you be if your place of work had fallen on top of you.

We made gentle chit-chat over the full Scottish breakfast: enough fat and protein to last a week. Bernie was delighted to be a granny. I think she rather envied my relative proximity to the boy, but was evasive about her plans. Our sons seemed well settled. Richard was devilling with a leading Glasgow advocate, and Neil, who was smart if not academic, had just become a partner in his uncle's electrical firm. Both were unaccompanied. I didn't ask about significant others.

There was no sign of Helen.

After a third cup of tea, I made my excuses and went over to Alison's table. Grant greeted me warmly. What a nice man. Reliable, if dull. He unashamedly dotes on Alison, who has him round her pinkie.

'This is all very grand,' I said. 'I hope I'm not paying.'

Grant beamed.

'Och no,' he said. 'Your mum's covered everything.'

'Mum?' I said. 'Are you sure?'

'I wrote to her,' said Alison, 'after Chris was born. She said that, as long as he was raised a good Christian, she'd turn the other cheek.'

Blimey. Mum would never have been this tolerant before.

'Astonishing!' I said. 'She must be mellowing.'

'Don't worry,' said Alison. 'She sent a tract about the scarlet woman of Rome along with the cheque.'

'Is Helen not coming?' I said.

'She should be here for the ceremony,' said Alison. 'Her boat's tied up in Lochmaddy. She's staying overnight, so you'll have lots of time to catch up.'

Just what I need.

'Where's the boy?' I said.

'Upstairs,' said Alison. 'With Miran.'

'Miran's here?' I said. 'Och, Alison, you're such a soft touch.'

'You think?' said Alison. 'If I'm to go back to work, we'll need an au pair, and Chris really likes her.'

'Has she said any more about where's she's from,' I said, 'or how she got here?'

'Och dad!' said Alison. 'Enough questions! How about you? Is Polly joining us?'

'No,' I said. 'She's got a lot going on at work.'

'That's a shame,' said Alison. 'I think she's really good for you. You are still together, aren't you?'

That is the question.

'I think so,' I said. 'But we're not seeing as much of each other as we'd like.'

'You only think so,' said Alison. 'You'd better make sure then.'

'Leave your poor father alone,' said Grant, winking at me.

Alison laughed.

'Sorry dad,' she said. 'I'm just looking out for you. You do know that, don't you?'

'Of course,' I said. 'Of course.'

Thankfully, I wasn't required for the christening rehearsal. I felt stiff and achy after a long day in the Land Rover, so, after breakfast, I decided to go for a walk. The ceremony wasn't for four hours. And if I missed lunch, so be it.

South Uist has textbook geology. Essentially, it's two north-south bands of gneiss, separated by a band of pseudotachylyte. In turn, the bands have east-west intrusions of igneous rock. Never mind. I think it's really interesting.

For a walker, the east coast is mountainous, the centre is a patchwork of lochans, and the west coast is machair: boggy sand dunes, ideal for sheep and golf courses. I guess that's why Ormacleit's now a resort, not a ruin.

I decided to head to Rubha Ardvule, the westernmost point on the island. From the map, it looks like it's actually not very far from St Mary's church, so, just in case I didn't make it back to the hotel, I went up to my room, and put my suit and smarter shoes into my backpack. Then I set off due west over the golf course. It was a sunny morning, with a light wind off a calm ocean.

I was about halfway along the coastal path to Bornish, when I heard two strangely familiar voices, coming from a nearby bunker. I stopped, and looked down, and was horrified to see the two American physicists, whose meddling had made our lives a misery before.

I was sure they would recognise me. I'd better recognise them first.

'Hello!' I called. 'Fancy meeting you here!'

Oh, was it them? As they puffed across the bunker, dragging their golf trolleys behind them, I began to realise that these Americans were subtly different. It wasn't just their timeless golfing uniform of black and yellow chequered sweaters, quite unlike the upmarket all-weather garb I'd last seen them in. Rather, they seemed genuinely puzzled to see me.

'I'm sorry, honey,' said the woman. 'But do we know each other?'

'Malcolm Nicholson,' I said. 'From the Rannoch Moor Visitor Centre. We met there a couple of years ago.'

'I think you've made a mistake, honey,' said the woman. 'We're Martha and Dean, from Southern California. And this is our first trip to Scotland.'

'Martha and Dean?' I said. 'Not Martin and Deanna from North Carolina? I'm really sorry. I got you confused. I meet so many people in my line of work. I can only apologise. So, what brings you here?'

'We're going to Glasgow for a conference,' said Dean. 'We thought we'd come over a few days early, and try some of your rustic golf courses. This one's really something to tell the folks back home about.'

'What's the conference about?' I asked.

'Quantum computing, honey,' said Martha.

'Is *Quantum Solutions* involved?' I asked, on a whim.

'Oh man!' said Martha. 'They sure are. They're the sponsors. Fancy you knowing them.'

'If you're from Rannoch Moor,' said Dean, too quickly, 'what are you doing over this way?'

'My grandson's christening,' I said. 'It's this afternoon.'

'That's just lovely,' said Martha 'Family's really important.'

'I'd best let you get on,' I said. 'I'm off round the point.'

'Enjoy your walk, honey,' said Martha.

The Americans set off back down to the green, and I carried on south.

Martha and Dean. There was a Martha and Dean. But that was *before*. I wonder if Helen remembers them.

Just in sight of St Mary's, I spotted the hotel mini-bus. Must be the rehearsal. I didn't want to talk to anyone quite yet. I made a sharp turn towards the point, and was immediately up to my ankles in mud. Cursing, I retraced my steps, and hurried along the coastal path to the Dun Vulan signpost, hoping no one had spotted me. Turning right, I was now heading straight towards the sea. The wind grew fresher, and the waves were flecked with white foam. Seagulls wheeled overhead, screaming at me: Beware! Beware!

The path to the point circled a small lochan. I took the clockwise route, past the stump of the broch, barely visible in the gorse. At the point, I halted and gazed out to the North Atlantic. Next stop Labrador. I suddenly felt a long way from anywhere. Yet people had made their homes here for thousands of years.

I checked my watch. Well past midday. I'd no time to get to the hotel. I completed the circle of the lochan, and hurried back to the church. Behind the grey stone building, I quickly pulled the suit trousers over my jeans, fastened my tie, and put on the jacket.

At the front of the church was a huddle of family.

'You made it!' said Bernie. 'What a state you're in! You haven't even combed your hair!'

I felt like a wee boy, as she straightened my jacket.

'Come on,' said Bernie. 'We're at the front.'

I smiled wanly as I passed cousin Helen in a rear pew. She gestured to me to join her, but I shook my head, and mouthed: later.

Sitting down, I picked up the order of service. The ceremony consisted of the christening followed by a Mass. Now, I'm pretty tolerant but I've really no time for this. How can a child have original sin? How anyone claim to speak on behalf of someone who can't see much further than the next meal? All those arguments with Bernie. All those baptisms.

As the priest droned on, I looked around the church. It was striking that, apart from the huge crucifix over the altar, and the stations of the cross on the bare stone walls, there was none of the idolatry my mum railed against.

Then I caught the priest saying, 'My dear friends, Christopher Malcolm Currie has been reborn in baptism...'

And I choked up. Christopher Malcolm. I knew it was Christopher for Grant's father. But me as well!

The rest of the day was pleasant enough. Meeting Grant's family again. Catching up with my own. Toasts and canapes, and then a lavish sit-down dinner. All the while, Miran hovered in the background. And Helen lowered.

I knew we had to meet. I knew I couldn't keep putting it off. But when I'd finally relaxed enough to talk with her, I saw her disappearing downstairs. After a decent interval, I got up and followed her, but was stopped on the landing by the Americans from the golf course, heading in the opposite direction.

'Mr Nicholson!' said Martha. 'No surprise to see you here, honey. And what a lovely family you have.'

'Thank you,' I said. 'I hope the rest of your game went well.'

'Seven over par,' said Martha. 'Maybe we'll do better tomorrow morning.'

'Good luck!' I said, trying to make my way past them.

'We wanted to ask you,' said Dean, without moving. 'We'd heard a story about *Quantum Solutions* setting up a facility on your Moor. Do you know anything about that?'

'Not really,' I said. 'I think it's still at the planning stage. But they do now have some presence.'

'Interesting!' said Dean. 'Maybe we'll pay you a visit, before the conference.'

'That'd be nice,' I said, without conviction. 'Now, if you'll excuse me.'

'Of course,' said Martha, stepping aside. 'Have a nice evening, honey.'

As I suspected, Helen was in the bar next to reception. Sitting down beside her, I declined a dram, so we settled for coffee, which she ordered. While we waited, we made polite chit-chat, as if postponing the inevitable. The waiter returned quite quickly, but seemed strangely unsteady as they filled our cups. Perhaps they'd been draining the leftover fizz.

'Malcolm,' said Helen, sipping her coffee. 'Those green stones we had. Have you still got yours? Does it ever glow like it used to before?'

Before I could reply, I started to hear the eerie music from the Lochmaddy quayside.

'Can you hear that?' Helen said, more alarmed than I've ever seen her.

'That weird music?' I said. 'Where's it coming from? It's just like when I came off the ferry and saw that ghostly figure.'

'Ghostly figure?' said Helen. 'Oh god, I really don't feel good.'

Then she clutched at her stomach and got to her feet. As she staggered out of the bar, I felt increasingly queasy, but it was a familiar feeling. Gingerly, I got up and found my way to my own room.

As I lay down on the bed, and the world began to dissolve around me, I remembered my last day at University. Coming back across the campus from the pub, a friend had spotted a fairy ring in the newly mown grass.

'Liberty caps!' she said. 'What a great way to celebrate!'

She bent over and gathered them into her straw boater.

'Here,' she said, passing the boater round. 'Have some.'

'Aren't you supposed to dry them and weigh them?' someone else asked, 'so you know how much you're taking?'

'No need,' said my friend. 'There's only a couple each, and they're better fresh.'

Now, I'd smoked a little weed, but I'd never taken mushrooms before. Still, it was my last day on campus, and I'd likely never see any of these folk again, despite protestations of undying friendship. So, when the hat reached me, I took two mushrooms and swallowed them down.

'You're supposed to chew them!' said my friend.

As we wove our way over the lawn, I suddenly felt ill, and threw up the evening's drinking. Everyone laughed sympathetically.

'Come on Malcolm,' said my friend. 'That shows it's working.'

I spent the next hour in the hall of residence common room, watching the coloured patterns playing on the walls. From the torrents of giggling, to an outsider it might have seemed like a shared experience, but, if I was anything to go by, everyone was inside their own heads. As the mushrooms wore off, I felt tired and heavy.

This trip felt very different. More of an immersive experience, like watching a film through a badly adjusted Virtual Reality headset, which exaggerated depth, and washed everything greeny-purple.

I was standing on a beach fringed with coconut palms, with soft sand sparkling underfoot. A little way off, I could see Helen, ghostly. I called soundlessly, and waved, but she was intent on a group of three shimmering men, sitting in rattan chairs on a raised dais. One of the chairs was slightly higher than the others. I got the impression of someone important and their entourage. I glided closer, to get a better look.

The man in the higher chair had a full head of white hair and an impressive beard. As I came near, I was struck by his beaky Roman nose, olive skin and dark eyes. Glowing threads ran from his fingertips, entangling the other men. He was speaking to the man on the left, who was bowed over, as if being admonished. I couldn't quite place his looks. Amerindian, perhaps? The third man, sitting bolt upright, was uncannily familiar. He turned and looked directly at me, piercing blue eyes in a very pale face. He smiled knowingly, and turned away.

Suddenly, I fell backwards onto the bed and was violently sick.

As I cleaned myself up, my head was bursting. It had to be the coffee. But who would do this to us? Was it the Americans, and some misbegotten *Quantum Solutions* shenanigans? But why would anyone think I was important?

And was I the sole target? A flask of coffee's too scatter-gun. They must have been after both of us. But what's Helen to them, if they can't remember me? Was it even the Americans?

And the trip, what was that about? I've been anxious about seeing Helen, and could make no sense of the weird man on the quay. Both must have been preying on my mind. But who were the other two, the leader and the led? From what little I know about it, that was far more like an out of the body experience than just hallucinating. I wonder what Helen saw. I wonder if she saw what I saw. I wonder if she saw me.

Chapter 9 - Malcolm

Sunday June 7th – Ormacleit Hotel, South Uist

When I came down to breakfast, Helen was sitting by herself on the far side of the dining room's tartan expanse. Bernie, and our sons, were right by the entrance.

'Hello!' I said. 'Nice to see you all again.'

'Come and join us,' said Bernie.

'I said I'd have a chat with Helen,' I told them. 'We haven't met for ages.'

Helen looked up as I got over to her.

'Christ I feel ill, man,' she said, much more calmly than I'd expected. 'What was that? Last night's coffee tasted weird, sort of bitter. I'm sure that's what did it.'

'You're not the only one,' I said, sitting down opposite her. 'I think someone drugged the coffee. I had what felt like a trip. Strange, vivid visions. How about you?'

'Same. But I can take a good guess at who made that happen.'

'You know who did it? Why would anyone want to drug us?'

'No idea why, man. But do you remember that weird music? If my brain is still working then I think you heard it too? Just before I conked out?'

'That's right,' I said. 'Like I heard on the quay in Lochmaddy, when I saw that strange apparition. They were in my trip, as well.'

'Apparition? Tall and pale, long white hair, bright blue eyes?'

I nodded.

'Well, that's Rial. Get this – they were in my druggie vision too! Either Rial does the music or it happens when they are around, not

59

sure which. They're on my ship, they work for the guy who's hired me. I can't tell whether they're man or woman, makes my brain hurt. My bet is they had something to do with this, though I haven't seen them about, and I've no idea how they could have got here.'

'What did you do to piss them off? And why would they go for me?'

'Here's the really bad news. Pretty sure it's green stone stuff. At least mine came back to life a few evenings back when that weird music was playing, so...'

Here we go.

'Green stone stuff!' I said. 'You're joking, aren't you! Mine's been glowing as well. It started when Ali turned up with Miran...'

'Miran? Are you sure that was the name? That's the second time I've heard it. Someone on the ship mentioned a Miran. A guy who was missing his girlfriend.'

'The Miran I met was really wet and bedraggled. Might she have come off your ship? She's here with Ali, you know.'

'No way can she be off the ship, man. When was that?'

'Must be three or four days ago,' I said. 'Wednesday.'

'Even an Olympic swimmer wouldn't have got herself to your part of the world from somewhere between France and Ireland, which is where we were on Wednesday.'

'Can't be the same woman. Did you see anyone else in your trip apart from that Rial person?'

'I'm not a tourist, man. I'm part of a crew, bringing a yacht over from the Caribbean for Mr Ross Peyroux, the guy I'm working for.'

'No, no, not that sort of trip. The drugs. Last night. Like LSD. Did you see anyone else?'

'Mine had Rial, like I said, and Mr Ross, and another of his guys, Cal, who's also crew, as well as a pain in the bum. And a druggie. He was the one who was going on about a Miran come to that.'

Suddenly, Bernie loomed over the table.

'It's nice to see you two getting on well together,' she said. 'I'm just off to Mass, so I thought I'd say goodbye to Helen. I need to talk to you later, Malcolm, don't run away.'

'Sorry we didn't have more time to chat, Bernie,' said Helen. 'I'll not forget the invite to Paris. Hope it works out with your new man.'

'Oh Helen!' said Bernie, flushing pink. 'That really wasn't for public consumption. I'll tell you about it later Malcolm, honestly.'

I looked Bernie full in the face, and said nothing. Bernie avoided my gaze, and hurried away.

'Oops, man,' said Helen. 'Sorry about that, thought she'd have told you by now.'

'Clearly none of my business,' I said.

As we sat in silence, a tartan-clad waiter approached our table.

'I'll take your order now. What would madam like?'

'I've gone off your coffee,' said Helen grumpily. 'Just some toast and some tea, please.'

'And Sir?' said the waiter.

'I'll have tea as well,' I said, 'and a boiled egg with toast. Four minutes, please.'

'Certainly,' the waiter said. And moved to the next table.

'Who's the bloke who was going on about a Miran?' I said, finally. 'Why was he in your trip?'

'Can we stop saying 'trip', man? Trips are what ships do, not people. Druggie visions is what people do. And Cal was having a druggie vision when he mentioned a lost girlfriend called Miran. Though he claimed he was *spirit walking*. As if. Spirit lurching more like. I looked it up and it's a Caribbean thing. And Cal says he's a Carib.'

'Spirit walking,' I said. 'That's where they visit the same dream realm, isn't it. There are Native Americans who take drugs to do that. Peyote mushrooms. Ayahuasca.'

Helen looked startled.

'Wow! Could that have been the stuff in my bike? You wouldn't credit this, man. I got here on a bike borrowed from the ship. I didn't look in the luggage slot until I arrived and there were three plastic packets of brown powdery stuff in there.'

'Bloody hell,' I said. 'That must have been a shock. What did you do with them? I don't suppose there are many police around here.'

'That's the thing. I was going to ditch them in the hotel bins, but I went to my room and dumped my kit first. When I got back, they'd gone. I bet that was Rial. And odds are some of it ended up in our coffee. That'll be the stuff Cal was on too.'

'Then I suppose we should be grateful this Rial person only targeted us' I said. 'Imagine if it had gone into the Reception coffee urn! So what's this Cal doing on the ship?'

'He's another of Mr Ross' people, same as Rial,' Helen said. 'Like I said, he was in my druggie vision along with Ross and Rial. On a Caribbean island. That's another Cal thing. He's always going on about *his island*.'

'That's crazy!' I said. 'I saw three men, on a tropical island. And I saw you.'

'Well I didn't see you, man,' Helen said. 'But if we both saw the same thing, then you saw Mr Ross Peyroux. Lots of white hair, dark eyes, very big-boss.'

'Sounds about right,' I said. 'So who is he? Oh, it's not the Peyroux of *Peyroux Holdings*, is it?'

'Right in one. That's what pays me – where have you come across it? I'm getting a bad feeling about this.'

'This really is crazy! *Peyroux Holdings* own the film company Polly's working for.'

'Octopus with arms everywhere then,' said Helen. 'By the way, let's get this right, Rial may not be a man or a woman. I'm not even sure they're human after last night.'

'What are they then?'

'Not a scoobie.'

'They seem to get about,' I said. 'My neighbour Glenys told me she saw someone who looked like Rial. Near our cottages.'

'Are you sure? When?'

'Wednesday as well,' I said. 'Same day Miran turned up.'

'They niver, man! Seems impossible from a ship out in the Atlantic, but hey, if Rial can turn up here as well, who knows? Really creepy.'

'Sir, madam, your breakfast.' We paused as the waiter deposited two sorts of toast, a bagel, butter, cream cheese, marmalade, jam, and two boiled eggs onto our table.

'The tea will be coming shortly – Assam, Darjeeling, Earl Grey? Or we also have a range of herb teas: camomile, mint...'

'Those aren't teas,' I said, tetchily. 'English breakfast, please. Strong. With milk.'

'Same please,' said Helen, making an obvious effort to smile.

Helen took a slice of toast and slabbed some butter and jam onto it.

'Green stones,' she said, as soon as the waiter left. 'Look, man, you're the only person I can talk to about this. You remember before the Incident. Before we got scooped up by those witchy-women from our own timeline and dumped in this one. Where things are just not right. Where I don't know whether I can trust my memory at all. All to get rid of the green stone. And now it's alive again. I can't take this.'

She angrily broke off a piece of her toast.

'Just not right?' I said. 'It is what it is. We just need to get on with things, I reckon.'

'Howay, mebbe it's OK for you sat on Rannoch Moor every day and doing the same stuff. I don't know whether I've been to all the places I remember being in, or met the people I remember meeting.

My bloke Wilf might not be the same Wilf I knew in the old timeline. When we met up after the Incident, it turns out he's got a cat when he never did before. This Wilf has had one for years!'

Why is this such a big deal? People change all the time. If something seems out of character, maybe we don't know the character as well as we think we do.

'I thought you liked cats,' I said, cracking a boiled egg and slicing off the top. 'For goodness sake! This isn't four minutes! The white isn't cooked properly!'

I sliced a finger of toast and stabbed at the egg. Helen chomped through her mouthful of toast and swallowed it hastily.

'The last time I liked a cat, *before*, it turned out to be not a cat at all but some witchy person-thing,' she said. 'Wilf's cat is a grey tabby that looks just like it. And I bumped into the Americans we met, remember them? Also before the Incident. They were in the bar last night just before I met you. Who else is floating around as same-but-not-the-same? It's like putting your foot down rabbit holes all the time. I want out of this.'

'I met those Americans too yesterday,' I said, scraping out the egg with a teaspoon. 'They're definitely not the same. I recognised them but they didn't recognise me. They're quantum physicists. What were the last lot?'

'They were some kind of physicists too – the same but not the same. Of course they didn't recognise you, man. Nor me neither. We got thrown back in time from where we were, you know this. None of that stuff with the *Fundamental Forces* lot before the Incident happened here-and-now.'

'But maybe there is a link,' I said, attacking the second egg. '*Peyroux Holdings* own the company who are trying to reuse the old *Fundamental Forces* plant up on the Moor. They're called *Quantum Solutions*. They're sponsoring the conference the Americans are here for.'

Helen looked as if she was going to choke on her next mouthful.

'It's all creeping up on us,' she said, spluttering crumbs. 'I want out.'

This really is deja-vu, Helen going off on one.

'What do you want to happen?' I said. 'If things go back to exactly how they were before, it'll be the same all over again.'

'We didn't have to remember our *before* though, did we? The witchy women asked us and we said yes. I want to ship out again and not remember. I want to be who I am and in my own time. The Incident's made me a mashed-up person.'

'But this is your own time now,' I said.

Before Helen could reply, the waiter arrived with the tea.

'Are the eggs to Sir's liking?' said the waiter, putting the teapot and jug onto the table.

'They most certainly are not...' I said.

'But the toast is very good,' said Helen, butting in quickly.

The waiter muttered apologies and backed away.

'Give the poor guy a break,' said Helen. 'I've been on too many ships with rude customers. It wasn't his doing.'

'Fair enough,' I said. 'I'll leave him a decent tip. Anyway, how could you possibly reset things?'

'What about our two stones?' said Helen. 'Mebbe we could summon those witchy women back with them? We know two stones can do stuff. We zapped a robot together, before the Incident.'

'They really weren't witches,' I said. 'More like aliens. And I absolutely don't want to see them again.'

'OK, I thought you might say that, man. Well, I can look for them on my own. Before the Incident I met one of them on Lewis. At the Calanais stones. And I took this gig because we are heading for Lewis, our next stop now, for refuelling. I'm going back to the stones.'

'But what about me?' I said. 'I'm not unhappy with how things are now. Why should I have to change? Anyway, Polly knows what happened. And I think the Wiccans do as well. Anyone who had an arrowhead pendant. Are you going to change all of them? That seems really selfish.'

'But you don't know that's what would happen. Last time our whole timeline was zapped and everyone – OK, nearly everyone – went down with it. Not our choice. Mebbe they could just move me. How do we know unless we ask?'

'You don't know either,' I said. 'It could just make things worse. Those women are a law unto themselves. Why should they go along with what you want? I don't want anything to do with this.'

'I'm sorry, Malcolm. I can't cope. I have to try.'

Helen got up and stalked out of the dining room. I followed close behind.

'Hello Dad!' said Alison, at the bottom of the staircase. 'Hello Helen! We're just off for breakfast. Have you had yours?'

'Hello Ali,' I said. 'Hello Miran. Where's the boy?'

'He's with Grant,' said Alison. 'They're just on their way. How was the food?'

'Hello Alison! The toast's good,' said Helen. 'Though Malcom might advise against their boiled eggs. Hello Miran. I think we met during the reception yesterday.'

I felt the stone buzz in my pocket.

Chapter 10 - Helen

Sunday June 12th – Ormacleit Hotel South Uist

I've had better chats than that one with cousin Malcolm. He can be such a gowk sometimes. I'm really grateful when we bump into young Alison as we leave the dining room – one more daft remark from Malcolm and I'd have bitten his head off.

A bit of blather and then I shoot off upstairs to get my act together for checking out. Leaving that odd young woman, Miran, with the same frightened rabbit look she gave me in yesterday's do. Another green stone connection. Just what I need. And she still could be Cal's missing girl friend.

I don't have to be back at the *Midsummer Queen* until five or so, which means I can get in a bit of walking on my way there. Nothing too strenuous as I don't have my walking boots and still feel way short of full fettle. But it should help clear my head after that noxious stuff last night. Lucky I made it to the loo before I threw up. And missed my dress uniform.

'Spirit-walking'. Hah! I saw people that I know. Assuming Rial is a person and not some kind of boggle or brag. And a generic 'tropical island'. No surprises there. Though the tangling up of Cal and Rial in glowing green threads from Mr Ross' hands was weird. Cal said he was a *slave* in his druggie rant. Does that make Rial a sort of slave too? What's really odd though is Malcolm saying he saw the same thing and saw me there too. As if my druggie vison beamed into his head. Could that have been a Rial thing?

I need to tackle Rial. If that's possible. But no sign of them here and no more weird music.

I manage to avoid meeting Malcolm again before I leave. But I have a nasty feeling he won't get out of all this as easily as he thinks and an even nastier one that I won't get out of it either. I can feel stuff closing in on us both. Better to take control if I can. My Lewis plan is still go.

I check the bike luggage slot again, and it's still empty. No packets of brown powder. Good. And off I go northwards, back up the road. Not as sunny as yesterday, with clouds blowing over from the sea, but nothing too drastic-looking. No traffic on the road.

A few miles along there's a small turning off to the right, along the top of the big loch. And not far along that a small car park, completely empty. I park, then take my backpack off and twine it round the handlebars. I'll be better without it and there's nobody going to half-inch it out here.

The first part of the walk is rather boggy, even with sections of boardwalk and a couple of small bridges. I begin to wish I had my boots, my trainers get all clarty. Still, I have some spare trainers back on the ship and I manage not to get my socks wet. Pure belta view of the island's mountains – if I had the kit and the time they'd be much more fun.

But after I go back across the main road towards the sea and onto the machair it all dries out and there's some great bird life. A golden eagle flies up almost in front of me. I think that's what it is anyway. Then there's an astonishing array of bits of rusty farm machinery just lying around, followed by a complete sheep skeleton.

The next bit of rusty rubbish is more interesting – looks like the nose cone of a rocket. With visible electronics. I'd like to poke around in that but I resist the temptation. Must be from the test station up ahead. The hotel concierge warned me not to carry on if there were red flags out. None visible though, and I continue. I'm feeling better, that heavy post-druggie daze has lifted at last. I stop for a minute and ferret in my fleece pockets for my bait: the biscuits and small water bottle I lifted from my hotel room.

By the time I am back on the road to the car park, admiring some small wild ponies along the way, I feel positively cheery. Until the car park is in sight, that is.

I can see there's another bike there. As I get closer, my first impression holds – it's just like mine but blue. Here comes trouble.

A man rises from the small wooden bench at the back and walks forward as I arrive. Yes, it's Boris. Who else?

'Hi, Yuri Petrovich,' I say, giving it my best customer service manner. 'What a coincidence. You out for a walk too?' I won't bother asking how he knew where to find me. The bikes must have GPS location beacons so the ship's guests don't lose them.

He's holding my backpack I see, and my dress uniform, e-reader and night things are scattered on the ground. Which is muddy, of course.

'Why you take red bike, McIver when Captain say blue bike?' He drops my backpack in the mud and takes a step forward.

'The blue one was out of charge,' I tell him.

He scowls. But as he'll have had to charge it to follow me, he knows that.

'Where is stuff?' he says in a most unfriendly manner, gesturing at the open luggage slot on my bike. And takes another step forwards. I tense, ready for a lunge or a punch.

'What stuff?' I say, trying to keep my face impassive and sound genuinely bewildered.

'You know what stuff, McIver,' he says. Ah well, that didn't work. I curl my fists, thumb outside in approved fashion. I reckon if he had a gun he'd have pulled it by now, but I really hope he hasn't got a knife.

'I divvent know, man,' I tell him. 'And if I did know it wouldn't be my problem.'

'Is very much your problem where is now. Where is it? You sell it to who? You will tell me.'

We're pretty much eyes locked on each other the way people are when a fight is brewing. Neither of us is prepared for the new voice over to our left.

'I think I might be able to help.' We both jump.

Rial moves into our vision. And yes, the eerie music starts up. It's definitely Rial that does it.

And all at once Boris' eyes lose focus. He starts to sway. Rial takes him by the shoulder and he does not respond. Shoulders him back to the bench and he slumps down on it, head bowed.

'What have you done to him?' I blurt out.

'Nothing very damaging,' Rial replies calmly. 'His mind is elsewhere.'

'And how did you get here?'

'It was the most probable place for me to be,' Rial replies. 'So I am here.'

That made no sense at all. But as for tackling Rial, somehow I don't think this is a good moment.

'Howay, what do we do now?'

'I will return Yuri Petrovich to Lochmaddy. He will not remember his trip here. I think you should return to the hotel for some lunch.'

I don't argue. Looks like it's better for your health to follow Rial's 'advice'. Anyway, the music gets on my nerves. Though it sems a bit more than that in Boris' case.

Rial touches Boris on the shoulder and he gets up like a zombie and walks to the blue bike. Rial gets on and Boris sits behind them, drooping but with his arms firmly round Rial's middle. Rather him than me.

I give them a good head start, picking up my stuff from the mud. I'll have to ask Elena to wash my dress uniform now. Then I also drive back towards the main road, turning left for the hotel and a late lunch.

I get back to the ship around four. Velho comes to fetch me in the tender and helps me get the bike back into the games room. The blue one is still not there. I hope Rial meant what they said and they haven't tipped Boris into a loch on the way. Not that I love the man, but I do want to get to Lewis, which will be tricky without a navigator.

The Captain meets me off the tender.

'Good to have you back, Helen,' he says, blasting me with that smile. 'I hope the family event was enjoyable.'

I give him a few highlights like the splashing on the head stuff and he listens patiently, but I can tell he wants to ask me something else.

'Have you seen Yuri Petrovich, by the way?' he asks with studied casualness. 'He went out on the other bike this morning and I was expecting him back by now.'

'Sorry, no Sir,' I say, watching him wince at the honorific. 'I hope he hasn't overdone it after his illness yesterday.'

Pound to a penny the Captain is in on Boris' drug shipment. I really hope he doesn't have it in for me as well. I don't want to end up 'accidentally' in the Minch.

Then around five, Velho is out again in the tender and brings Boris and the other bike back. Boris does look ill. Hard to be unhappy about that. So much for us sailing for Stornoway after the evening meal as originally planned. I expect we'll have an early start instead to make our refuelling slot.

Boris misses the evening meal and does not go into town afterwards. Elena does, looking rather cheerful. This time Velho goes too, and I'm left in charge. Plenty of chapters in the Swords and Sorcery on my e-reader to keep me going.

Journal June 11

Don't know where to start this journal entry, eventful days.

Well, Rial. More questions than answers.

Rial saved my bacon with Boris, but why? And now I owe them one, which is not a happy thought.

Though mebbe they also set me up? What if Rial knew about the drugs and switched the bike chargers the previous night? Did they also make off with those packets? Apart from dosing the coffee Malcolm and I drank? And again, for why?

I should have asked them – but to be honest after what Rial did to Boris, I was pretty keen to be elsewhere. A bit of that weird music and looks like people do pretty much what Rial wants. Though it didn't work like that on me, or on Malcolm either come to that.

Hmm, we've both got green stones, Rial will know that if the stones 'call to them'. Mebbe that's *why* they turned up for the white knight act – though the *how* is more worrying. My very own Rial beacon, and even the thought of ditching it brings me out in a sweat. Malcolm never had that with his. And Malcolm is really annoying: he thinks just because the Incident was no problem for him it can't be a problem for me.

On the more cheery side: I sent a long email to Mam and Dad about the christening with a few pics and just had one back from Dad. The bairn is doing OK in his incubator and Dad tells me proudly he is actually Michael David – the middle name after him. After a bit of dithering I sent a shortened account to Wilf as well. I didn't promise him email, only a Friday meet on WhatsApp, so mebbe that will make things less chilly between us.

Stornoway tomorrow now, after an early start, assuming Boris recovers. At our speed that can't be more than a couple of hours. But refuelling will take the rest of the day – if not longer – given the amount we need. Those gas turbines drink it down like water and our tanks are huge. And we have to dump our waste out as well.

Then the Captain says we have a booking on Tuesday with a specialist to investigate our navigation system problem, and if they need parts, we'll sit until they arrive. That should mean a day or two of shore leave when I'll be able to get myself up to the Calanais stones. I'll hire myself a car though – no more trackable bikes.

It's going to be déjà vu all over again on Lewis. The last time I was in Stornoway was in the run-up to the Incident, with a body on board, though in that lumbering Marine Scotland vessel. I must be the only human being in any world who remembers this.

But then there were all those trips to visit the grandparents when we were kids, with Dad growing up there. Every Easter hols. Not the best time if your grandparents are seriously religious. No escape on Good Friday or Easter Sunday. What seemed like hours in church both days. The fun came in the summer visits, long northern days me and Donnie would spend in the grounds of Stornoway Castle. Great memories, those.

Well, the grandparents are dead now. I know this is still true from chatting to Mam and Dad. I started to poke around my family history with them, just to make sure I was well up on here-and-now Hulkie and not going to make embarrassing mistakes. Back then, before that Marine Scotland visit, I was there for Ganny McIver's funeral. That shed-load of cousins, what with my Granda being third of seven children. Dozens of cousins – sounds like a slogan.

Part of my current plan is to chase up cousin Steven. Of course, I might never have come across him again but for the dead body and him being in the police. *That* Steven knew a lot of the old ladies who live by the Calanais stones and their stories about those stones.

According to him, Ganny McIver's great grandma was a witchy person who lived over there and the women have a story she's still about in some form. Creepy, or creepy? Was she the old woman I met at the stones before the Incident, or was that one of the Big Three who cut off our timeline? Dad was pretty reticent about the witchy ancestor when I asked him. Sounds like Ganny McIver really hated it and he got teased about it at school.

Anyway, I'm going to try and pick Steven's brains this time round too. I already googled him, and he is still in the police here-and-now. Lucky for me he didn't become a schoolteacher instead. My note took a while to write – reminding him about the funeral and asking if we could meet up. He might not remember who I am, since here-and-now Steven hasn't met me – assuming we did meet – since the funeral. And that was seven years ago.

I'll hand it in at the Police Station for them to pass on to him. I hope he's not off on leave or in some big, complicated case, though that does seem a bit unlikely in a place as small as this.

At some point we're off to Jura and we finally get Mr Ross on board. He has business there and apparently Jura is short of decent places to stay for rich business types. Neither the video meeting nor the druggie vision warm me to the man, though I guess the vision bit was just my unconscious telling me to beware, as if it needed to. I don't want to end up clagged in Ross spider-web stuff like Cal and Rial seemed to be. Whatever that really means.

More hindsight sooner would have been handy, as I'm on an open-ended contract. Which means there's a penalty if I close it without client agreement. Which would appear in my Seafarer's Book. Yes, that was a first-class blunder, but then I thought it was all going to be simple and short. Hah! Wrongo, Hulkie!

Chapter 11 - Malcolm

Sunday June 12th – Ormacleit Hotel, South Uist

Was that it? Was Helen really not going to discuss things further? After what she'd just announced, how could she possibly stand there, calmly chatting with my daughter, as if nothing had happened?

Angry and upset, I manoeuvred through the throng, and returned to my room. There was supposed to be a final luncheon, but more strained jollity was the last thing I wanted. I packed my bag, went down to reception, and returned my room card. The family had dispersed, and there was no sign of Helen.

As I left the hotel, the strange music welled up and subsided. I looked around and saw, beyond my Land Rover, the shimmering shape of who I now knew to be Rial. I ran over the drive towards them, but only caught the briefest glimmer of a Cheshire cat grin. There was nothing untoward in the back of the Land Rover. I should have checked the front.

I got in, belted up and set off out of the hotel.

Bernie. Bernie has something to tell me.

At the main road I turned south to St Mary's church. I'd cut it very fine. As I arrived, Grant's parents and Bernie were just boarding the hotel mini-bus. I hooted the horn. Bernie waved and came across. I gestured to her to join me.

'This is really uncomfortable,' said Bernie, clambering into the passenger seat. 'Couldn't you buy a Range Rover?'

'Nice to see you too, Bernie,' I said. 'I do need to get going, to catch the ferry. What was it you wanted to tell me?'

'Can't we go somewhere more civilised?' said Bernie. 'There's lots of time to talk before lunch.'

'I really don't want to get sucked back in,' I said. 'Besides, I've checked out.'

'But we're your family!' said Bernie.

'I know,' I said. 'I know. Though, to be honest, I'm not so sure about you.'

'That's unfair,' said Bernie. 'I did what I could. You know that.'

Let's not go there.

'What do you want to tell me,' I said. 'I gather you've met someone. That's not really my business, is it?'

'He's more than someone,' said Bernie. 'I think he really understands.'

'Let me guess,' I said. 'French. A psychiatrist. He couldn't be called Thierry, could he?'

'How can you possibly know that?' said Bernie, shocked. 'I've not told anyone.'

Big mistake. That really is privileged knowledge.

'Lucky guess,' I said. 'Besides, Helen isn't nobody. Not that she's said anything to me.'

'That's a cheap gibe,' said Bernie. 'Helen's my close friend. You know that.'

'Fair enough,' I said grudgingly. 'I hope it works out.'

'He's asked me to marry him,' said Bernie.

'What's stopping you?' I said, nonplussed. 'I offered you a divorce, years ago. You said no.'

'It's not that straightforward,' said Bernie.

'I thought you just applied to the Pope,' I said.

'Don't be flippant,' said Bernie. 'This is a big deal for me.'

'And it isn't for me?' I said.

Bernie shrugged.

'I've no idea any longer,' she said. 'Can't we discuss this amicably? Please? You're not coming back, are you.'

'No,' I said. 'No.'

'That's clear then,' said Bernie. 'Well, we'll need a civil divorce first.'

'Always practical,' I said. ' Look, so long as I'm not to blame, just send me the papers, and I'll sign them. We still have the same solicitor, don't we? We can split the costs.'

'Thank you,' said Bernie. 'I'll get on it. What about the house?'

'It's fully paid up,' I said. 'I don't really want it. You could buy me out. Or we could sell it. But I don't need the money immediately. Do you?'

'No,' said Bernie. 'But you know Alison and Grant are living there.'

'Well,' I said, 'let's wait until they've got somewhere of their own.'

Bernie heaved a big sigh.

'Thank you, Malcolm,' said Bernie. 'I've been dreading this. You've no idea.'

'I am sad,' I said, feeling far more relieved than I'd ever imagined. 'Really. But, like you say, let's just get on with it.'

I put the Land Rover in gear, and we drove back to the hotel in silence.

The journey north to Lochmaddy was uneventful, and the ferry, for once, was on time. As we pulled out of the harbour, I realised that the super-yacht beyond the breakwater must be the one Helen was working on.

Helen. She really was totally barking. Awful things happen to loads of people. They can't turn back time. They get help, and mostly get over it. Why couldn't she?

Yes, the worlds changed. Yes, that's mind boggling. Yes, it's perpetually weird things not having happened, or having happened differently. Yes, I trip myself up all the time, with things that I might have forgotten, even though I never knew them, and things that weren't, even though I remember them.

Like giving Alison the arrowhead. Not in this world.

Like Thierry. He was from that other world. But Bernie doesn't remember. I don't suppose he does either. I bet Helen does, though.

Helen wants everything to stay the same as it is now, but to no longer remember *before*. How's that going to work? When the witches changed the worlds – if they were even witches – things went back to pretty well how they'd been, before *Fundamental Forces* opened up their transilience gate. That was back to a known world. But is there a world where nothing changes except Helen's memory? How's that going to work? I just hope she gets over it, and gives up this crazy idea of going to Lewis to find the so-called witches.

But suppose she doesn't get over it. Suppose the witches try to change things for her, and it all goes pear shaped. What happens to me? Does my world change again? Would I have to go through all this nonsense with Bernie again? Would I even have met Polly?

Oh. Polly. Oh.

I drove back down the Trotternish Peninsula to Portree, and stopped at the harbour side cafe.

'It's you again,' said the proprietor, before I'd even sat down. 'Did the police find your friend?'

'My friend?' I said. 'Who do you mean?'

'Nando,' said the proprietor. 'The guy who got out of the back of your wagon.'

'I didn't even know he was there,' I said.

'Pull the other one,' said the proprietor.

'He was a stowaway,' I said. 'What do they want him for?'

'They didn't say,' said the proprietor, 'but it'll be drugs, you'll see. I gave them the CCTV footage. They'll probably contact you. Anyway, what'll it be?'

I made my order, sat down, and phoned Polly, which went straight to voice mail. I left a moderately, but not very, concerned, message, adding that I had some good news.

When my tea and scones arrived, I wolfed them down, and headed on home. It's a four-hour drive, but I was tired of travelling, and hammered down the road.

On the far side of Glen Coe, I noticed that I was running out of fuel. So, instead of taking the Achallader turnoff, I carried on off the Moor to the *Tartan Trading Post*, and topped up the tank.

'Hello Malcom,' said Jennie, the attendant, when I went into the booth to pay. 'Did they find the guy who was with you?'

This is getting serious.

'He wasn't really with me,' I said, defensively.

'I know that,' said Jennie. 'I showed the police the CCTV. It's pretty obvious you didn't see him. But I think Dougie'll still want to interrogate you.'

'Mercilessly, no doubt,' I said. 'I'd best turn myself in.'

Jennie laughed.

'Turn yourself into what?' she said.

'Och, you Wiccans will have your little joke,' I said. 'How much is that, please?'

I'd just parked up, when Dougie came out of the next-door cottage.

'Malcolm!' he said. 'A wee word please.'

I knew it was serious. He usually calls me Malco.

'What's it all about?' I said.

'Let's talk inside,' said Dougie.

'Of course,' I said. 'Your place or mine?'

'You're just back,' said Dougie. 'Why don't you come to ours. Leave your things in the Land Rover, please. I'll need to search it.'

'Do you want to do that now?' I said, suddenly worried about what Rial might have stashed away.

'No, no,' said Dougie. 'Come and have a wee cuppa. Glenys has made a fruit loaf.'

'That sounds nice,' I said. 'Lead on.'

We went into Dougie and Glenys' cottage, and along the corridor to their living room. Glenys got up to greet us.

'I'll get the tea,' she said. 'And leave you to it.'

'Thanks,' said Dougie. 'God, I hate doing this with pals.'

'For the second time, as well,' I said.

'The first time,' said Glenys quickly, as she left the room.

Whoops. Another time slip.

'Oh yes,' I said. 'That speed infringement hardly counts.'

'Amazing that you managed it, in that old crate of yours,' said Dougie. 'Let's not beat about the bush. You had an unknown passenger from Crainlarich. You discovered him in Portree. But you treated him to scones. I'd have thrown the book at him. What's that about?'

'I felt sorry for him,' I said. 'That's all. He'd done me no harm.'

'Did he give a name?' said Dougie.

'Nando,' I said.

'Like the chicken chain,' said Dougie. 'You're quite sure he didn't emerge before Portree?'

'Quite sure,' I said. 'Anyway, he paid for his scones. Look.'

I fished out the silver coin.

'Interesting,' said Dougie. 'I've an app for that.'

He moused up his mobile, and pointed the camera at the coin.

'What are you doing with a numismatic app?' I said. 'Money's for spending, you always say.'

Dougie ignored me, and scrutinised the screen.

'King James shilling,' he said. '1605 to 6. It'd be worth around four hundred quid, if it was original.'

'What do you mean, original?' I said.

'It's pristine, isn't it,' said Dougie. ''It's obviously a fake. Or at best a modern striking. He doesn't seem like a counterfeiter. If he can make coins that good, what's he doing cadging rides?'

Blimey, Dougie's a good cop. As well as a good cop.

Dougie handed the coin back to me.

'Not evidence?' I said.

'Of what?' said Dougie. 'A prank? Where did he say he was heading?'

'Islay,' I said.

'That's helpful,' said Dougie. 'What was he after on Islay?'

'He was looking for the Lord of the Isles,' I said.

'That'll be right,' said Dougie. 'Come on. I need to check the Land Rover.'

We went back down the corridor, and across the yard to my cottage. There was no sign of Glenys.

'Keys, please,' said Dougie, holding out his hand.

'It's unlocked,' I said. 'You know that.'

'Sorry,' said Dougie. 'Routine.'

He let himself into the front of the Land Rover and systematically searched under the seats and the pockets and the glove compartment. Then he went through the back.

'Find anything?' said Glenys, coming round the side of my cottage.

'Nothing,' said Dougie. 'Where's ma tea, Mrs Wumman?'

'In the tea bag,' said Glenys.

Dougie laughed. A well-worn routine.

'I'd best let it out, then,' said Dougie. 'You're in the clear, mate.'

He handed me the keys, and returned to their cottage.

'Good thing I got there before he did,' said Glenys.

'What do you mean?' I said. 'Did you find something in the Land Rover? What did you find?'

'Later,' said Glenys, tapping the side of her nose. 'Come and have some fruit loaf.'

Chapter 12 - Helen

Monday June 13th – Stornoway, Lewis

I help Velho start the turbines up at seven as per orders, given we are due for our refuelling slot at 9.30. There will be at least one road tanker's-worth just for us. Then breakfast on the move, with Monsieur in a grump according to Elena, as he had to get up even earlier than normal to do his fresh pastries. As usual no sign of Rial; as usual Cal gets through more than his share of the pastries.

Boris is up on the Bridge of course, and Elena takes him his breakfast. Rial got me out of one hole but I'm guessing Boris does still remember of his shipment is missing and probably still blames me. I plan to watch my back around him. Come to that, could be the whole of the permanent crew are in on it, in which case I'm not flavour of the month with any of them. Mebbe Monsieur is hockling in my coffee.

We arrive in good time before nine, after hanging around near the harbour entrance for ten minutes to let a ferry in ahead of us. They turn rightwards for the ferry terminal and we move left to the Esplanade Quay for the fuelling station. We're tying up for the first time since the Azores.

Different quay to my last visit and a great view of Stornoway Castle across the inlet, though it's largely hidden in the summer green of one of the few woods on this island.

Then there's the usual tying-up faff. Our quay is right by the Port Authority Office and a guy arrives rather promptly to check our seafarer's books, passports and all the other ship paperwork. He sits at a table in the lounge and we go up one at a time. I'm a UK national anyway, but none of the permanent crew are, and without a seafarer's book they'd need visas.

As Cal has been enrolled as cabin boy, he has a seafarer's book, but I watch to see what will happen with Rial. Rial hands the guy something and he nods, but it didn't look like a seafarer's book to me. And there was a split-second of weird music as well, though nobody else seems to hear it.

After the Port Authority guy has gone back ashore, we have to attach the fuel line. I help Velho, and eventually we start refuelling. It's a smelly business, and naturally all the usual precautions must be followed: no naked lights, no using mobile phones, and no cooking. So the Captain gives us all shore leave for the day except himself and Velho.

After we get our black bags out on the quay that is – all the food waste and rubbish from our trip since the Azores. As usual, Cal moans all the time we are lugging them. Rial is nowhere to be seen again.

Finally we can go ashore.

'Coming for a coffee?' Elena asks me.

'I'll look for you later, man,' I tell her. 'Got a family errand to run first – my folks come from round here.'

I head off up the streets to the police station to hand in my note for Steven.

There's a bit of a queue at the desk, but as the conversation is in Gaelic I can't earwig on it. Eventually I hand my note over to the uniform. I tell him I'm a visiting relative and he tells me Steven is about, though in a meeting. That's good. The note has both my mobile number and my email. If he wants to get in touch, he can.

I exit, wondering whether I can track Elena down for the coffee – there's bound to be a place near the quay and it's only ten minutes back. My phone's map app gives me a selection and I head for *Coffee n'Cocktails* as the most likely. Sure enough I can see Boris, Elena and Monsieur, heads together in conversation round a table inside. But as I enter all three stop talking, and look at me. No smiles or welcome. Guess who they were talking about?

'Hi,' I say. 'Can I get you guys anything?'

'No,' says Boris, rather shortly.

I get myself a large cappuccino and sit down.

'So McIver,' Boris begins, at half his usual volume. 'You visit the police here, yes? Why is this?'

I guess I should have realised someone might follow me. No wonder they all look so jumpy.

'Well, Yuri Petrovich, my family come from Stornoway and I'm hoping to meet up with some of my relatives here. The cousin I know best happens to work for the police, and as I've lost his contact details, I dropped off a note for him at the police station.'

'Is good story,' says Boris, looking as if he doesn't believe a word of it.

'It's a true one,' I tell him, looking him straight in the eye. Time to clear this one up. I lower my voice and lean in.

'Look, Yuri Petrovich, I do know you guys have stuff on board you'd rather the police didn't know about. For one thing, Cal has been at your supplies. But you think I want to be on a ship where the police find something like that? Does me no good at all. So stop looking at me as if I plan to be a snitch.'

'What is "snitch"?' Boris asks aggressively.

'This is someone who tells the tales,' says Monsieur helpfully. 'She is saying she will not tell the tales on us.'

'She better not,' Boris says.

I glare at him in a 'you-and-whose-army sort of a way' but keep my mouth shut.

'Would a little recompense help?' says Elena, looking at Boris.

'No thank you,' I say sharply. Bad enough I know about this, but if things go pear-shaped and I'm in on the deal, I'll be in real trouble.

'Just move it off the ship, man, get it delivered, and I'll be happy.' But not very. I don't say that.

'Don't worry, it's in hand,' says Elena.

In some of those black bin bags mebbe? I really hope so. I don't say that either.

There is a silence.

Then Monsieur finishes his coffee with an expression of distaste and gets up.

'It is for me to see what the local supplies can offer us,' he says. 'Perhaps some venaison, or faisan. And whether there is anywhere with a better quality than this for lunch.'

Elena follows his example. 'I'm for shopping,' she says. 'There's bound to be cashmere or tweed somewhere in this town.'

And before I can worry about being left on my own with Boris, he looks at his watch. 'I go also,' he says.

Good, he isn't going to ask about the two missing packets. Oh – could be he thinks Cal took them after what I just said. Oops.

I finish my coffee slowly, then decide to go for a walk round the inlet to the Castle. It'll get me out of the way of the crew. Though it is also what I did on my pre-Incident visit. Déjà vu all over again.

Unlike the South Uist castle, Stornoway's isn't ancient – some Victorian Lord had it built. I wander around the woods for a long while, remembering how Donnie and I rampaged about in made-up stories of wars and adventures. Then a shower blows in, driving me into the Castle itself. I didn't make it in there on my pre-Incident trip.

There's a café and a museum; I decide to get myself a soup and sarnie. I'm about to roll into the café when I see of all people – Boris! – at a table with a young woman. He doesn't half collect them. She looks rather smart and corporate, and I wonder what they are talking about. Then my eye catches a well groomed young man two tables away who to my surprise takes a very quick pic with his phone pointed right at Boris and his squeeze. He could easily be a cop. I really hope this isn't the prelude to some real police bother.

Boris is high up a list of people I don't want to meet right now. I back off quickly and do the museum.

It has not a lot in it – mostly placards about endless clan wars and some old bits and pieces plus lots of tweed. Then a trail of school trip children and noise takes me down the far end to The Exploratorium.

That turns out to be one of those hands-on science things a lot of museums have these days to bring in the punters. This one has the usual stuff around gravity and momentum – basically dropping and banging things: kids love that. To my surprise it also has a 'Quantum Corner'. Not something I know that much about, but after listening to the Americans, and with Malcolm telling me Mr Ross has a company in the area, I decide to find out more.

No hands-on in this section – of course. But some natty animations driven by touch screens and just a few kids stabbing them randomly to see what they do. One covers light being waves and particles at the same time: I vaguely remember that from school. And electrons jumping into orbits round an atom, a very pretty animation. Schrödinger's cat, alive and dead also at the same time until you take a look; a bit hard to take. Seems Schrödinger thought so too and was trying to debunk the whole thing.

But wait a minute – this animation shows it does work if the world splits and the cat was alive in one world and dead in another depending on which one you ended up in. Though what it doesn't point out is what *I* know: *you* split too, and since you remember different things you get to be different people in the different timelines. Howay, I could tell the Americans a thing or two. Of course, they'd never believe me. You bet I keep quiet about the Incident.

Then I'm pulled up by the last placard: 'The Exploratorium Thanks Our Quantum Corner Sponsor: *Quantum Solutions*.' The very Mr Ross company that Malcom mentioned. Spooky!

I suddenly wonder whether Rial's weird reply to me, about being in the most probable place, was a riff on quantum stuff. After all, Rial is Mr Ross' Personal Assistant. If electrons can jump position, mebbe someone-or-something like Rial can too? Like turning up in the hotel and then bailing me out with Boris? Well, that's mebbe a bit wild. Though given the Incident, what's not wild?

It's mid-afternoon and I decide to go back to see how the refuelling is going. As I leave, my phone rings – and not with a number it knows.

Yes, it's Steven. Would I like to come out for a meal this evening? With him and his girlfriend. In the Arts Centre restaurant at 7. It's on the tip of my tongue to say we had lunch there a couple of years back, but I catch myself in time. That was pre-Incident, and not this Steven. I tell him I'll check with the Captain, but hope to be there.

The girlfriend bit is a pain. It will probably be hard to ask Steven about my ancestor and all that with a random person present. Though good for him – the pre-Incident Steven seemed too wrapped up in his work to be much of a dating man.

Walking back through the town I realise my dress uniform is still in the wash after Boris' attentions, and I don't have any other special occasions gear. That means I have to do something I hate. Clothes shopping. Lucky for me, my phone says there is a vintage clothing store near the harbour. I come away with a smart silk tunic that fits me, if in a rather vivid Chinese paeony pattern.

When I get back to the *Midsummer Queen*, refuelling is still going, but Velho tells me we are on the last 1000 gallons or so. And there's bad news about our specialist navigation trouble-shooters, due the next day. It seems the ferry that came in just before us this morning also has a navigation problem. And they get first dibs, because with no ferry, things are in a shambles for the whole town. So we have to wait. Which of course suits me.

Refuelling didn't finish in time for Monsieur to cook, and the Captain tells us all to get our evening meal in town. Boris says he'll get the two of them a take-away and stay onboard. Given how much he likes his nights ashore that's pretty fishy, but not my problem. Rial leaves with Cal, who looks glum. Given my earlier slip I'm glad Rial is keeping an eye on him. I announce I am eating with my cousin and his girlfriend. Good luck if they follow me this time.

The Arts Centre looks much the same as pre-Incident, to my relief. A big modern building with a glass-topped tower. Steven is waiting in the foyer looking very posh in yes, a tweed jacket. His girlfriend is a small, slender woman with dark hair cut in that elegant way you get in a pricey salon. She's wearing what looks like a designer trouser suit and carrying a Gucci handbag. Not short of money then. She also has one of those too-perfect make-up jobs they do in beauty salons that make the victim look like an android. At least, I think so.

But I have to make a big effort to keep my face neutral. Because she is the woman Boris was talking to in the Castle café. I wonder whether Steven knows about that?

'Helen, good to see you again,' says Steven. 'You've not changed at all since we last met. This is my girlfriend, Lucy Lopez. Lucy, my cousin Helen McIver. Our grandfathers were brothers.'

'Steven has told me so much about you, Helen,' says Lucy. She has a mid-Atlantic accent and is clearly not Russian. 'I've been *dying* to meet you since he told me you were in town.' She says that with a little too much emphasis. Mebbe she thinks I'm playing gooseberry.

We go upstairs to the restaurant, with its view over the harbour. I can see this morning's ferry is still down there but our quay is not visible. The menu is mainly seafood, but it looks OK. We order a bottle of white wine too.

'What brings you to Stornoway, Lucy?' I ask. 'I guess from your accent you didn't grow up here?'

'Lucy's been visiting us often,' Steven chips in. 'She's been organising an exhibit at the Castle Museum that her company have sponsored. My good fortune, given she's based in Glasgow.'

'Oh, you must be with *Quantum Solutions*,' I say quickly. 'I was at the exhibition this afternoon. You and your company have done a great job.'

'Why thank you, Helen,' she says. Mebbe she always sounds over-enthusiastic. 'We're a small but growing high-tech company and it's so good to find you have heard of us. I must have missed you this afternoon, I was over there myself checking our displays out. But I was going to ask you the same question, Helen. You don't sound in the least like Steven.'

She gives him what looks to me a rather proprietorial smile.

'My family moved to Wearside,' I say. 'I was born in Sunderland.'

'Oh, so you're a Geordie?'

Red rag to a bull is that! I put her right. 'No, Geordies are from Newcastle. We're known as Makems.'

'Oh Helen, how cute!'

'And are you a quantum physics person yourself?' I say quickly, trying not to let that last remark get to me.

'I did my PhD in quantum physics,' she says. 'My topic was *A Spin-Optical Quantum Computing Architecture*. I am so lucky, Helen, to be working for a company that is turning the theories I investigated into practical devices.'

'Are you guys building quantum computers at Rannoch Moor, then?'

'Helen, you are right in one. But we only recently opened at Rannoch, so I'm surprised you've heard about our new plant. Has our fame spread to Wearside already?'

'My cousin – well also Steven's – works over on Rannoch Moor', I say. 'He's a ranger.'

For a moment her assured mask seems to slip a little and I can see real surprise.

'Not Malcolm Nicholson?'

'Yes, do you know him? Small world and all that.'

'Goodness me, Helen, I was speaking to your cousin Malcolm only last week. What a coincidence! And what a nice helpful man he is too.'

Really? That doesn't sound like Malcolm. But I don't say that of course.

Our starters arrive and Steven looks relieved – he hasn't managed many words in edgeways.

There's less chat as we eat, but I gather Lucy should have left on the ferry that is stuck in the harbour. Today's flight was full, so she's leaving on tomorrow's. She's getting *QS* to pick up her car from Ullapool for her; sounds like she's pretty senior. I wonder whether she knows Mr Ross but decide not to ask. I say as little as possible about the ship. I do not mention Boris.

It turns out that Lucy is good at annoying remarks. For example, how on earth do I manage for clothes as a taller woman? With a look at my tunic that suggests she wouldn't be seen dead in it. Is the *Midsummer Queen* a nice place to work? Does working at sea mean I am not allowed to use make-up? How do I cope with all those men in crews? Steven tries to keep up with her, smoothing things over. She does not mention Boris.

After the main course Lucy announces she will just go and fix her face.

'Uaireannan! Lucy is very high powered,' Steven says once she is out of earshot. 'She can come over larger than life sometimes.'

'No problem,' I say gently. 'I'm used to all sorts. I often deal with customers a bit like her.'

Time to get my plan on the road.

'Steven, is there any chance we could have a short family chat while I'm here? This isn't the time or place, but I'm doing some family history research and I'd love to pick your brains.' Family history research makes a useful cover story.

'Dè an co-thuiteamas. I was also hoping to have a quiet word with you. Nothing official you understand. Just we don't get big private yachts like yours here so often and it makes us curious when one turns up.'

Oh, that sounds tricky. Just what my crewmates don't want. But how am I going to get what *I* want otherwise? And am I going to tell him about Lucy meeting Boris?

'Well, nothing to hide,' I say brightly. 'Do you have a slot tomorrow? We're waiting for some repairs, but they're busy with the ferry it seems.'

'I'll text you,' Steven says.

'Conspiratorial cousins is it?' Lucy is back. 'Family secrets? Do tell!'

'Just boring stuff about my niece's christening this last weekend,' I say, not meeting Steven's eyes.

By the time I get back to the ship, I am exhausted. Lucy is hard to keep up with. There's nobody about, so I turn in and read.

Journal June 12

Steven just texted me: a meet for a coffee tomorrow at 10. Not, I'm relieved to see, at *Coffee n'Cocktails*. It's a tricky one. I can't grass on my crewmates, but I'm not a fan of outright lies either. Nor do I want the crew to know about the meeting, but if Steven gets wind of that he'll know I'm hiding something. I'll just have to play it by ear. Hoping to get myself off to the Calanais stones in the afternoon.

I wonder what Lucy and Boris were talking about? I wouldn't put Boris down as a museum-funder. Poor Steven looks like a hooked man to me. It's a dilemma whether to mention the meeting when I see him – if he doesn't know, then it isn't kind, but there again, Boris is bad news and he ought to know about it.

Nearly time to get my head down. But I'm getting more and more stressed by the weird dreams I get in the early morning. They are waking me and I have trouble sleeping again afterwards. That's the

Hulkie who has been regularly compared to a log for ability to sleep through a racket.

Last night I dreamed about the pre-Incident three witchy women and their huge mesh of timelines, with blackness surrounding the one we were in then. They said they had to kill it before it poisoned even more around it. And then I was out on the moor again with reality somehow cracking up around me. The Incident. It feels like the green stone is eating at my brain.

After that I was in the druggie vision again. Ross, with his sinister spider web around Rial and Cal. Rial staring straight at me. And after that something Malcolm didn't mention in his one. I'm able to fly and I lift off from the beach and fly out to sea. But the sea rears up in front of me into a terrifying whirlpool, and I'm sucked right into it. I try to fly through it, I see a light at the end. The first time it turned into the ceiling light in the hotel bedroom. This time, I woke up.

Chapter 13 - Malcolm

Monday June 13th – Rannoch Moor

I awoke with a splitting headache and a ferocious thirst. Dougie's fulsome apology for policing me involved far too many samples from his substantial collection of malt whiskies. Glenys was hospitable as always, but said nothing further about what, if anything, she'd found in my Land Rover. I'd need to catch up with her.

I drank several mugs of water, took a couple of paracetamol, and had a shower, which revived me enough to feed the increasingly disgruntled cat, and assemble a large greasy breakfast.

As I ate, I worked through the pile of post that had accumulated on the hall table. So much for the Internet being the death of paper. There were a few letters from the banks and the utility companies, but nothing that seemed urgent. The rest was all advertising, for mortgages, insurance, home extensions, and private medicine. I was about to dump these in the paper recycling, when my eye was caught by a mailing from the *Peyroux Investment Fund*, guaranteeing 15% return on any sum, with unlimited withdrawals. Perhaps *Quantum Solutions* were really onto something?

Replete, I set off up onto the Moor for what I hoped would be the start of a quiet week of wrangling visitors. I'd had enough family for now, and more than enough of weird coincidences.

Outside the Visitor Centre was a large cardboard box. It must have arrived on Friday, after I'd left. Thank goodness it hadn't rained. I wasn't expecting anything, though. I unpeeled the polythene wrapped delivery notice. Inside was Lucy Lopez's business card. The back read: *Enjoy!*

I tried to pick up the box. It was absurdly heavy. I unlocked the Visitor Centre, went through to the storeroom, and emerged with the trolley. Then I manhandled the box onto the platform, and wheeled it into the reception area.

Inside the box was a large Italian coffee maker. This was crazy! Where on earth could it go? It would have to be plumbed in. And who would pay for the installation? Let alone the coffee. My budget barely stretched beyond stationary and cleaning products.

But Lucy Lopez seemed to have thought of everything. Nestled next to the coffee machine was a brown envelope, with a cheque for £1000 from *Quantum Solutions*, made out to *Rural Resources*. This felt tantamount to a bribe, though for what I'd no real clue. Surely our attitude to the power cable was pretty well irrelevant, set against what seemed to be an international conglomerate, who must have the ear of government. I'd need to check all this with head office in Fort William.

I wheeled the box through to the storeroom. Then I sat down at the counter and fired up the laptop. One message, from head office. Please could I come for an urgent meeting. Maybe tomorrow? I'd no timetabled visitors.

There's a coincidence. Just what I needed.

I acknowledged the meeting. Then I checked my phone. I should have turned it on first thing. There were two missed calls from Polly, and a text. Please would I get in touch. I immediately called her.

'Malcolm!' said Polly. 'Where have you been? I was getting worried.'

'It's a long story,' I said.

'It always is,' said Polly. 'Is everything all right?'

I gave her the edited highlights of my weekend. I didn't mention the stowaway, or the trip. Or Bernie's bombshell. Maybe I should have done.

'It sounds like I was wise not to come,' said Polly. 'Anyway, I think I can get away this weekend after all. Are you free?'

'I thought you were going to Jura,' I said. 'And I was going to join you.'

'It's all up the air,' said Polly. 'Look, suppose I come to you.'

'That sounds really nice,' I said. 'To be honest, I've had enough travelling for a bit.'

'It would be good to spend some time together,' said Polly. 'And I could catch up with Glenys.'

Really? Not just Megan?

'I didn't realise you were in touch,' I said. 'You've barely met.'

'Oh no,' said Polly. 'We've been in regular contact for ages. She's been incredibly helpful.'

'Helpful?' I said. 'How's she been helpful?'

'With making sense of it all,' said Polly.

Oh, right.

'But you can talk with me,' I said, 'can't you?'

'Of course I can!' said Polly. 'But this is different. She's got a really interesting take on how it all works.'

'Do you mean the Wiccan stuff?' I said. 'But you're a scientist. Wicca's hardly rational.'

'I don't see any conflict,' said Polly. 'Just different views of the same thing.'

'Well,' I said, 'if it helps, of course. But I am very surprised.'

'Let's talk about it at the weekend,' said Polly.

'When do you think you might come?' I said.

'Let's aim for Friday,' said Polly, 'but I trust we'll talk before then.'

'For sure!' I said. 'Big hugs!'

'Big hugs!' said Polly.

And ended the call.

After a quiet morning, briefly broken by an Austrian family in a camper van asking about wildlife, I drove up to the *Altnafeadh Hotel* for lunch. Dougie's police car was parked outside, and I could see his silhouette, framed in the bay window.

'The usual,' said Jeannie, the waitress.

That was a statement. I smiled and nodded.

'Malco!' said Dougie, as I sat down opposite him. 'Last night was a blast! I hope you got home all right.'

'Thankfully, my boots knew the way,' I said.

Dougie's radio phone rang.

'I better get this,' he said.

He got up and walked over to the door. All I could hear was his exasperated muttering.

'Sorry, Malco,' Dougie said, clipping the phone back onto his jacket, 'but I need to ask a favour.'

'Sure!' I said. 'But can't it wait until we've eaten?'

Jeannie was approaching with a laden tray.

'I'm afraid not,' said Dougie. 'A couple of tourists have got themselves bogged down on the Moor. No one else is available to help them. My steed's all tuckered out. And you're the ranger.'

I felt satisfyingly smug. Dougie's car certainly wasn't up to cross country driving.

'I'll put this aside for you, then,' said Jeannie. 'Let's hope it doesn't coagulate.'

'Come on pardner,' said Dougie. 'Let's hit the trail.'

Dougie's addiction to post-war Westerns was an endless source of slang. Yes, that war. The big one, last century.

We took the gravel track that ran west from the Hotel, over the Moor, towards Rannoch Station. Past the *Black Corries Lodge*, still shuttered, the gravel gave way to dirt. This was where *Quantum Solutions* wanted to lay tarmac.

The Moor was at its summer best. All the songs are right. The bracken really was golden, and the heather bloomed purple on the mountain flanks.

'How far are we going?' I said.

'The Menzies Stone,' said Dougie.

'Which side?' I said.

'Ours, unfortunately,' said Dougie. 'Not that it matters. There's no one free on the other side, either.'

'I wonder what they were trying to do,' I said. 'You need a 4x4 if you've any chance of making it right across.'

'They're in a 4x4,' said Dougie. 'Electric. The battery's flat.'

We both laughed. Electric car failures, especially on single track roads, were the bane of Dougie's duties.

'Look!' said Dougie. 'There they are!'

Up ahead was a Mercedes, bogged down in the drainage ditch to one side of the track. Two familiar figures were waving excitedly at us. The Americans. Dean and Martha.

'Malcolm Nicholson!' said Martha, as I got out of the Land Rover. 'So nice to see you again, honey! How was the christening?'

'You know these people?' said Dougie.

'Sorry,' I said. 'Dougie, this is Martha and Dean. I met them on South Uist. Martha and Dean, this is Dougie, our local policeman.'

'Nice to meet you, Dougie.' said Martha. 'Thank you for rescuing us.'

'We should have charged up in Fort William,' said Dean, 'but this looked like the right route.'

'The right route to where?' said Dougie.

'To the *Quantum Solutions* plant,' said Martha. 'They invited us to visit them before the conference.'

'Conference?' said Dougie. 'What conference?'

'That doesn't matter right now,' I said.

I got back into the Land Rover and reversed up to the Mercedes. Then I unhitched the hook from the stay, crawled under the car, and found the hitching point.

'All right,' I said. 'Let's give this a go. One of you needs to get in and steer. The others should push.'

Martha climbed into the Mercedes through the front passenger door. Dougie and Dean went round to the back.

I put the winch into gear. As the cable took the strain, Dougie and Dean put their backs into the boot, and the car lurched out of the ditch, onto the track.

'We'll tow you back to Crianlarich,' I said. 'You can recharge there.'

'But we've almost made it to the road,' said Dean.

'The road's miles away,' I said.

'No,' said Dean. 'It's just here.'

On the far side of the Menzies stone, fresh tarmac came to an abrupt halt.

'You knew about this!' I said to Dougie. 'Didn't you! That's why you went to Tulliallan. Why didn't you tell me?'

'Not now,' said Dougie. 'Not now.'

We slowly made our way back to the A82, Martha and Dean in the Mercedes. Dougie sat beside me, uncharacteristically quiet.

'I'll drop you here,' I said to Dougie, when we reached the *Altnafead Hotel*.

'No,' said Dougie. 'I'd best see this through.'

'What the fuck is going on?' I said, speeding up onto the main road. 'They don't have planning permission, do they.'

'It's private land,' said Dougie. 'As far as the Stone. They can do what they like.'

'It's a National Park, for fuck's sake,' I said. 'Someone must have OKed it.'

'They did,' said Dougie.

'That's why you were at Tulliallan, wasn't it,' I said.

'Yes,' said Dougie. 'I was going to tell you, but then there was all that nonsense with your stowaway.'

'What are the polis worried about?' I said. 'Littering?'

'Traffic management,' said Dougie. 'There's a consortium wants to promote what they're calling the Central 400, to rival the North Coast 500.'

'What's the route?' I asked.

'A loop out of Pitlochry, up to Inverness, and down the Great Glen,' said Dougie.

'That's never 400 miles,' I said.

'400 kilometres,' said Dougie. 'The stretch from the Stone to the Hotel's the last link.'

'Why go over the Moor?' I said. 'They could just carry on down to Tyndrum and round.'

'Search me,' said Dougie. 'If it goes through, there'll be a big increase is traffic in both directions. Great for local business, of course.'

'That's not what they're saying about the NC 500 in our Northern office,' I said. 'It's all about people ticking off their bucket lists. They don't give a stuff for the locals. Who's in the consortium?'

'I doubt you've heard of them,' said Dougie. 'The main backer's *Peyroux Holdings*.'

Why am I not surprised?

'They bankroll *Quantum Solutions*,' I said. 'It all fits together.'

'How do you know that?' said Dougie.

I told him about Lucy Lopez.

'She sounds like a piece of work,' said Dougie. 'Still, decent coffee would be a big improvement on that rubbish instant.'

I turned off the road at the *Tartan Trading Post*, and manoeuvred the Mercedes up to a charging point. Dean hooked it up, while Dougie took the American's details from Martha.

'Why on earth did you think you could get across the Moor?' I asked him.

'It's on the map,' said Dean.

'Map?' I said. 'What map?'

He scrabbled amongst the sheaf of papers in the driver's door pocket.

'Here,' said Dean, handing me a glossy brochure. 'On the back.'

The schematic map showed the *Quantum Solutions* plant in the centre of the moor. The A82 and A9 ran north-south on either side, both marked as thick red lines. Another thick red line ran east-west, from the Hotel via the plant to Pitlochry.

'If you build it, they will come,' said Dean. 'Surely half-assed to leave it unfinished. So like you Brits.'

'Where did you get this?' I asked.

'It came with the conference pack,' said Dean. 'Months ago.'

Bastards! It's all stitched up.

'Can I hang onto it, please?' I said.

'Sure thing,' said Dean.

I looked at the bottom of the brochure.

'Lucy Lopez!' I said, surprised.

'Who's she?' said Dean.

'The conference contact,' I said.

'Do you know her?' said Dean, suspiciously.

'Not really,' I said. 'She came to visit me a few days ago.'

'What was she wanting?' asked Dean.

'She works for *Quantum Solutions*,' I said. 'She's interested in the Moor, given where their plant's situated. Do you know her?'

'No,' said Dean, too quickly. 'No.'

'We're done,' said Dougie, closing his notebook.

'Thank you, officer,' said Martha. 'Which way should we go, honey?'

'Follow the road to Killin,' said Dougie, 'and then head for Pitlochry. On the other side of town, take the road west to Rannoch Station. Then ask someone. I've no clue how the new road connects. I doubt it's on sat-nav yet.'

Dougie turned to me.

'Come on,' he said. 'I'll buy you lunch.'

I folded up the brochure, and put it away in my inside jacket pocket.

Lunch was subdued. I was sure there was more Dougie wasn't telling me, but he wasn't volunteering anything, and I wasn't asking.

I returned to work, and wrote up a report for head office. That's standard when we're asked to help the emergency services. Apart from anything else, it looks good on the annual returns, and justifies keeping the Visitor Centre open. I hope.

The rest of the day was quiet. In the summer, traffic's often nose to tail, all the way up the Moor to Glencoe. North bound traffic must cross the carriageway, and it's a nightmare trying to get back onto the road in either direction.

Back at home, after a round of too long delayed chores, I was settling down on the sofa, when the phone rang.

'Dad!' said Alison, before I'd had time to answer. 'Have you heard from Miran?'

'Alison!' I said. 'What's happened?'

'She's disappeared!' said Alison. 'First thing, I heard Chris crying, which is unusual, as she's always been so attentive, and when I went to wake her, she was gone.'

'Sorry,' I said, 'but she's not come here. Would she even know how to get here? Was she all right at the christening?'

'I think she was a bit freaked by Helen,' said Alison. 'I've no idea why.'

Green stone stuff, no doubt. Why has this come back to haunt us?

'Did she leave a note?' I said.

'That's the strange thing,' said Alison. 'She didn't, but there was a shiny coin on her pillow. All silvery.'

'What does the coin look like?' I said.

'It's got Latin writing on it,' said Alison. '*Iacobus Rex.* That's King James, isn't it. But there hasn't been a King James for hundreds of years.'

'Did she say anything more about her boyfriend?' I asked.

'Not much,' said Alison. 'But she's desperate to find him.'

Must be the Cal bloke that Helen mentioned, the one I supposedly saw when I was tripping. But he didn't look anything like my stowaway.

'Have you told the police?' I said.

'What can I tell them?' said Alison. 'I don't even know her family name. All I wanted to do was help her. She seemed so gentle. I suppose if the police find her, they'll try to deport her. That's the last thing I want.'

'I could ask Dougie,' I said. 'He's mostly discreet. Have you got a picture of her?'

'There are tons of christening photos,' said Alison. 'I was going to make up an album for you and mum. She's in quite a few. But I'll send you one over right now.'

'I'll see what Dougie says,' I said. 'And don't worry. I'm sure she'll turn up.'

'Thanks dad!' said Alison. 'You know, she's a strange one, isn't she.'

'Why do you say that?' I asked.

'It's as if she'd never seen everyday things before,' said Alison. 'She seemed frightened of the car, at first, and was fascinated by the electric lights when we got home. It's as if she's from another time and place.'

'Hmm,' I said. 'That is strange.'

I heard yelping in the background.

'Oh,' said Alison, 'that's Chris. I better get going.'

'I'll be in touch soon,' I said. 'Love to you all!'

'And to you,' said Alison. 'Thanks again!'

Chapter 14 - Helen

Tuesday June 14th – Stornoway, Lewis

We're stuck here in Stornoway until the Comms company arrives to fault-analyse our navigation system. No news on that yet, the Captain tells us at breakfast.

'Well guys, enjoy a short break today. But be ready to come back if I text you,' he tells us, using his caring voice, accompanied by one of those brilliant smiles.

Velho has found some obscure and rather messy engine maintenance task, which seems to be his idea of a short break. Thankfully he doesn't need me. Boris and Elena are off on the two motorbikes and Monsieur says he has some game recipes to practise. Rial is absent again and Cal looks gloomy and says nothing at all. I say that I need a present for my sister-in-law and new nephew, which is true enough. It covers me for a wander round town and meeting up with Steven.

The café in Steven's text message was *An Taigh Cèilidh*, which is Cèilidh House according to my sketchy knowledge of Gaelic. Dad grew up speaking it and the grandparents were patchy in English so we kids picked up bits and pieces. Most of what I know these days though is the Gaelic equivalents of swear words, the ones Dad still uses. The Steven I met pre-Incident was indeed a rather showy Cèilidh dancer, but I don't expect much dancing at 10 am. I assume his choice has something to do with being out of sight of my crew.

It's another blowy day, with clouds westwards that look like rain, and I'm glad of my fleece. On the way I buy some prem-size babygros in the one kids' clothes shop my phone knows about. They look like dolls' clothes. When I walk into the café, I get a 'madainn mhath' from the guy behind the counter. I feel smug saying it back and showing that at least I can do good morning in Gaelic. I also feel happy Steven is already here, since I am a lot less sure I can order a coffee successfully in Gaelic.

'Welcome, Helen. I still remember that evening with us all after Old Mrs McIver's funeral – I think you made quite an impression on us.'

Hmm, that will have been the evening of single malts when a bevy of cousins, including Steven, kept asking me about my travels, and I spun some yarns.

'Oh, you know how seafarers can go on a bit,' I tell him.

When we're settled with our coffees, I wait for Steven to get started. Best do his stuff first, then mine.

'I hear your yacht is owned by a Russian?' he begins, in a casual tone. But I know when I'm being interrogated, even in a friendly way. This is Steven-the-detective.

'Yes, man, but I'm working a short contract for a guy in Glasgow who chartered it,' I tell him quickly. 'Mr Ross Peyroux, big wheel in Scotland I'm told. He's involved in a film project on Jura and there aren't any big-wheel type hotels there. He had his yacht brought over from the Caribbean so he can stay on it. That's rich people for you, man. He pays well too.'

'I've heard the name. He owns *Peyroux Holdings* I think. But not a Russian crew?'

'Only the mate, Yuri Petrovich. We've a skeleton crew really, five from the owner, two of us hired by Mr Ross, plus his PA.'

I decide to drop my bombshell. Steven has to know.

'I was surprised to see your girlfriend seems to know Yuri Petrovich, though. They were having coffee together at the Castle Museum together yesterday, I noticed.'

Steven-the-detective is not as good at a poker face as he ought to be I see. He looks like I slapped him on the neb with a wet fish.

'She didn't mention it,' he says finally, obviously struggling to get his voice under control. 'I can ask her about it.'

There's a pause as he makes a visible effort to get his questions back on track.

'Helen, I'll be open with you, why not? Our local masters are worrying about Lewis being a drugs gateway. And my mainland colleagues are worried about a big increase in a new drug called ayahuasca, a psychedelic thing from South America, similar to magic mushrooms. A yacht like yours would be one way of bringing it in.'

Now he's looking at me very directly, obviously to see if I flinch or colour. Full marks for professionalism I'd say.

'Well man, I'm only an electronics officer and a newbie in the crew. I've not noticed any drugs lying around, but there again I haven't been searching the ship either.' I look back with what I hope is a totally guileless expression.

'Just interested that you came up here to Stornoway when you are actually heading for Jura?'

'There's a fuel facility here and we haven't refuelled since the Azores. We came up west of Ireland and this was probably the closest UK facility. But I don't plot our course. You'd have to talk to the Captain.'

'Well, perhaps we will. That's not up to me.' He relaxes slightly. Steven-the-detective is done.

'Anyway, enough business. You said you were on a family history hunt?' He still sounds battered, minus his puppy enthusiasm. I feel a bit of a heel. But apologising is only going to make it all worse. I can see Lucy is on the way out as a girlfriend.

'My Dad set me off. He mentioned a famous ancestor, Margaret MacAskill. He said she came from over near the Calanais stones. Then clammed up as if he didn't much want to talk about her, which isn't like him.'

'A Thighearna, yes. She's well-known in these parts. The grandmother of old Mrs McIver that we buried, so not a relative of mine, but your great-great-grandmother. Not liked by the more religious-minded, and I'm guessing old Mrs McIver was sensitive on the topic. I recall my own grandfather claiming yours was wrong to marry her with such an ancestor.'

I'm pleased to see this has shaken Steven from his misery.

'But why wasn't she liked, man? What did she do?'

'Oh, she made prophecies. They'll be written down somewhere, folk used to take them seriously. Because she was said to be a bana-bhuidseach. Hmm, a female sorcerer, a witch I suppose you could say.'

This is what pre-Incident Steven told me too. And there were prophecies, which sort-of came true. Creepy stuff.

Steven is in his story-telling stride now.

'She did indeed live by the stones, and the old ladies over there say she is still about, if you can believe that. Some of them are your cousins too, though distant ones. That's how Lewis is, a small pond.'

'I'd love to talk to them! But I'm guessing they are Gaelic speakers and my Gaelic is just a few phrases. Do you know any family historians I could collar for a visit over there?'

'Given I suppose you will be away soon, probably nobody I can round up as quickly as that.'

'Aye, well.' Disappointing, though I'll still go and poke around.

Then Steven looks decisive.

'But I've an idea. Today it happens I'm to drive over to Carloway to interview some tourists, I'll be passing the stones. I can break the journey at one of your cousins and then leave you to walk the area until I come back. I expect Carloway to be a short session. Will this help?'

'Steven, you're a marra! A real friend, I mean. That would be great.' I have to hand it to him, I wouldn't have been nearly as helpful if someone had just busted up my love life. There again, Steven-the-detective may get another bite at the cherry as well on the way.

Here-and-now Steven has a nice car, a black BMW, just like pre-Incident Steven. He drives much the same way too, quite fast but with precision. And, of course, he asks more questions in a casual way. I tell him Boris and I are not on great terms because Boris is prejudiced against women in tech roles and thinks I don't know how to fix our navigation system. I tell him that the Captain is unnervingly charismatic, and Velho is a great engineering colleague. He can make of all that what he will.

It's not a long drive, and in half an hour we get to the cottages by the stones. Steven has rung ahead, and says Mrs Morrison is expecting us. Steven tells me that like a lot of old ladies she loves visitors, and she'll insist on feeding us, and to be patient about my questions. I realise, with a slight chill, that I know the name. After my last visit to the stones, before the Incident, when we got soaked in a storm, it was a Mrs Morrison who dried us off and gave us tea.

Mrs Morrison is bustling and active, grey haired, with eyes that look like they don't miss much. And she is indeed a here-and-now version of the woman I met before. No slips now, Hulkie!

Sure enough, she has plates of sandwiches and some tea for us, and I dig out my limited Gaelic to praise both. She beams, but her responses are that fast I can't make out very much. When we finish the sandwiches and are onto biscuits with more tea, Steven tells her about my family history quest. She rattles away back at him.

'Mrs Morrison says that she is 'of the blood' too,' Steven tells me. 'Round here that's status. And she says that Margaret MacAskill can only be seen by those of her own blood.'

'*Seen*? Has Mrs Morison really *seen* Margaret MacAskill? Who's been dead for a hundred and fifty years or so? Surely not, man.'

'Didn't I tell you that locally they think she's still about? Sorcerers are said to live on in some other form when they die.'

'Then what does she look like? When has Mrs Morrison seen her?'

I'd dismiss this whole thing as far-fetched, a figment, had I not met an old lady up at the Calanais stones myself before the Incident. Though she was one of the three witchy women I think, not a ghost of Margaret MacAskill. A witchy woman would be better, but a sorcerous ancestor might still be able to help me.

Steven asks my question, and then it's clear Mrs Morrison is telling him a story. I can hear the drama in her voice but frustratingly understand almost nothing, except the Calanais stones get several mentions.

'A Thighearna mhor!' Steven said finally, turning to me. 'That was some story. Margaret MacAskill is thought of as an answerer-of-difficult-questions, like an oracle. But only to be invoked in real need, or bad luck follows. And only by those of the blood. Now Mrs Morrison has a son in the British Army.'

I detect a note of disapproval in Steven's voice.

'His unit was sent to Afghanistan and Mrs Morrison wanted to know whether to press him to leave in case he was killed there. So she sought out Margaret MacAskill.'

'How? What did she do?'

'She says she went up to the great stone in the centre of the Calanais ring and said a summoning. That she cannot repeat to me because I am not of the blood. The sky darkened and then a mist rose from the ground. A woman she didn't know came out of the mist with a white linen headscarf like women used to wear and a shawl over her shoulders. She looked neither old nor young, Mrs Morrison says. She asked her question.'

'And did Margaret answer?'

'Mrs Morrison says that she did, but the answer is always a prophecy, not a 'yes' or a 'no', and prophecies must always be interpreted. It was something like...' Steven pauses, looking for the right English words I assume.

'...five moons shining blood falling, three suns rising life growing. Which she interpreted as meaning he would be wounded but survive.'

'And what did happen to him?'

'Mrs Morrison says she warned him, but he took no notice. Not being a believer in MacAskill and prophecies. But he was caught in an IED explosion in his first six months. Invalided out of active duty back to the UK. Now, she says, he is not so sceptical.'

Mrs Morrison nods solemnly. I guess she does know some English. I'd still be sceptical if I were her son, knowing the kind of thing that happened in Afghanistan with or without prophecies.

Steven thanks Mrs Morrison for the food and the story. I think. He gets up.

'Helen, I must go. I am due in Carloway in half an hour or so. I'll text you when I'm leaving to return.'

I get up too, but Mrs Morrison grabs my arm and motions me to sit down again.

'See you later,' I tell Steven.

Chapter 15 - Malcolm

Tuesday June 14th – Fort William

I was opening up the Visitor Centre when I heard a familiar vehicle drawing up. Sure enough, it was Dean and Martha's Mercedes. I got up to great them as they came into the building.

'Dean! Martha!' I said. 'I hadn't expected to see you again. How can I help you?'

'We just had to come back, honey,' said Martha. 'We really didn't thank you enough for all your help yesterday.'

'That's right,' said Dean. 'We might still be stuck on that god-forsaken Moor if it wasn't for you.'

'All part of the job,' I said. 'Did you make it round to *Quantum Solutions*?'

'No, honey,' said Martha. 'We were totally wiped out, and needed a break. We might head over there this morning.'

'We'd like to thank you properly,' said Dean, looking around. 'This whole place is pretty spartan. Maybe we could help with some renovations. Maybe we could start with a proper coffee machine, instead of that antiquated kettle of yours.'

Not another! Just what we need.

'That's very decent of you,' I said. 'But that's really not necessary.'

'Don't you just love that British reserve,' said Martha. 'Here, get in touch if you can think of anything.'

She dug in her bag and fished out a card:

Dr Martha Gellman, Co-Director, Sub-Atomic Systems Laboratory, Redwood Corporation

'Redwood Corporation?' I said. 'I thought you were academics.'

'We are, honey,' said Martha. 'These are our funders. We're sure they can find the price of a paint job.'

'And what would you want in return?' I said.

'Just keep your eyes and ears open,' said Dean. 'You could let us know if you hear of any new developments up at *Quantum Solutions.*'

'Or if Lucy Lopez comes back,' said Martha.

I quickly put two and two together.

'Are *Quantum Solutions* your rivals?' I asked.

'Oh no, honey,' said Martha. 'We're all scientists, all singing from the same hymn sheet. Come on Dean, let's get going. Thank you again.'

I set of to Fort William late in the morning. A summons from my boss was rare. It must be something serious. Carol was always professional, but could be a bit perfunctory.

The *Rural Resources* Central Highland office is well situated to the north of the town, just before the T junction with the Road to the Isles, in the grounds of the Old Inverlochy Castle. The office itself is a cruciform of four repurposed shipping containers, which is far nicer than it sounds. The two closest to the road form the visitor area and café. And the two behind house offices, and a decent sized meeting room, which is opposite the café, and great for ceilidhs, if you like that sort of thing. Enclosed corridors run between the containers, and the whole assembly is covered by a steeply pitched roof, essential in wild weather.

Carol has the office at the far end, with picture window views of Ben Nevis and the River Lochy. Lesley, her PA and bidie in, has the office next door. Lesley's door was open.

'Hello Malcolm,' she said. 'Long time no see.'

'Hello Lesley,' I said. 'Out of sight, out of mind.'

'Never!' said Lesley. 'What brings you this far north?'

Of course she knew.

'I've been summonsed,' I said. 'I hope it's nothing bad.'

'Oh no,' said Lesley, brightly. 'If it had been, you'd have got a letter from HR, not an email. I'll just check if she's free.'

Lesley picked up the phone handset and pressed a red button.

'That's Malcom,' she said, and put the handset down.

'In you go,' she said to me. 'See you later?'

'Hope so,' I said.

I knocked on Carol's door and let myself in.

'Hello Malcolm,' said Carol, from behind a huge computer monitor. 'Could you come round, please? I've some things to show you.'

Not one for small talk, Carol.

'Sure,' I said.

I trundled the office chair round the desk, and parked it next to Carol's mobility scooter.

'This is just between us,' said Carol, mousing up a spreadsheet.

'Of course,' I said.

'These are our visitor returns for the last five years,' said Carol. 'You can see that Glenfinnan's still enjoying the Harry Potter bounce, and we're pretty solid here. Your numbers are down a bit, but still healthy. The problem's Kyle. We'd gambled on people stopping to view the bridge, but they just blithely zoom over to Skye. We really can't go on subsidising them out of our core funding. But if we close Kyle, then Glasgow will say that we're not viable with only three centres, and they'll merge us with Grampians. I don't know about you, but I don't fancy commuting to Inverness.'

'No,' I said. 'No. But before we go any further, might I tell you something, please? I think it's germane but I didn't want to put it in writing.'

'Fire ahead,' said Carol. 'But keep it brief.'

'Have you heard of *Quantum Solutions*?' I said.

Carol beamed.

'Indeed I have,' she said. 'What are they to you?'

I told Carol about Lucy Lopez's visit, and the coffee machine. Then I gave her the £1000 cheque.

'This is wonderful!' said Carol. 'They really are serious!'

'You knew about this?' I said. 'You might have told me.'

'Well not exactly this,' said Carol. 'But Dr Lopez came to see me just after she saw you. She just barged in unannounced, and made us a proposition that I can't in good conscience refuse.'

'She told you about the road across the Moor?' I said.

'She certainly did,' said Carol. 'That's the key. Of course I said yes.'

Blimey!

'Is that really your call?' I said. 'What do Glasgow say?'

'It's nothing to do with Glasgow,' said Carol. 'We're a federation, remember?'

'But what about local sentiment?' I said, forlornly.

Without someone like Henry making a fuss, I feared no one would mind much.

'She says they'll be sensitive,' said Carol. 'That's why I wanted to see you. We need to show that we've done due diligence, and you're just the person.'

'You must have known I'd be against this,' I said. 'It'll ruin the Moor.'

'That's why you'll be taken seriously,' said Carol. 'I'd like you to visit Cruachan, and talk to the engineers. Be as Bolshy as you like. And report back to me. I've fixed up a visit for you for tomorrow morning. And Dr Lopez says they're sponsoring a conference in Glasgow on Thursday. I'd like you to represent us. And I'd like you to visit *Quantum Solutions* on the Moor. That'll be Friday.'

Blimey squared!

'Why can't you go?' I said. 'You know I'm not a political animal.'

Carol said nothing, and tapped the arm of her mobility scooter.

'Fair enough,' I said. 'I suppose I can do the conference, but I'm not sure I'm up for Cruachan. It's all underground. Can't someone else go?'

'No one else is free,' said Carol. 'Come on, you'll be fine. Look, you can have a few days off in lieu.'

'What about the cheque,' I said hopelessly. 'I can't just keep it, can I?'

'Leave it with me,' said Carol. 'I'll sort out the paperwork and add it to your budget. Maybe you could buy that data projector we've been talking about? But it's up to you. Just be sure to send in the receipts. Thanks for coming in. It's all for the best. You'll see. Email me on Friday with your report, please.'

She picked up her handset and pressed her red button.

'Lesley,' she said. 'Malcolm's just leaving. Please send him the details of the meetings he's going to.'

And returned to her screen.

Lesley ushered me along to the café, asking inanities about the christening. I'd hoped to ask her a bit more about Lucy Lopez's visit, but she parked me with a cup of tea, and went back to her gate keeping.

Surely I wasn't on my own here. I decided to have another go at Henry, and phoned him.

'Malcolm!' said Henry. 'What a surprise! We were just talking about you.'

'Nothing good, I hope,' I said. 'I'm in Fort William, and I wondered if I might drop by on the way back to work.'

'Of course,' said Henry. 'How about now. You could join us for lunch.'

'That sounds nice, thank you,' I said. 'Can I bring anything?'

'I don't think so,' said Henry. 'I'd better give you address and directions. You've not been here before, have you.'

Well I have, but not that Henry's likely to remember.

'Just the postcode'll do,' I said. 'I'll bang it into *Google* maps.'

'I'll text you the whole address,' said Henry. 'See you soon!'

Henry and Megan lived in a row of converted cottages, on the far side of Port Appin, which is a bit under an hour due south of Fort William. The settlement is a huddle of twisty little roads, all the same, but I'd actually been there twice *before*, so, this time, I managed to thread my way along the single tracks without getting lost. I parked up at the front of the house, and walked round to the back.

'You found us!' said Henry, standing in the open doorway. 'Welcome! It's Megan's turn to cater, so you're in for a treat.'

I groaned inwardly. Megan had many skills, but cooking wasn't one of them.

'Sounds good!' I said, summoning enthusiasm. 'Is it a full house?'

'No, thank goodness,' said Henry. 'The kids are all away at their grandparents. That's my parents. In Edinburgh. Come on in. Would you mind taking your shoes off?'

The house was utterly changed from what I recalled of my last visit. Before, there had been piles of variegated stuff along every wall and on every surface. Now it was almost spartan. The walls were freshly painted white, and the wooden floors had been sanded and sealed, and covered in thick Tajik rugs.

'Gosh, this is cosy,' I said, levering off my work boots.

'We like it,' said Henry. 'Nice and simple. This way.'

He led me through to the kitchen.

'Malcolm!' said Megan, hugging me tightly. 'How good to see you! It's been far too long. We were just saying that to Polly.'

'Polly's been here?' I said.

'Oh yes,' said Megan. 'For the weekend. Didn't she say? She was so sorry to miss the christening. Do have a seat.'

I have no idea what's going on.

'What brought Polly here?' I said, sitting down at the stripped pine dining table.

'The solstice,' said Megan. 'We're making plans.'

'I didn't realise she was that involved,' I said.

'Oh yes,' said Megan. 'She's a regular visitor. Soup? It's foraged mushroom.'

The soup tasted as grey as it looked.

'What are you planning?' I said, spreading lumpy peanut butter onto even lumpier whole meal bread. 'Back to the quarry?'

'We've not decided yet,' said Megan. 'But Polly's discovered what looks like a system of dispersed standing stones. They're all in places called Tarbert.'

'Right,' I said. 'Why's that significant?'

'It's from the Gaelic,' said Megan. 'An Tairbeart. A crossing place, where you can portage a boat between two lochs, like an isthmus.'

'Goodness,' I said, brain suddenly firing on all cylinders. 'There are lots of Tarberts. If you include Tarbet. And Tarbat. I wonder if there's a geological connection.'

'Interesting!' said Megan. 'The stones are all singletons. Maybe they're all made of the same material. We thought they might be portals.'

'Surely they're just to mark the crossing point,' said Henry. 'You wouldn't want to lug a boat any further than you had to. We're not all Fitzcarraldo.'

'The Hebrides are hardly the rain forest,' said Megan. 'Not since they cut down all the trees. More soup?'

'Thank you, but no,' I said. 'That really hit the spot. Portals between what?'

'Different worlds, maybe,' said Megan. 'We just don't know how to invoke them.'

'An excuse for more prosecco, no doubt,' said Henry, winking at me. 'You and the girls must get through gallons of the stuff.'

Megan raised an eyebrow.

'So long as you're paying,' she said. 'Dessert? I've made a bramble pie.'

'Yum!' said Henry. 'Is there custard?'

'In the freezer,' said Megan. 'Could you find some, please?'

Henry got up, and disappeared down the passage that ran along the back of the conjoined cottages.

'How did Polly make the Tarbert connection?' I asked, as Megan chiselled out three portions of pie.

'Location spotting,' said Megan. 'For Henry's film.'

'How's that going?' I asked.

'You'll need to ask Henry,' said Megan. 'I'm sick of the whole thing. I wish he'd stuck to the books.'

'How does Polly seem to you?' I asked, cautiously.

'Good,' said Megan. 'Good. And to you?'

'I'm never quite sure,' I said. 'We've not seen so much of each other, since she got the film job.'

'That's a shame,' said Megan. 'She's really fond of you. You must know that.'

Oh! Oh!

'What must he know?' said Henry, returning with an iced-up plastic tub. 'Shall I bang this in the microwave?'

'Go for it,' said Megan, opening the microwave door. 'That the film's taking longer than you expected.'

'You're not joking!' said Henry, punching at the buttons, shutting the door, and sitting back down. 'They keep changing their minds. I'm not even sure it's going to be a film anymore. It was supposed to be 120 minutes. Then they thought about TV and suggested six 30 minute episodes. Then they wanted three 60 minute episodes. Then four 45 minutes. TV's a nightmare. You need a cliff hanger every 15 mins for advert breaks.'

'Aren't there cliff hangers at the end of every chapter?' I said.

'You'd think so, wouldn't you,' said Megan. 'Apparently not.'

'They're quite different media,' said Henry, pompously. 'It's not one to one.'

The microwave pinged. Megan opened the door to a flurry of steam.

'Should be good and hot,' said Megan ladling glutinous pink sludge onto each slice of pie. 'Here you go. Help yourself.'

'All right,' said Henry, tidying up the crockery. 'What brings you here?'

'The road,' I said. 'It looks like a fait accompli.'

'What road?' said Megan.

I recounted Dougie's tale of the Central 400.

'That's deeply shitty,' said Megan when I'd finished. 'Is there really nothing you can do?'

'Nothing,' I said. 'Not so long as I work for *Rural Resources*. We have to be seen to be neutral. That's what I want to talk to Henry about.'

Megan looked at Henry. Henry avoided her gaze.

'You haven't told him,' said Megan. 'Have you.'

'Told me what?' I said.

'I'll leave you to it,' said Megan, getting up. 'Gies a shout when you're off, Malcolm.'

'For sure,' I said. 'Thanks for lunch.'

'You're always welcome,' said Megan, and left the kitchen.

Henry filled the kettle and placed it on the range.

'Tea?' he said. 'Or coffee?'

'Tea, please,' I said. 'Come on. Out with it. Why can't you help?'

'I can't help,' said Henry, 'because, although I work for *Great Alien Plum*, on paper I'm a *Peyroux Holdings* employee.'

'But I thought film production was the gig economy,' I said. 'Everyone on piece work, apart from core staff. That's what Polly said.'

'Well,' said Henry, '*GAP* said that if the film's successful they might make another, so they offered me a retainer to give them first refusal. It's a lot of dosh. And five kids don't come cheap. *GAP* manages a budget on behalf of *Peyroux*. The contract says that the retainer makes me staff.'

'And *Peyroux* bankrolls *Quantum Solutions*,' I said. 'OK. I get it.'

'I'm really sorry, Malcolm,' said Henry. 'I'm in the same position as you.'

'What about all your connections?' I said. 'There must be someone who can make a fuss.'

'I could give them a go, I suppose,' said Henry. 'But I'd need some evidence.'

A sudden thought.

'Will this do?' I said, fishing out the brochure Dean had given me. 'The back page.'

Henry scanned the map.

'Excellent!' he said. 'Just the job! Leave it with me.'

'Thanks,' I said, as the kettle's whistle grew more insistent. 'How about that tea?'

Chapter 16 - Helen

Tuesday June 14th – later – Calanais Stone Circle, Lewis

Well, here I am walking the long avenue of pairs of stones at the Calanais towards the central circle. And feeling pretty nervous, if truth be told. The sky is still sun and cloud, though the wind has dropped. Last time I came, before the Incident, I got caught in a terrific storm up here. But that's not what makes me so nervous.

That's down to nearly an hour with Mrs Morrison – Sorcha. Yes, we are on first-name terms. Because after Steven went, the first thing she said in very halting English was – 'I know you'. And she reached inside her thick woolly and drew out a chipped flint arrowhead.

My face must have been a picture. How could she know me from my previous visit? That timeline no longer exists, and its population went down with it.

But there again, the last time I was here, the witchy woman I met said the arrowhead was 'the sign of Wicca'. Then that makes Sorcha some kind of a witch too. And it's the arrowhead, so the witchy women said, that preserved my memory of where I came from. Feeling a total gowk I drew my own arrowhead out. And she nodded.

Arrowheads aren't much use at language barriers: *Google Translate* works better. I got my phone out and that's how we managed our laborious conversation, along with my fragments of Gaelic and Sorcha's fragments of English.

Sorcha thinks because I am 'of the blood' I am entitled to summon Margaret MacAskill if I have a question I really need her to answer. So she taught me the summoning. I promised solemnly never to tell anyone else not 'of the blood'.

Hopefully I can manage the Gaelic – we went over it enough times. It helps that I know approximately what it means in English and one or two of the words already: 'By sky and sea and stones and our shared blood', and all that. And I've to hold up the arrowhead. According to Sorcha, all the women 'of the blood' are 'children of the Cailleach' which must be a Gaelic version of Wicca, like Elena's term was for a Greek one. But I don't want to be a witch, that's for sure! Just Hulkie the seafarer, like I used to be. I'm a bit scared Margaret McAskill won't appear, and also that she will.

As I walk down the avenue, I can feel the green stone in my pocket begin to vibrate. That happened the last time too. And I saw new green stones being 'born' in a stone circle at Kilmartin before the Incident. This doesn't make me feel any better.

And now I am standing by the central stone. Here goes. I extract my arrowhead, hold it up, and say the summoning.

Nothing, and I think I've been had.

But wait a minute.

Wisps start to rise from the ground as if it is steaming. I shiver.

Come on Hulkie, it's only mist.

In a few minutes it's thick and white, the inside of a cloud.

A shadow appears in it, comes towards me, becomes a person. A woman, neither old nor young, with a white linen headscarf, a shawl over her shoulders, and the striped skirt I remember seeing on very old ladies when I was a kid, visiting.

'*Halo a ghràidh*' it – she – says. Ganny McIver used to say that – hello my dear.

I stumble through one of my laboriously prepared phrases: '*Chan eil mòran Gàidhlig agam*' – I don't speak much Gaelic. Even to a – what, a ghost? – this must be pretty evident. This is dreadful, how can I communicate? Not with my phone, surely?

The figure gestures at me, and I'm conscious my green stone is vibrating like a wasps' nest and becoming warm. I take it out of my pocket. The figure smiles.

The stone glows so brightly I can hardly look at it, and forms a green enclosure in the mist encompassing us both. The figure speaks again, again it's in Gaelic, but suddenly I can hear the same voice in my head, in a kind of English. Hearing double, like seeing double.

'Child of my blood, why you have called me?'

111

'You are the answerer of questions and I have a question.'

'I answer when there is need of an answer. So ask.'

I've thought so hard about how to ask my question but now it comes to it, what do I say? Do I have to explain all about the Incident? Surely not?

'I was brought into this time from a different one. But my mind is scrambled between the two. How can I become one person again?'

'This is truly your need? The children of my blood can know many times.' She shows me that she too has a flint arrowhead round her neck.

'It's truly my need. This child cannot live with a mind in different times.'

'Then the stone will take what the stone gave.'

'When? How? What should I do?'

'When the two take the path of the whirling waters.'

I'm pretty sure I'm not going to get any more than this after what Sorcha told me. And badgering this apparition doesn't seem a good move. But before I can say anything at all, a strange voice breaks in. For a moment I feel I might keel over altogether.

Rial has stepped into our green enclosure. Who else would it be?

'Greetings to the right-hand of the Cailleach,' they say. Calmly! 'Will you permit me also to ask a question.'

Margaret McAskill turns to look at Rial, and I wonder just what she will do as she stretches her arm out towards them.

'Greetings spirit of air, bound as you are.'

As she points, I see the same green spider webbing as in that druggie vision form around Rial's pale body.

'I know your questions and will answer. My daughter here cannot free you herself, two are needed. When the dark is least then the binder shall be bound. And the Cailleach will not be mocked. You are answered.'

She looks back at me.

'Farewell, daughter of my blood. Go well.' Then she turns and walks into the mist, becoming a shadow and fading out. As she does my stone fades and the mist turns white again.

Before I can ask Rial what the fuck they are doing here, they give me that intense blue-eyed stare and say:

'I came because there was an anomaly. You must know I see across times. And now I must be elsewhere.'

'Wait!'

But Rial takes no notice and walks off into the mist, also becoming a shadow and vanishing. I don't feel like chasing after them either. Spirit of air? That certainly doesn't sound very human.

I feel a wind on my face and the mist starts breaking up, blowing into twisty shapes. Not to my surprise, there is no sign of anyone but me among the stones. And before I can start trying to digest a truly weird experience, my phone pings.

It's Steven saying he'll be with me quite soon. I walk back down the stone avenue and then to the main road. Trying to fix everything that was said into my memory. I'll worry about what it means and whether it actually gets me anywhere later.

When I get to the main road, I find the day's surprises are not done. There are Boris and Elena, on the two electric motorbikes. Boris is peering at his phone, and Elena is pointing up the road I just walked down from the stones.

Elena jumps as she catches sight of me and says something to Boris. Who looks up and scowls. I do hope Elena is still in peacekeeping mode and I don't have to try out my unarmed combat skills with Boris.

'Hello shipmates,' I say breezily. 'If you're looking for the stone circle it's just up the hill.' I point back along the road. 'Very impressive it is too. I used to come here as a child when I was visiting my grandparents.' All true.

'How you get here?' Boris demands.

'My cousin gave me a lift, man,' I tell him. 'He's about to come and fetch me back to Stornoway.'

And would you believe it, right on cue, that's when Steven arrives.

Well, Boris and Elena can hardly make off without looking really rude, or indeed rather suspicious. And naturally, Steven gets out to say hello to them.

'The *Midsummer Queen*'s first mate, Yuri Petrovitch Lisov,' I say to Steven. 'And this is…' I have to think what Elena's official name is, oh yes, 'Eirini Nomikou, our chief steward. Shipmates, this is my cousin Steven McIver.'

Elena gives Steven a nice smile, while Boris does not.

'Good to meet you both,' says Steven. 'Helen was telling me how much she enjoyed being part of your crew.' He does lie very convincingly.

'Our excellent Electronics Officer,' Boris says grudgingly. Not such a good liar.

'I hope you have seen some of our island today,' Steven says. 'Have you been up to the Ness? Our most northerly point, and very dramatic with its cliffs. And there's a lovely little art gallery at the port.'

'Oh yes,' says Elena, 'we just visited that. Lovely prints and paintings.'

I feel that there was some purpose to that question of Steven's. His bounce and enthusiasm can hide just how keen a policeman he is.

'Excellent,' he says now. 'Well, I must get back to Stornoway with your Electronics Officer. Don't miss the Calanais stones now you are here, they are spectacular.'

We get into the car. I notice Steven checks his rear-view mirror, perhaps to see whether Boris and Elena do go up the road to the stones.

'What did Mrs Morrison want to say that she kept you there?' he asks after we start off.

'Nothing much, man,' I say. 'I think she felt she hadn't done her duty to a relative on the tea and biscuits front. It's hard to chat when you don't really have a common language.'

'So you didn't summon Margaret MacAskill then?' he asks.

'Well, wasn't all that a story?' I say. 'You think that really happened?'

'I've known Mrs Morrison a long while,' he says after a pause. 'She sees further than the average old lady.'

I decide to change the subject.

'Howay, Mr Policeman, you weren't checking out my shipmates' movements just then by any chance?'

'Interesting pair,' he says.

'Oh come on!'

He laughs. 'You come clean with me, Helen, and I'll come clean with you. As long as you promise to keep it to yourself.'

Well, I do need to know if the police are going after the crew I'm a part of.

'OK, man. Yes, I did summon Margaret MacAskill. Believe it or not as you choose. And asked a question about a private family matter. Her answer was, as Sorcha told us, open to interpretation. Your turn. I promise not to tell.'

'I thought so. And I do believe you, as I believe her. It's said there's more in heaven and earth than we know. So I gather you and Mrs Morrison ended up on first-name terms. Good going for two people without a common language, taking tea and biscuits.'

That was me told. Seems like I am not a good liar either, though I suppose Steven has had lots of practice in detecting lies.

'Here's my side,' he goes on. 'I was interviewing some tourists along in Carloway. Russian tourists, unusual for these parts. Tourists are usually Sasunnach, with a few Americans. There was a tip-off that they might be of interest to our anti-drugs mission. So it's interesting that your Russian colleague passed through Carloway earlier today. Worth pursuing perhaps. Is there anything you'd like to tell me about Yuri Petrovitch? Other than he obviously cannot stand you?'

I bite my tongue and do not remind him about Lucy meeting Yuri Petrovitch.

'Look Steven, what do you think getting mixed up in that kind of stuff would do to my career? And I'm on contract for some while yet. If I walk away without due cause, that goes on my seafarer's book and likewise hurts my career.'

'I hear what you're saying. You should know I can keep confidences. If you do come across anything that would help us, I promise I will be discreet.'

'I'll bear that in mind.'

'If you do want to help, you could mention the name 'Nando' and see if Yuri Petrovitch reacts to it. That's a strange young man picked up by our colleagues on Islay we think might also be involved.'

'OK Steven, I get the point.'

I lapse into a grumpy silence until we get to Stornoway, going over again what Margaret MacAskill – if that's what she was – had said. And Rial. How much of our conversation did Rial hear? I really do need to collar them. If that is actually possible. As for Steven – what have I done to deserve a cousin in the police?

I'm hardly aboard the *Midsummer Queen* when the Captain finds me.

'Ah, Helen, just the person! The electronics specialist is here at last and he wants to talk to you.'

Just what I need with a head full of weirdnesses.

I find the specialist, a young man from the mainland, in the Bridge. He complains he could not recreate the fault. Could I show him please. I sit at the console and show him how the plotted course spreads out. Looking up I see Rial is out on the main deck again. Is that the elsewhere Rial said they had to be? Who knows?

'There,' I tell the young man.

'Oh, now I see. Odd. That wasn't happening earlier.'

'Transient faults are the hard ones,' I say, and he nods mournfully.

Then the Captain comes onto the Bridge.

'Helen, I've been talking to the company Damon here represents. They say they should replace the translocator altogether.' Damon nods.

'They normally ship by ferry, and that would be a number of days after it comes into stock, which should be late tomorrow. But if I send someone over to collect, we could fly the component back much quicker, as soon as they have it. I wondered, Helen, whether you would catch a flight over to Glasgow tomorrow and help us out?'

Now, that was not in fact a question, just how this Captain likes to issue commands.

'Aye, aye Sir,' I say. And he winces.

A day away from Boris and co seems such a good idea. I can tackle Rial when I get back after all. Glasgow it is.

Journal June 13

Steven's interest in Boris is one more to add to my growing list of worries. Were Boris and Elena distributing the drugs round Lewis? If those Russian tourists really are Boris contacts and mixed up in this, it's a matter of time before the police latch on and then follow up with our crew.

But that's not my main worry. Margaret MacAskill reckoned that remembering stuff in your past across different timelines was something many people did, not just me. Malcolm's neighbour Glynis for example? But I can't hack it. Does that make me some kind of failed witch? Like it or not?

There again, she also seemed to say I could become whole again. 'The stone will take what the stone gave' – that must be my stone surely? 'When the two take the path of the whirling waters' – like the whirling waters I saw in the druggie vision and keep dreaming? But which *two*? Rial and Cal? Mebbe Rial wasn't making it up when they said they could help me? Mebbe Rial knows what Margaret's answer to my question actually means?

And it seems like Rial thinks I could free them – whatever that means. Remove those green spidery bindings? Which according to the druggy vision come from Mr Ross. A man I for sure do not want to come up against. But surely that 'when the dark is least then the binder shall be bound' would be about Mr Ross then?

Still, Margaret MacAskill said it would take more than me. That must be someone else with a stone, which would be Malcolm? Good luck with that one, Rial. Cousin Malcolm just wants to be left alone.

116

A wild idea on the nav system problem. Could it be something Rial does? No music this time, but Rial seems to drift between places at will – could they fuzz position data just by being there? Hey – I could test that with the GPS data output on my phone! But not until I am back from Glasgow.

And mebbe a trip off the ship will help to clear my head. I'll take the babygros to Glasgow with me and post them from there. Another email from Dad tonight – all's going well. And a reply from Wilf to my email as well. Gossip about our friends, doings of his cat, and saying he misses me. Do I miss him? I wish I knew.

Chapter 17 - Malcolm

Wednesday June 15th - Cruachan

When I got home last night, Lesley's email was waiting for me. I was to be at Cruachan at 10.00. It's only a 40 minute drive to the west, on the road to Oban, so, this morning, I had a leisurely breakfast, and missed what passes for rush hour traffic.

Cruachan's a pumped storage hydroelectric scheme. The turbines are inside the mountain, with the reservoir on top. When there's excess electricity on the grid, the turbines pump water from Loch Awe up into the reservoir. And when there's excess demand, or they need to restart the grid, the water's sent back down to drive the turbines. Although I must have passed the site hundreds of times, I'd never actually visited it.

I stopped at the gatehouse, and had my name checked by a security guard. He directed me to a parking space, and told me to look for Dr McCrone in the offices above the visitor centre.

Dr McCrone, a woman of around my age, was the *Quantum Solutions* project lead. Her rear office wall was filled with a huge diagram of the Cruachan scheme. On the side walls were black and white photos of pylons.

'My hobby,' she explained, noticing my curiosity. 'Most people loathe them, but they have a rare aesthetic. Very strong. Yet gracile.'

Dr McCrone moused up a map of central Scotland, and patiently explained where the new cable would have to run to service *QS*. As we talked, I took copious notes.

I asked lots of questions about impact, and she reassured me that it should be minimal, especially as *QS* had said that money was no object. Indeed, they were paying for the long-delayed expansion to the Cruachan scheme itself, in exchange for a guarantee of uninterrupted supply.

Dr McCrone also said that she shared my concerns about the road, but that was a matter for *QS* and the landowner. In any case, her understanding was that it would be single track, which was hardly suitable for the Central 400.

'Is there anything else?' said Dr McCrone.

'No,' I said. 'You've been most thorough. Thank you.'

'Right!' said Dr McCrone. 'Time for the tour.'

'The tour?' I said.

I really didn't like the sound of that.

'Oh yes,' said Dr McCrone. 'You've not been here before, have you?'

'Well, no,' I said.

'Come on, then!' said Dr McCrone. 'This is my favourite part of the job.'

She led me out of the building to a small electric golf buggy.

'Hop in!' she said, handing me a hard hat.

I fought back waves of panic as Dr McCrone drove the buggy round the building, and into an archway in the side of the mountain. But the tunnel was well lit, and I found being enclosed by a vast mass of granite far less oppressive than I expected. Perhaps this wouldn't be so bad.

At the far end of the tunnel, Dr McCrone parked the buggy, and led me up to the viewing gallery. Down below, four huge yellow drums thrummed on the floor of the chasm.

'Those are the turbine housings,' said Dr McCrone. 'Astonishing, aren't they!'

'They certainly are,' I said.

But I was more taken by the mural running along one wall of the turbine hall, depicting the life and times of Cruachan. At the start of the mural was the figure of an old woman. I was sure I recognised her.

'Who's that?' I asked, pointing down at the mural.

'That's the Cailleach Bheur,' said Dr McCrone. 'She's supposed to be the guardian of the waters. All superstitious nonsense, if you ask me.'

'Where does the water actually go?' I asked.

Big mistake.

'That's a great question,' said Dr McCrone. 'It's all hidden away from visitors. Health and Safety. But, seeing it's you, I'll show you the flow-way.'

'There's no need,' I said. 'Really.'

But Dr McCrone had already unlocked a large steel door in the side of the viewing gallery. The chasm echoed to the roar of rushing water.

'Come on!' she said. She switched on a fluorescent strip light, and ushered me through the door into a narrow corridor. I stopped and stared down the corridor in horror.

'On you go,' said Dr McCrone.

'There's really no need,' I said.

'It's well worth it,' said Dr McCrone. 'Come on.'

Increasingly anxious, I made my way along the corridor to the gantry at the end. Straight in front of us was a vast cascade of water.

'It's even more impressive in the dark!' shouted Dr McCrone. 'I'll leave you alone for a couple of minutes, so you can soak up the atmosphere!'

This can't be happening! This can't!

But before I could stop her, Dr McCrone went back down the tunnel, turned off the light and shut the door.

Panic overwhelmed me. My head was bursting, and my chest contracted until I could hardly draw breath. This was it! This was it! This was it!

Unearthly music.

And a familiar disembodied voice said: 'Use the stone, Malcolm.'

I fumbled for the green stone, and held it up. The space was bathed with green light. Hovering in front of the wall of water was Rial, evanescent in the dancing spume.

'Better,' said Rial.

It wasn't a question.

I took a deep breath, and my body relaxed.

'Thank you,' I said. 'Thank you. How did you know I was here?'

'The wise woman told me,' said Rial, 'that all will be well when the two take the path of the whirling waters.'

'What wise woman?' I said. 'Anyway, you can't think that's us. That's absurd.'

'No, not you and I,' said Rial. 'What do you know of Miran and Nando?'

I was utterly thrown.

'It can't be a coincidence you're here,' I said.

'Miran and Nando,' said Rial. 'They are the key. What do you know of them?'

The light came back on. I turned as the door at the far end of the corridor opened.

'How was that?' said Dr McCrone, rejoining me. 'Amazing, isn't it!'

I turned back to the water. Rial had vanished.

'Amazing,' I said. 'Truly amazing.'

I was still in shock, but, strangely, far calmer than when we entered the tunnel. Rial had made it go away. I wondered if there might be a permanent fix.

Dr McCrone led me back to the buggy, and drove me to my car.

'I hope that was useful,' she said, handing me her business card. 'Do get in touch if you've any more questions.'

'I'm to write up our meeting,' I said. 'Would you like a copy?'

'Yes please,' said Dr McCrone. 'And the hard hat.'

Dr McCrone returned to her office, and I climbed into the Land Rover. At the gate house, on a whim, I turned off the engine and got out.

'Excuse me,' I said to the guard, 'but do you have CCTV, please?'

'Of course,' said the guard, putting down his magazine. 'What's it to you?'

I turned on my phone, and found the photos Alison had sent me after the christening.

'Have you seen this woman?' I said, showing the guard a picture of Miran with the boy.

'I may well have done,' said the guard. 'Four or five days ago. Hang on.'

The guard moused up the security archive, and fast forwarded through the footage.

'Here,' he said, freezing the frame. 'That's her, isn't it?'

'Certainly looks like her,' I said peering at the slight figure at the site entrance. 'Has there been anyone else recently?'

'There was another,' said the guard, scrolling forward, 'a couple of days after the woman.'

Nando, caught in time.

'That's him,' I said. 'Did you contact the police?'

'There's no point,' said the guard. 'Happens all the time. Folk get lost coming down from the mountain. We've given up telling them off. You're not police, are you?'

'No, no,' I said. 'Not police. Thank you. You've been really helpful.'

'Why are you after them?' said the guard.

'They're visitors,' I said, thinking quickly. 'They left some stuff behind. I was here anyway. And you've got the only CCTV for miles around.'

'Fair enough,' said the guard, going back to his magazine. 'I hope you find them.'

It was mid-morning, so I drove straight on up to the *Altnafeadh Hotel* for lunch. Dougie's car was parked up opposite the entrance, and Dougie was parked up in his favoured dining room window seat.

'Malco!' said Dougie, as I sat down. 'We've got him!'

'Who have you got?' I said, pantomiming my order to Jeannie.

'Nando,' said Dougie. 'Your finger lickin' stowaway.'

'Where did they find him?' I said, tiring of this trope.

'On Islay,' said Dougie. 'Just like you said.'

'What's he charged with?' I asked.

121

'I've no idea,' said Dougie. 'I'm sure they'll think of something.'

'Rough justice,' I said.

'All I know is that it's part of some huge drugs operation,' said Dougie. 'Coming in from the Caribbean through the Hebrides.'

Whoa! That's where Helen's just come from. And that's where Helen's moored up. Is Rial the connection? I really don't want anything to do with this. But Rial made it go away. I really need to speak with Helen.

'What drugs are they bringing in?' I said. 'Cocaine?'

'Strangely not,' said Dougie. 'It's a hallucinogen called ayahuasca. Gives you a short, sharp trip.'

Whoa! That must have been what Helen and I took. But who would want to do that to us?

'There can't be a lot of demand for that round here,' I said, tentatively.

'I've not come across it before,' said Dougie. 'Yer man must have spotted a market opportunity.'

'He's not my man,' I said. 'And he didn't strike me as a likely drug runner. Not that I spent any time with him. But he did seem intent on finding someone he called the Lord of the Isles.'

'Could be the head honcho's moniker,' said Dougie. 'The Lord of the Isles sounds just like a Caribbean bad ass.'

This is crazy!

'Where are they holding him?' I asked.

'I'm not sure,' said Dougie. 'Glasgow, most likely.'

'I'm off there tomorrow,' I said.

'You're the main man!' said Dougie.

'No, no,' I said, wearily. 'Work. A conference. *Quantum Solutions.*'

'Is that about the road?' said Dougie. 'I heard that your pal Henry's been stirring things up.'

'That seems unlikely,' I said. 'He's on the *QS* payroll.'

'*Rannoch Against Quanta*, they're calling themselves,' said Dougie. 'God knows how it got out so quickly. You're sure he's not involved?'

'Quite sure,' I said.

Though I wasn't.

Back at work, increasingly intimidated by the coffee machine, I surfed for plumbers, and made several phone calls. Eventually, a firm in Inverness said they'd come next week. Expensive, but *QS* are paying.

All through the afternoon there was a trickle of tourists. Not enough for show and tell, but too many to focus on anything else. Still, it's good for the numbers. I didn't envy Kyle.

I was shutting up shop when Polly phoned.

'Hello Malcolm,' she said. 'How are you doing?'

'Hello Polly,' I said, wondering why I still can't talk about my innermost fears. 'All's good. And yourself?'

'Busy as ever,' said Polly. 'Are we still on for the weekend?'

'I do hope so,' I said. 'But I've got to go to Glasgow tomorrow. When are you coming?'

'Sometime on Friday,' said Polly. 'Depends when I can get away. When are you back?'

'Should be Thursday night,' I said. 'But you've got a key. If I'm not there, just make yourself at home.'

'I'll do that, thanks,' said Polly. 'And I can always catch up with Glenys.'

Of course.

'Are you staying for the solstice?' I said.

'Who have you been talking to?' said Polly. 'That'd be lovely, but I'm pretty sure I'll be on Jura by then. Can you still come?'

'I've got a couple of days in lieu,' I said. 'Maybe we could go there together.'

'Let's see,' said Polly. 'Sorry, but I've got to get on with things now. Another rewrite to wrangle. Bloody Henry. See you soon! Big hugs!'

'Big hugs!' I said, wondering when there might be some actual hugs.

Midsummer on the moor is magnificent when it isn't raining. The sun stays high well into the evening. And it's warm. Yes, midges, but they don't bother me as much as lots of folk.

When I got back home, an enticing smell of barbecue was wafting over from Glenys and Dougie's side of the non-existent fence.

'Malco!' called Dougie, who must have knocked off early. 'Come and join us!'

'Are you sure?' I said.

'Of course we're sure!' said Glenys.

'Thank you,' I said. 'Can I bring something?'

'Just yourself,' said Glenys. 'The cat's here already.'

'I'm sure we could use some beer,' I said. 'Hang on. I'll just get myself sorted out.'

'Don't be too long,' said Dougie. 'The salmon's beginning to catch.'

'Quick as I can,' I said, going into my cottage. 'I need to make a call.'

I sat down on the sofa and phoned Helen. Of course she had no time for me. And not on her ship as I expected, but to my surprise, busy with Bernie. Sooner her than me. So I said what I hoped were persuasive words:

'Rial. Nando. Miran.'

There was a pause. Unusual for Helen.

She must be in Bearsden for some reason. I suggested meeting the next day, and said I would text her details as soon as I had the full conference programme.

We ended the call, I found a six pack of *Druid's Ruin* in the kitchen cupboard, and went back out to join my neighbours.

Chapter 18 - Helen

Wednesday June 15th - Glasgow

From the airport bus, Glasgow is looking almost beautiful in the morning sunshine. Plenty of time to take it in too as we crawl across the Clyde. The Erskine bridge is well-clagged with the motorway's morning rush-hour traffic.

I don't feel very sunny. I thought I was going to get a fun morning wandering round the town and a quiet lunch. Then off to *TransWorld Navigation* - Damon's company - to pick up the part. But late last night the Captain tells me that Mr Ross, hearing I'm in town, wants a quick in-person.

Ominous, or ominous? I really hope it's just some employment contract minor issue. But big bosses leave that stuff to their HR, so probably not. Though a standard big boss doesn't have someone or something like Rial working for them, trussed up in green spiderweb. My working life seems to have taken a sudden swerve into total fantasy.

I could leave the gig right now and go home. But Mr Ross wouldn't need green spiderweb to get me blacklisted by all the cruise companies. And here I am, getting off the airport bus at Central Station.

Peyroux Holdings have their offices down on the Broomielaw, by the river, in the IFSD – International Finance Services District. 'Glasgow's Wall Street' they claim, though if you've walked the real thing like I have, that only makes you smile.

The building is all glass and pot plants, and Reception sends me up to the top floor of eight. I announce myself to the young woman in the office there.

'Mr Peyroux is expecting you,' she says, pointing at the door opposite the one I came in by.

Come on Hulkie, he can't eat you. Pull yourself together!

I walk into a penthouse office with a glass wall looking out over the river. It's full of sunshine. Mr Ross gets up from an imposing desk. As well as a computer screen, I notice it has a large black book open on it, with a small glass paperweight that seems to flicker different colours.

'Ah, Ms McIver, how good to see you.' I grit my teeth – not my favourite mode of address, that. He points at a couple of easy chairs round a coffee table. 'Do take a seat.'

'Nice to meet you Sir,' I say in my best customer service mode.

He's not all that tall, mebbe an inch less that I am, but has that air of energy and power I noticed in the video. And similarly snazzy tailoring – this time a turquoise jacket with darker blue trousers. I shift the offered chair round a little, so the sun won't be in my eyes, and sit down. So does he. He moves like a much younger man than his neatly styled white hair and beard suggest.

The door opens and the young woman brings in a tray with coffee things and sugar biscuits. There are some minutes of fussing while she organises a cup for each of us. I feel a bit paranoid, thinking of the coffee that gave me the druggie vision, and decide not to drink it.

'Thank you for all your work up to this point,' Mr Ross says. 'My Rial tells me you are very competent.'

'That's very nice of them,' I reply, as you do. I wonder exactly what Rial has been saying about me.

'I like competent people,' he says. 'I always have room for them in my organisation. I'll get straight to the point. I'd be gratified if you would consider a permanent post with *Peyroux Holdings*.'

Stunned silence on my part for a moment. Then I vigorously supress my first reaction, which is 'you must be joking!' and hope my face didn't give it away.

'That's very good of you Sir, but I enjoy being able to free-lance and work for a variety of organisations.'

'I doubt other organisations have the kind of remuneration package *Peyroux Holdings* offers competent people like you.' He names a figure that makes me blink. 'And given our range of activities, we can certainly offer variety.'

Under his smooth manner he doesn't sound pleased. There's more than one way of tangling people in green spiderweb.

'I'm sure that's all true, Sir, and a very generous offer, but I must respectfully decline.'

His face sets into sternness. He leans forward, lifts a hand towards me and says – something. It's not English, it's quiet, and I feel as if my stomach has dropped several floors in a lift. There's a strong vibration against my leg – the green stone in my pocket. The air suddenly feels charged with something.

But the moment passes.

'I'm sorry Sir, I didn't quite catch that,' I say, deadpan.

'Ah,' he says, 'just expressing my disappointment. My first language is not English. Still, I hope you may reconsider later. I will be joining the *Midsummer Queen* in a couple of days. You could let me know at any time.'

Oh joy. Yet another complication on the ship. Still, I bet he'll make mincemeat of Boris if Boris is arsey.

He gets up and so I do too. The interview is done. He holds his hand out and I try not to hesitate. Nor do I flinch at the firmness of his grip or the slight jolt, like a small electrical shock I also feel. And I look him straight in the eyes. Very dark eyes.

'Your strength of character is admirable, Ms McIver,' he says. But he does make it sound more like an obstacle.

After that I get my wander round the town. I do the City Art Gallery and the Cathedral with its Necropolis. In between I get a decent steak in the Merchant City. I feel as if I've survived an ordeal.

TransWorld Navigation are in what turns out to be a pretty desolate industrial area over the river, a bit of a hike. Their daily stock delivery comes in at 4, so I turn up at 3.30. I have my e-reader in my fleece pocket and settle down in the stock distribution office with a new Sword and Sorcery while I wait.

It's almost 4.30 when the stockman in his brown coat emerges from the alleys of shelving behind his counter.

'*Midsummer Queen*?' he says loudly. I get up and move to the counter.

'Sorry pal, item's nae in the load. Been ontae them. Loading error their end, ken. Tomorrow they reckon.'

Sod's law in action. But there's no point in swearing at the man and I don't. I ring the Captain back on the *Midsummer Queen* for further instructions. The Captain does not swear either, just heaves a deep sigh. He asks me whether, now I'm in Glasgow, I'd mind staying the extra day. Not really a question of course.

He says he can ask Mr Ross to get a hotel sorted out for me, but I've had plenty of Mr Ross for one day. I tell him I have family here and can stay with them, and hope that is true.

Bernie told me at the christening she was stopping on for a few days in her old house in Bearsden because Alison and Grant are there just now. Anyway, if push comes to shove and they've no space, I'd rather get my own room. But in fact it all pans out. Bernie is delighted when I ring her, tells me Alison says there's a spare bedroom I can have. Bearsden it is. Along the way I'll buy myself a toothbrush.

When I look at my phone, from where I am to Bernie's house is more than an hour by public transport – that not being Glasgow's strong point. When I get closer to the town, I hail a taxi and arrive in just over twenty minutes.

In my own memory, I was last at Bernie's not long before the Incident, but that was to see pre-Incident Bernie, and not in this here-and-now house. I'll need to be careful what I say. Still, it seems to have the same address I remember and looks much the same too, with immaculate white harling, and a well-manicured lawn in front of it. Alison opens the door.

'Welcome, Helen! Come in. Bernie's through in the lounge with the boy.'

The lounge still looks very smart, though the big sofas don't have the floral fabrics I recall. There are pictures of the kids when they were young in silver frames, expensive-looking ornaments, and patio doors out into a neatly organised back garden. Bernie is on one of the sofas with the bairn draped over her.

'Hi Helen,' she says quietly. 'Can't get up! Come and sit down over here. We need to keep our voices down, he's just gone off.'

But Alison lifts the bairn off her and lays him carefully down in a pram in the corner. We all of us hold our breath. He doesn't wake.

'Glass of white wine?' Alison asks us. She brings us a glass each and then says: 'I'll leave you to it while I get our tea on.'

After a bit of quiet-voice chat, Bernie pauses and then looks at me rather seriously.

'Helen, I wanted to ask you something.'

'Anything.' Though I hope this isn't about Wilf.

'Did you tell Malcolm what I told you on Saturday about Thierry?'

'Only what you heard, Bernie. I'm really sorry I put my foot in it. I should have realised it was still under wraps. But that was all.'

'So not that he's called Thierry and is a psychologist?'

128

'No. Malcolm didn't ask about it and I'd have said no more if he had.'

Bernie pulls a face.

'Malcolm came out with that later, and he said it was you that told him.'

Oh dear, cousin Malcolm getting confused by pre-Incident events and using me as a scapegoat. Because Thierry actually came to the first run of Alison's wedding with pre-Incident Bernie. That means Malcolm knows about it without anyone telling him. How do I deal with this?

'I guess someone else told him and he decided to land me in it rather than them.'

At this point I hear a buzzing. But it's not my green stone, just my mobile, which luckily is on vibrate. And guess, what? It's Malcolm.

I get up to take the call outside the room.

'Hi Malcolm. Not a good moment for a chat, man. I'm in Bearsden with Bernie.' After what Bernie just told me I may sound a little sharp.

'But we need to talk.'

'And this isn't a good moment.'

'Rial. Nando. Miran,' he says.

Oh.

Rial and Miran we both know, but how come Nando? Steven's potential drug smuggler? Weird. And I do really need to talk to him about Rial. Wait a minute, I thought Miran was helping Alison with the bairn. But I haven't seen her.

'So you're in Glasgow,' he says, before I can decide what to say. 'I'm there tomorrow. Can we meet, please?'

Well, I suppose, as long as I get back to *TransWorld Navigation* before four, we could meet. Though after our last conversation, can't say I feel happy about the idea.

'Text me where you'll be,' I tell him. 'I'll get back to you.' And I end the call.

I go back into the lounge. 'That was Malcolm,' I told Bernie. 'I'm probably meeting up with him tomorrow.'

'Don't be too hard on him,' says Bernie. 'Wherever he got it from, it gave us both a wee push to tidy things up. I know you've been telling me to move on, and whatever happens with Thierry...' there's such a hopeful look on her face '...it is time we did that. But enough about me, Helen. You haven't mentioned Wilf once to me, whether tonight or Saturday. Have you broken up with him?'

'No,' I tell her. 'We're still in our sort-of together. Different flats but staying over from time-to-time.'

'You're not a wee bairn Helen, and I'm not such a good example myself to be handing out advice, but you and Wilf can't last like that. I ken your Mam rubs you up the wrong way with her you-should-settle-down, but even so, there may come a time when you want to but there's nobody to do it with. You do seem to be fond of Wilf. Bring him to Paris!'

I can't tell Bernie how my broken-up memory bugs me and how I have to try to sort it.

'Mebbe I will,' is all I say.

Journal June 15

A good evening. Alison made us all a tasty pasta bake, and after that, Bernie got to bath the bairn with me as assistant. Babbies and water – a fun combination. Then Grant suggested I read the bedtime story. It brought home what I know but haven't been thinking about – if I want a bairn I've only got so much time left. So mebbe Bernie does have a point about Wilf.

I asked Alison what happened to Miran, and Alison says she just vanished. And then asked me if I said something to her at the christening, as she freaked out right after she met me. I told her I didn't say a thing, she just clocked me and backed off fast. But why did Malcolm mention her in that call? Along with Rial and Nando? Has she been arrested as well? I can just about make a link between Rial and Nando via those packets of drugs, but Miran? If she's Cal's missing girlfriend, will she turn up at the ship?

Malcolm's text says he's at a conference in the University tomorrow, and to meet him there after their lunch. It sounds like that's the *Quantum Solutions* event the Americans mentioned, but I still have zero idea why Malcom is into quantum physics all of a sudden. Could be it's to do with his mention of Rial. Who said at the Calanais stones they could 'see across times' which, if it's true, sounds like a quantum-y thing. If you can do that, could you give a timeline a push by turning up in it?

I need to tell Malcolm about the Calanais stones, Margaret MacAskill and what she said. Yesterday she tells Rial they need Malcolm as well as me, and today Malcolm mentions Rial. Some coincidence that.

Then there's my biggest worry right now. Mr Ross. Why did he want me to work for him? Given a choice, you'd be crazy to work for a man like that. But it looks like neither Rial nor Cal do have the choice. I think he tried some witchy stuff on me to make me say yes and it failed. That was why he was disappointed. Rial's music doesn't seem to work on me or Malcolm either. It must be the stone. I really hope so.

Chapter 19 - Malcolm

Thursday June 16th – Glasgow

I took the morning train to Glasgow: there's no way the Land Rover would satisfy the emissions requirements, and parking's a nightmare. I'd planned to read a novel, but ended up just gazing out of the window, watching the world go by.

I'd not been to Glasgow for quite a while, and I can't say I'd missed it. Perhaps that's just the traditional east coast disdain: I grew up in Edinburgh. But all fur coat and no knickers seems like a better description of Merchant City than Morningside. Behind all the glitzy new developments, there's the same old seediness and poverty.

The conference was in an ultra-modern University block to the east of the City Chambers, a short walk from Queen Street Station. It was easy to find the location: the building was festooned with huge banners proclaiming *Quantum Solutions* sponsorship. The train was forty minutes late, but I'd allowed for that, and still arrived well before the opening ceremony.

I registered at the conference desk, and was given a hessian booty bag containing a paper copy of the programme, a data stick with all the presentations, and a wad of bumph about Glasgow and *QS*. Of course the handles were too long, so the bag dragged along the floor. Of course the handles were too short, so the bag wouldn't ride comfortably on my shoulder. And they'd spelled my name incorrectly on the badge, so I just popped it into the bag.

I found a relatively quiet corner, and skimmed the programme. The morning sounded pretty dull, with lots of technical stuff about system design and performance. But there was a complimentary buffet lunch, immediately followed by an interesting-sounding talk called *Taking Many-Worlds At Face Value*. I reckoned I could slip away after that, so I texted Helen the location, and suggested that she meet me in the atrium just after the talk was due to finish. She replied almost immediately with a thumbs up.

The lecture theatre was surprisingly full. Perhaps quantum computing really has got some traction. I was looking for a seat at the back, when a beaming Lucy Lopez collared me.

'Malcolm!' she said. 'Welcome! I'm really glad *Rural Resources* sent you. Dr McCrone told me that she felt you'd got a solid feel for the project, so I'm sure this will round that out. If there's anything you don't understand, do ask questions. After all, we're all here to learn, aren't we.'

To my mortification, Lucy led me to the reserved seats in the front row. About halfway down the aisle, we passed the two Americans, who waved cheerily at me. I forced a smile.

Lucy plonked me down next to her seat, and mounted the stage, joining a group to one side.

A younger woman in jeans and a 'No cat jokes!' T-shirt approached the microphone. She introduced herself as head of the university's quantum computer team, told us about the absence of fire alarms, and pointed out the emergency exits. After a brief preamble, she introduced Lucy Lopez as representing the conference sponsors. Lucy thanked her, and, in turn, introduced the President of *Peyroux Holdings*, P. Ross Peyroux. The commanding man I'd seen in my strange vision joined Lucy at the microphone. To my consternation, he glanced down at me as the green stone vibrated softly in my pocket.

Peyroux spoke briefly but succinctly. He was delighted to be supporting this venture, especially as his subsidiary *Quantum Solutions* were commissioning the first commercially viable, all-British, indeed all-Scottish, quantum computer. Accuracy was very high, and scalability seemed unlimited. Even as he spoke, field trials were underway to confirm that it was close to achieving quantum supremacy, that is, of solving problems that would defeat a conventional computer.

Muttered scepticism rippled through the lecture hall.

Peyroux smiled, and said that he fully understood that quantum computing, like AI, had been grossly overhyped. Nonetheless, their machine was based on sound research. Anyone who doubted the *QS* claims was welcome to come and inspect their set-up. Dr Lopez would be happy to facilitate this. He finished by misquoting Shakespeare's tired old saw:

We are the stuff that dreams are made of.

Then he thanked the audience, and bowed to them. As applause mounted, Lucy ushered him off the stage, and the conference proper began.

There were three sessions before the break, all way over my head. At the break, Peyroux buttonholed me. Lucy Lopez hovered nervously in the background.

'You know who I am,' Peyroux said, proffering a hand. 'And who are you?'

'Malcolm Nicholson,' I said without thinking, as we shook hands. '*Rural Resources*. Rannoch Moor.'

'Ah,' said Peyroux. 'That's two things we have in common. I'm sure we have lots to talk about, Mr Nicholson. But not now.'

He turned away.

Two things. What two things? The Moor, for sure, but the stone? Or Polly? Or Helen? But they're not things.

To clear my head, I took a quick stroll round George Square. Same old statues. Same old pigeons.

After the break there were three more sessions. The only one that I could begin to follow was about the geomorphology of quantum computing installations, which had unexpected effects on device behaviour. High concentrations of graviton energy seemed to enhance quantum stability. Maybe that was why *QS* had chosen Rannoch Moor.

The buffet lunch was the usual selection of deep-fried breaded protein, nonetheless catering for all diets: carnivorous, vegetarian and vegan. It was a sunny day, so I thought I'd take a picnic back out to George Square. But, just through the entrance, I saw Lucy Lopez and the two Americans heading in the same direction, deep in conversation.

Bloody hell! What's going on? Why did the Americans imply they didn't know LL? Or was that my false implication?

With no desire for any of their company, I headed up the hill and found a bench beside a modernist rendition of the Callanish stones, in the middle of the university campus.

Yes, I checked my stone. No response.

After lunch, I returned to the conference venue. Just beyond the revolving door, I saw Lucy Lopez again, but with someone I didn't recognise. He seemed to pass her something, which she popped into her conference bag.

The lecture theatre was almost deserted. The woman with the T-shirt returned to the microphone, accompanied by an older woman, introduced as Dr Irene Popescu from Transylvania, currently the holder of a Hambledon Fellowship at Broxburn University, in the Department of Applied Meta-Magical Anthropology.

Dr Popescu proved a highly excitable and animated presenter. Her central thesis was that quantum physics was just another belief system, given plausibility by an apparent fit to what we perceive of as reality. Nonetheless, as with all belief systems, it had been appropriated by the dominant class for their own ends.

Quantum systems were a contemporary form of oracle, used to make believable predictions about the future. And the close fit of their predictions to reality made them particularly dangerous, far more so than nonsense about General Artificial Intelligence. We already knew how to make real intelligence. She had a daughter to prove it.

I laughed. She beamed at me. Lucy Lopez sat down beside me, wryly shaking her head.

Dr Popescu continued. We worry about the ethical implications of AI, but we have no idea about how to constrain the use of these new systems. So, why should we be concerned?

She gave a brief outline of interpretations of quantum physics, focusing on the Everett hypothesis, that reality continually bifurcated between many worlds. For physicists, this was a metaphor, but supposing we took this literally, just as ancient peoples took the shadows cast by standing stones literally as portents of what was to come?

I sat up straight in my chair, intent on her presentation.

'Of course standing stones can be used tell the time, or mark the seasons, but they can't predict the future. Still, people behaved as if they did. Now, suppose people could be persuaded that there really were many worlds, not just at the quantum level, but on our macro scale. Suppose people truly believed that quantum computing, backed by science far more plausible than shadows, really could predict the future? This would give whoever controlled it extraordinary power. Power for evil as well as good. Why should we grant such power to rapacious plutocrats, plutocrats like P. Ross Peyroux, whose plans for world domination were masked by his performance of disinterested philanthropy...'

Lucy Lopez leapt up onto the stage and took the microphone away from a highly agitated Dr Popescu. Then she gesticulated to two servitors, who gently led Dr Popescu to the wings.

I'd had enough. I picked up my goody bag and headed up the aisle. Helen was sitting in the back row.

'That was weirdly relevant, man,' she said. 'I came in late. I'm sorry I didn't hear all of it.'

'I can let you browse the transcript,' I said.

I fumbled in the goody bag and came up with two identical data sticks.

'Looks like there's a duplicate,' I said. 'Why don't you take one.'

'Thanks,' said Helen. 'Let's get out of here. Do you know anywhere decent for a coffee?'

I led Helen down through Merchant City towards the Clyde.

'I guess you're staying at Bernie's,' I said. 'How are they all?'

'In fine fettle,' said Helen. 'But you've confused the hell out of Bernie. And thanks for dropping me right in it over her new squeeze.'

'If she's changed her mind about our divorcing,' I said, 'then she should have told me first.'

'Fair enough,' said Helen. 'But naming Thierry. That's just what I've been talking about, man. Confusing *before* and now. That can't go on.'

'That was a mistake,' I said. 'I was really angry. Anyway, it could be a lucky guess.'

'That'll be right,' said Helen.

I stopped outside a wee café just off Albion Street, that Bernie and I used to like. The cafe was quiet, and we quickly found a table towards the rear. Once the waiter had taken our order, Helen didn't waste any more time.

'Why did you mention Nando?' said Helen. 'According to cousin Steven, he's a drug dealer the police have just picked up.'

Helen looked increasingly incredulous, as I told her about Nando stowing away, and how I'd discovered that he'd been at Cruachan, around the same time as Miran.

'Oh! Whirling waters!' said Helen. 'The prophecy!'

'Bloody hell!' I said. 'A prophecy? That's what Rial told me!'

'You met Rial again?' said Helen. 'Where on earth was that, man?'

I explained about my panic attack at Cruachan, and how Rial had appeared and calmed me down.

'That Rial's a piece of work,' said Helen. 'Now we're both in their debt.'

136

But it was my turn to be incredulous, as Helen told me how Rial had rescued her from her shipmate on South Uist.

'Is your ship running drugs?' I asked. 'That doesn't seem at all like you.'

'If I'd known that,' said Helen, getting crosser and crosser, 'I'd never have taken the gig, would I! And the odds are the police are going to bust me along with the others.'

'Why does Rial need both of us?' I asked, as our order arrived.

'It's a long story, but you've got to know, man,' said Helen.

Helen recounted an increasingly wild tale about ancestors and witches and prophecies. But it all felt worryingly familiar, as if the past had come back to bite us. Well, rather, she'd sought it out, just as she said she would.

'Rial needs us,' concluded Helen, 'because of the prophecy that two stones are needed to free them from Mr Ross.'

'You mean Peyroux?' I said. 'How is Rial in thrall to him?'

'I think Mr Ross is some kind of sorcerer himself,' said Helen. 'Remember we both saw Rial all bound up in green stuff, in that druggy vision? I saw that again at the Calanais stones. And I saw Mr Ross yesterday, and I'm sure he tried to work something on me.'

'He sought me out after his speech,' I said. 'He seemed quite urbane, but from what you're telling me, maybe he was trying to threaten me. So, is he in on the drugs? That seems unlikely, surely. Is there any link to Nando?'

'I don't think so,' said Helen, 'but Steven did ask me to mention Nando to my shipmates. I've not had time yet.'

I thought quickly.

'What about Miran?' I said. 'I'm sure she's been at Cruachan at the same time as Nando. You said she was another shipmate's girlfriend? She said she was looking for someone. Could that have been Nando?'

Helen reminded me that Cal had definitely mentioned Miran. In any case, like her, he was employed by Peyroux, not part of the charter crew.

'What if there's a connection between Nando and Peyroux?' I said.

'No way, man,' said Helen. 'Not if he's a drug runner.'

'Fair enough,' I said. 'That would jeopardise Peyroux's investment in *Quantum Solutions*.'

I told Helen about the *QS* plan to link Cruachan and their plant with a road across the Moor. When I mentioned Lucy Lopez, Helen became quite excited.

'Lucy Lopez!' said Helen. 'She's Steven's girlfriend. Or she was. I met her on Lewis. She gave me big spiel about her PhD in quantum computing.'

'Quantum computing?' I said. 'She told me it was in materials science.'

'You know what,' said Helen, 'she met my drug running shipmate on Lewis. Steven wasn't amused. Now ex-girlfriend, I think.'

Jesus Christ!

Helen's phone buzzed.

'That's the part,' said Helen. 'It's finally turned up. I better go and collect it before they lose it.'

'You can't just leave things hanging!' I said.

'Sorry, man,' said Helen, getting up. 'Duty calls. Let's do email.'

Chapter 20 – Helen

Thursday Jun 16th - Glasgow

I decide to hell with the expense and call a taxi to take me back to *TransWorld Navigation*. The part's come in early and I might be able to get the flight before the one I'm booked on. I'm standing there on the street waiting for it to appear when a familiar voice says:

'Hi, honey.'

It's Martha the physicist. And there's Dean in tow. But what can she possibly want given we haven't really met in this timeline? Surely they don't remember me from the lounge in the *Ormacleit Castle*? Given I was earwigging, I really hope not.

'Can I help you?' I say, turning on customer service mode.

'We saw you in the conference,' she says, 'with that nice Mr Nicholson. He did us a good turn when our automobile ran out of power on Rannoch Moor. And honey, I couldn't help noticing your logo.'

She points at the *Midsummer Queen* badge on my fleece.

'Is that Mr Peyroux's ship?' she asks.

'Not his as such,' I say. 'He's chartered it.'

'Owned by a Russian, then?' Dean asks in a much less friendly voice.

'So I was told,' I say. 'I've not met the owner. I was hired by Mr Peyroux, just for the charter.'

'But you've Russian crew then?' Dean asks.

'Only the first mate,' I say. Martha and Dean exchange a look. I don't like the way this conversation is going. Come on, taxi!

'And you've sailed into Glasgow?' Dean says.

'No, I've flown over from Lewis to collect a part we need,' I say. And then add, though I'm not sure why: 'Mr Nicholson is my cousin and so I thought it would be good to do a bit of family stuff while I was here. I'm not a quantum person.'

Ooh dear, they share another look. What is going on here?

'And do you know our good friend Lucy Lopez too, honey?' Martha asks.

I'm tempted to lie at this point. I have this feeling Lucy is bad news, especially when her name comes up just after my mention of Boris. But I don't. Better not if you don't have to.

'I met her briefly,' I say. 'She seems to have organised a good event here, I hope you've both enjoyed it.'

Phew, that's the taxi, at last!

'Nice to have met you both,' I say, hailing it energetically. 'Must dash, I've a flight to catch.'

I ring Elena back on the *Midsummer Queen* from the taxi – she made my travel booking. She says she'll try to move my flight to the earlier one that I still ought to be able to make. I feel I need brownie points with the crew for showing enthusiasm right now. I go over my conversation with the Americans but can make nothing of it. The pre-Incident Martha and Dean were into industrial espionage – maybe these versions are too? Well, if they are, it's not my problem, though maybe it's one for Mr Ross.

I get the taxi to wait when we get to *TransWorld Navigation*, collect the carrycase with the part in it, and we're off to the airport. The case should fit in the overhead lockers and I've no other luggage because the original plan was same day.

The traffic is terrible enroute to the airport and I start to worry I should have left my booking as it was. I also have plenty of time to think about that meeting with Malcolm as we inch along. Seems like my second Lucy Lopez bombshell hit home. He looked almost as upset as Steven. I wonder whether she has a PhD in anything other than making it all up. And whether Mr Ross knows whatever it is she is doing with Boris. If not, I wouldn't want to be in her shoes when he finds out. Oh – maybe the Americans know. That man sneaking a pic of them could be one of theirs and not our police at all.

I don't scare easily, but Mr Ross really is quite scary. Having him on the ship is going to be a nightmare. Mebbe I should have said more to Malcolm about him. Underlined the sorcery bit. Did he really see how ominous it was that Mr Ross came up to him specially? Malcolm needs a bomb putting under him if you ask me.

Well, I'd still put money on Rial managing to recruit him. I hope so, because if Rial is going to help me I bet they must be free of Mr Ross first.

I'm out of the taxi like greased lightning when we get to the airport. Oh joy, the board shows the flight has a thirty-minute delay. And Elena has texted to say I am on it. I might just make it back for our evening scran. You can get used to Monsieur's haute cuisine.

Though I've flown a great deal – most of my cruise gigs started somewhere distant – I'm not a fan. Especially in small planes like this one. I'm happy when we touch down after a very bumpy hour in the air. Give me a ship any day.

Ten minutes in another taxi and I'm back at the *Midsummer Queen*.

Not quite hail-the-conquering-hero but the Captain tells me he is very pleased to see me. In his warmest tone, with one of those dazzling smiles.

'I asked Damon if he could stay on and install the fix tonight,' he says. 'So it's great, Helen, that you got the earlier flight. We need to sort this before Mr Ross joins us. He is due tomorrow around midday, and wants us to start for Jura in the afternoon. We'll overnight at Barra, but after that there's some tricky navigation between islands.'

'Happy to help,' I say, in best customer service style. But I wonder whether the part will help if it turns out it's Rial that's fritzing the navigation system. And feel a bit cold inside at the speed with which Mr Ross is joining us. We could easily have picked him up from Islay in a day or two.

At least I've made it for the evening meal.

Monsieur has been working hard with his local ingredients and we have wild salmon terrine followed by game pie. Good stuff. Everyone seems rather cheery. Except for Cal of course. Rial is absent yet again and I try to recall whether I have seen them eating anything at all since they joined the ship.

Not sure how it comes up, but the conversation turns to our working names. I give them the story of how I came to be Hulkie – it involved stopping an almost-punch-up in my Nissan prentice days between a Mackem workmate and a stuck-up Geordie foreman.

'But don't you think it's a little fierce sounding to your colleagues?' Elena asks. I point out I've worked on very large cruise ships where things are not always sweetness-and-light like small private yachts. I give Boris a big smile as I say this. And for sheer devilment I decide to do Steven his favour.

'You think my name is odd,' I say, 'well, I came across someone called 'Nando' like the chicken chain. I bet he gets plenty of requests for "extra-spicey."' I'm watching Boris as I say it but see no reaction from him other than an eye roll that goes with the groan from Elena and Velho.

But to my surprise there is a sharp intake of breath from next to me, which is where Cal is sitting. He starts to say something but stops himself, and when I turn to look at him, his face is like thunder. The others stare at him, but he just puts his head down and focuses on his food.

After an awkward silence Velho valiantly picks up the conversation and tells us his working name means 'wizard' in Finnish. He got it because his mother is a Sami, people native to the part of the far north called Lapland in English, and reputedly all wizards.

'You magic us mended navigation system then,' Boris says. 'Is all dumb stuff I think. We have real names, we use those.' Well, he'd soon learn if he was on a cruise ship that it doesn't always work like that, but I don't comment.

I wait for Cal to leave at the end of the meal and then follow him out. He heads for the main deck and I'm pretty sure he knows I'm behind him. He stops by one of the rails, looking out towards Stornoway Castle over the inlet. The woods look green and peaceful in the evening sunshine. I join him, leaning on the rail next to him.

'Cal, I'm sorry if I upset you. I had no way of knowing my mention of someone called Nando would be a big deal for you. Do you want to tell me why?'

'First tell me how you know the name. Maybe it's not him. Because how could he be here?'

I tell him what Steven said about the arrest, and then what I just found out from Malcolm about Nando coming from Cruachan and stowing away in his jeep. Cal turns to look at me as I go through all this and looks more and more horrified.

'Me cago en Nando! It's him! He's after Miran!'

'Is Miran your girl-friend? Because she came out of Cruachan too. She was at the christening in South Uist.'

Right away I wish I hadn't said that. Cal's face crumples up into an inarticulate sob.

'Oh Miran, Miran, mi amor, mi vida! She was there, so close, and I didn't know,' he finally manages to say. 'Now Nando will find her, and I'll never see her again.'

'Whyever is that, man? Is he a threat to her?'

'Only to me. He loves her. He took her away from me.' His face changed suddenly. 'Mr Ross mustn't know. He's looking for them.'

'Mr Ross? Why? What are they to do with him?'

'Of course, you don't know. Miran is his daughter.'

Oh.

'You were instructed not to discuss this,' comes a new voice, from behind us, making us both jump. Rial. Who else?

Cal flees back inside the ship immediately.

'And was there an 'anomaly' here too?' I ask as cuttingly as I can manage.

'There are things of which I can speak and things of which I cannot speak,' Rial says. Looking uncomfortable, I'd swear.

'But why is Mr Ross looking for his daughter and her boyfriend?' I ask. Rial says nothing. OK, that's not a surprise. Green spider web stuff I expect. Well, I can imagine why they'd rather he didn't catch up with them. I expect he has views on his daughter's boyfriends and I'm sure you'd prefer not to be one he didn't like. Imagine Mr Ross in a radgie...

But Miran and Nando are important. They must be the 'two' of the whirling waters in Margaret MacAskill's prophecy. Not Rial and Cal. Hmm, Cruachan's over on the mainland, somewhere near Rannoch. Goodness knows how we get them back there. This reminds me of problem-solving computer games I have played where you have to be in the right place at the right time with the right people and objects. I was never much good at those.

Let's try a different topic while I've got Rial here. I whip out my phone.

'Rial, I think our faulty navigation equipment might actually have something to do with you?'

'With me?'

I fire up the GPS sensor display from an app I installed.

'Stand still for a moment if you can.'

I can see the GPS readings are jumping all over the place. I walk backwards away from Rial. Still jumping horribly but at first glance the range may have narrowed a little. I walk right up to them. Yes, the range gets wildly worse.

'Well Rial, I'm not sure how you do it, but you are definitely fritzing my phone's GPS sensor. No wonder our navigation system is having trouble locating us accurately. I bet sticking the new translocator in won't help one bit. Can't you stop whatever it is you are doing?'

'Can you stop breathing?' Rial says.

'I can hold my breath for a while,' I tell them. 'We need the kit to work to get us to Jura safely, it's not like sailing across the wide-open Atlantic.'

'It means going blind,' Rial says, sounding very unhappy. 'Not seeing across the timelines. Being only here.'

'I suggest you cover your eyes for a while then, man, however that works. And stay put. At least tonight while Damon does his stuff and goes away happy, and then when we sail until we get to Jura. Or do you want us to hit something between islands?'

Rial doesn't answer, but I think they've got my point.

Journal June 16

Too much is happening. I'd like a day off please – which is what I wanted but didn't get in Glasgow.

Wow, Mr Ross is Miran's dad. I guess I need to tell Steven that Nando is her boyfriend. It could mean Mr Ross is in on the drug smuggling after all. I really hope not given he's my employer. I'll text Steven. And I really need to tell Malcolm as well. Should I just email him or gave him a call?

Blowing his mind twice in one day seems a bit harsh, it can wait until tomorrow.

Now here's a question: if Rial can 'see' so many things, how come they haven't helped Mr Ross round up Miran and her lad already? Rial certainly must have clocked Miran at the christening, after all. They could easily have known she was staying with Malcolm's daughter as well. That might not have been good news for Alison. Just as well Miran scarpered.

And here's an answer: Rial already knows – or has seen – something about them which fits their own escape plan. Mebbe the prophecies weren't all news to them after all. And Rial could always 'play the daft laddie', as Dad sometimes says, and not tell Mr Ross things unless he asks directly. 'Devious' would be Rial's middle name – if they had one.

How long was Rial there when I was talking to Cal? Did they hear what I said about Nando? Did they already know where Nando was too, or have I just told them that? I hope not.

Just now, and just for fun, I googled for Lucy Lopez AND PhD. The only relevant result from that is a *Quantum Solutions* webpage listing her as public relations consultant. Then I did one on the words I remember from the title she quoted me: 'spin-optical quantum architecture'. Bingo! It brings up an academic paper and her name is not in its author list. Hah!

Chapter 21 - Malcolm

Friday June 17th – Rannoch Moor

Helen's call woke me up. In more ways than one. As I showered, I tried to get my head round what she'd told me.

Miran's Peyroux's daughter. And she's looking for Nando. And Nando's looking for her. But they arrived together. Or maybe they didn't? I should have checked the time stamp on the Cruachan CCTV footage more carefully. Well, he certainly appeared after her. And she's not Cal's girlfriend. But Cal's somehow in thrall to Peyroux.

And what about Rial? They behave like an independent agent, but they still seem tied to Peyroux. And Rial and Miran and Nando and Peyroux all trigger my stone. They must have some connection to some other world, like *before*.

Dougie said Nando's in custody. I needed to speak with Dougie, and try to make sense of it all.

My visit to the *Quantum Solutions* plant wasn't until mid-afternoon, so I went to work as usual. On the road up onto the Moor, I got stuck behind a long convoy of new age travellers. Other drivers were less patient than I am, and I finally pulled off at the Visitor Centre to a cacophony of horns.

I spent the morning sorting through the accumulated post. The plumber confirmed the date for fitting the coffee machine, but running new pipes was going to make quite a mess. I'd need to locate a decorator. I hoped there'd be enough of *QS*'s bribe left over to spruce up the display cases, if not for a new data projector.

At lunchtime, I went up to the *Altnafeadh Hotel*. Dougie, in his usual seat, looked hot and bothered, constantly checking his mobile.

'What's up?' I said, joining him.

'Those bloody travellers,' said Dougie. 'I've been told to monitor them. What a bloody hassle.'

'I really don't mind them,' I said. 'So long as they clean up after themselves, and they usually do, they're far more welcome than rubber-neckers dumping fast food packaging all along the road.'

'That's as may be,' said Dougie, 'but there's still a lot of hostility to them. We really don't want the locals stirring up trouble.'

'Where are they heading?' I asked.

'I've no idea,' said Dougie. 'Bloody right to roam. They can go pretty well wherever they like.'

Jeannie approached, bearing my unstated order, as if by telepathy.

'Thanks,' I said, as she plonked it onto our table.

'What have you been up to?' said Dougie. 'We've not seen you for a couple of days. The cat's been asking after you.'

'Sorry,' I said. 'I hope it's not a nuisance.'

'Och no,' said Dougie. 'Glenys dotes on it. Where have you been?'

'I'm supposed to be checking out *Quantum Solutions*,' I said. 'I've been to Cruachan and then Glasgow. I'm off to their plant this afternoon.'

'Busy man,' said Dougie. 'Is that about the road?'

'Due diligence,' I said, 'but it's a waste of time. I reckon it's a done deal. Still, I get time in lieu, and I'm maybe going to Jura. Depends on Polly.'

'Glenys says she's here tomorrow,' said Dougie, 'but I expect you knew that.'

Oh, right. Aye well, I should have called her. Or maybe she should have called me.

'Sure,' I said, vaguely. 'Anyway, what's happening with Nando? Has he told you anything useful?'

'No,' said Dougie. 'He didn't seem to understand why he was being held. And then he was released to his uncle.'

'Who's his uncle?' I said.

'A Ross Peyroux,' said Dougie.

Whoa. Miran and Nando are cousins. Is that even legal?

'Peyroux's behind *Quantum Solutions*,' I said. 'And Henry's film. I wonder how Nando fits into everything.'

'Not a scoobie,' said Dougie. 'Thank goodness it's the weekend.'

After a leisurely lunch, I set off south. The *QS* plant is in the middle of the Moor. I thought I'd take the main roads there, down to

Crianlarich, northeast up the side of Loch Tay, north on the A9 to Pitlochry and then back west on the minor road to Rannoch Station. After my visit, I'd try to find that strange section of new road to complete the loop.

As I turned off the A9, I noticed a shiny black SUV behind me. It kept its distance, and stopped at Rannoch School. Probably some posh parent visiting their benighted child. At Rannoch Station, I carefully crossed the tracks of the West Highland line, and let myself through a gate marked *Quantum Solutions*. Beyond the gate was fresh tarmac. That hadn't been here before. The road led down the north bank of Loch Laidon to the low cluster of buildings at Tigh na Cruach. All around, the moor was unbroken wilderness, the peaks of Glencoe rising stark to the west.

As I parked up, a man in a suit, accompanied by a security guard, came out of the nearest building.

'Mr Nicholson!' said the man, in a northern European accent. 'Welcome to *Quantum Solutions*. I'm the site director, Gustav Heinz. And I've heard all the jokes about 57 varieties, thank you.'

The security guard silently handed me a clipboard.

'It's an NDA,' said Heinz. 'Standard procedure.'

I signed the form and returned it to the guard.

'There's not a lot to see,' said Heinz, leading me into the nearest building and summoning the lift. 'The main assembly's in the old mine workings below us.'

The lift arrived. Two buttons: *G* and *L*. Heinz pressed *L* and we slowly descended.

The door opened onto a large chasm of aisles of identical card frames, filled with racks and racks of identical boards. There was a loud hum from the air conditioning units that lined the walls.

'How do you get everything down here?' I asked. 'The lift's far too small.'

'There's an access shaft at the rear,' said Heinz. 'Big enough for a forklift truck.'

We walked down the central aisle. Banks of switches flickered. We could have been in a 1960s science fiction film.

'This is our first-generation system,' said Heinz. 'If all goes well, the next generation will be quadruple the scale but take up about the same space.'

'But it's really hot now,' I observed.

'Yes,' said Heinz. 'That's why we need more power, for the cooling as well as the processing.'

147

'How does it all work?' I asked.

'I thought Dr Lopez explained this,' said Heinz. 'Superimposition of states. Entanglement.'

'You've lost me,' I said. 'Is there something about the materials the system's built from?'

'That's an astute guess,' said Heinz. 'A lot of people would pay good money to know the details. But it's all commercial in confidence.'

'I'm most interested in the road,' I said.

'Of course,' said Heinz. 'Let's go up.'

When the lift arrived, a curiously familiar man got out, and headed into the machine room. As the lift ascended, I realised I'd seen him at the conference, passing something to Lucy Lopez. Must have been work related, then.

Back outside the building, Heinz walked me to the Land Rover.

'Look,' said Heinz, pointing along the new road. 'You can see it has minimal impact.'

'I get that you need all-weather access from the east,' I said, 'but why do you need to extend all the way west? Can't you just cut and cover the cable?'

'It's not that simple,' said Heinz. 'I understand that Dr Lopez briefed you about the new room temperature superconductor. We've no idea how it will perform when deployed at scale outside the laboratory. It's likely there'll be intermittent failures. If we're constantly sending vehicles out to fix it, we'll chew up the track, especially if it's wet.'

I laughed politely at this sally.

'That's reasonable,' I said. 'But how will you restrict access? There's all this talk of a Central 400.'

'We'll put in gates,' said Heinz. 'And there'll be CCTV monitoring. But, yes, we don't want floods of visitors, and we certainly don't want breakdowns. Let's see how it goes. If the cable proves durable, we can revisit the need for the road.'

'I'll just write all this down,' I said, finding my notebook. 'For my boss.'

'Please send me your report,' said Heinz.

'Of course,' I said.

I stood and silently scribbled. Heinz inspected his smart watch.

'Is there anything else you'd like to know?' said Heinz. 'I need to get back to the coal face.'

'What are you actually doing?' I said. 'In words of one syllable. I gather it's some sort of search engine.'

'It's far more than that,' said Heinz. 'It's more like a forecasting system.'

'For the weather?' I said.

'That's a trivial example,' said Heinz.

Just wow!

'Essentially, we can explore the probabilities of different developmental trajectories. As we scale up, we can model arbitrarily complex systems.'

'Like the stock market?' I said.

'That's one of our early benchmarks,' said Heinz. 'But, ultimately, we want to explore the fundamental nature of reality.'

Just wow cubed!

'Possible worlds?' I said. 'Predict the future?'

'Oh, you don't want to believe that nonsense,' said Heinz. 'It's all scaremongering. Reality's far too big to model.'

'But if weather forecasting's trivial,' I said, 'you're implying that you can handle quite substantial subsets.'

'That's the hope,' said Heinz. 'To capture deep properties of increasingly large neighbourhoods.'

'Neighbourhoods?' I said. 'Of what? You've lost me again.'

'Well, all right,' said Heinz. 'Possible worlds, if you must. But quite sparse ones.'

'You mentioned trajectories,' I said. 'Is that like timelines?'

'I suppose that's one way of looking at it,' said Heinz. 'If it helps. Anyway, it works best if we know what's important. What to focus on.'

Why is Peyroux interested? Lightbulb moment.

'Can you track people?' I said.

'That would be wholly unethical,' said Heinz.

That's not a denial. Maybe there is something in Irene Popescu's fears?

'Surely,' I said.

'Anything else?' said Heinz. 'You can always contact Dr Lopez. Her PhD's in science communication, so she can probably explain this more simply.'

Helen was spot on. Lucy Lopez has everyone fooled. What's her game?

'Nothing more,' I said. 'Thank you. You've been very helpful. Is it all right if I just carry on along the new road?'

'Of course!' said Heinz. 'Have a good day.'

The new road was well laid, and I made good time onto the open Moor. As I approached the Menzies Stone, I heard the noise of another vehicle. Checking my rear mirror, I saw the black SUV accelerating towards me. Before I could pull over, its bull-bar caught my driver-side rear bumper, and spun me off the road.

Dazed and frightened, I staggered out of the Land Rover. The SUV had pulled up behind me. As I turned to confront the driver, I was pinioned by my arms from behind, a cloth bag was forced over my head, and my wrists were bound with what felt like a cable tie.

'Where's the memory stick?' shouted a mid-Atlantic male voice.

'What memory stick?' I stammered.

'Don't mess with us, or it'll be worse for you,' shouted the man. 'The one in the conference bag you stole.'

'But I didn't steal a bag,' I said.

'Sure you did,' said an older Deep South male voice. 'I bet it's still in the jeep.'

'It's a Land Rover,' I said, weakly.

'Whatever,' said the older man.

I heard a car door open.

'Here it is,' he said. 'Still on the passenger seat.'

'Tip it all out,' said the younger man.

I heard the sound of objects landing on some surface.

'Looky here,' said the older man. 'You're not Lucy Lopez, are you?'

'Of course I'm not!' I said.

'Then why have you got her name badge?' said the older man.

Jesus Christ! I'd taken the wrong conference bag.

'Isn't the memory stick still there?' I said.

'There's one in the bag' said the older man, 'but it isn't the one we need. What have you done with the other one?'

'The duplicate?' I said. 'It's just conference proceedings, isn't it?'

'Don't tell us you didn't check it first,' said the younger man. 'Come on. Where is it?'

'I gave it to my cousin Helen,' I said without thinking.

'Cousin Helen, eh?' said the younger man. 'Is she part of your gang? Come on. Let's go find this cousin Helen.'

I was shoved backwards into the heather.

'Don't hurt him any more,' said the older man. 'There'll be the devil to pay if it gets back to Martha and Dean.'

And the black SUV drove off.

I rolled over, and fumbled around until my fingers felt tarmac. Then I crawled onto the road, and groped around some more until I encountered a Land Rover wheel. Must be the front nearside; I could tell by the dished in hub cap. I hauled myself up, and felt my way to the passenger door. Swinging round onto the seat, facing backwards, I rooted in the glove box for my Scots army knife. Once I'd extracted the small blade, I carefully worked the knife round, and cut the cable tie without damaging myself. Finally, hands free, I untied the bag over my head.

I felt very badly shaken up. I really shouldn't be driving in this state. But I had to warn Helen. I got into the driver's seat, fired up the engine, and edged the Land Rover back onto the tarmac.

These were professionals, and they were obviously after whatever Lucy Lopez had been given about the plant, on the other memory stick. What on earth did it reveal that made it worth attacking me?

Maybe I should I tell Dougie? But what could he do? Send CID round to interview me? I suppose the black SUV might be on *Quantum Solution*'s CCTV. But it was the weekend, and that could all take days. Helen was in danger now.

At the Menzies Stone, the tarmac ran out, and I was back on the familiar gravel track. Just shy of the *Black Corries Lodge*, I saw smoke rising from the heather. Must be the new age travellers. Any other time, I'd have checked them out.

I stopped where the track met the road, and felt in my pockets for my phone. My phone wasn't there. I don't think they took it. It must have fallen out when they pushed me over. I couldn't face looking for it now. I'd call Helen from the landline when I got home, and go back for the mobile first thing tomorrow.

At the front door, the cat sat stoically, beaming disappointment. I let us both in, petted and fed the beast, and ran a bath. As it slowly filled with warm brown peaty water, I phoned Helen.

Chapter 22 - Helen

Friday June 17th – Stornoway, Lewis

I get hold of Malcolm really early, he sounds only half-awake. But he's duly gob-smacked by my news about Miran. I wonder whether somehow she knew I was working for Mr Ross and that was why she ran off at the christening? And why she also ran off from Malcolm's daughter? Poor thing, to be so desperate to get away from her father.

I don't have much time to wonder though as it's all-hands-on-deck time as soon as breakfast is done. We have to look good when Mr Ross arrives. Yes, it does include scrubbing the deck and polishing everything in sight. Boris predictably slides out of doing any of it and just gives the orders. Cal is so deliberately inept, I follow him around and do it right for him.

He glares when I gently point out he's left smears of polish on the brass rails as I rub them down for him.

'It's all right for you,' he says, keeping his voice right down. 'You're not a slave. You can leave.'

'Why don't you contact the authorities then, man,' I say, also very quietly. 'Modern slavery is illegal in the UK.'

'Soy imbécil,' Cal says. 'It's not that kind of slavery, don't you know that by now? And where would I go, he stole my island.'

He has a point. Explaining green spider web to a lawyer seems unlikely. I decide this could be a good moment to get to the bottom of the stolen island, but before I can ask another question, Boris sees us with our heads together. 'Is problem?' he asks.

'No problem, man,' I say, 'just talking types of polish.'

'You polish then. Not talk,' he tells me and stalks off.

Cal moves off in the opposite direction and my chance goes. For now.

We finish soon before midday and scatter quickly to get our dress uniforms on. Captain Tucker wants as formal a reception party as a skeleton crew can manage. I'm guessing that he has never met Mr Ross in person but for one reason or another wants to impress him.

Soon after midday, when we are assembled back on deck, one of those extra-large taxis with sliding doors pulls up on the quay. Rial has gone to meet the flight and leaps out of the front. Before the driver can get there, Rial opens the back door. Mr Ross emerges, dressed in yet another fancy jacket, this one in a tasteful shade of violet. To my surprise he's walking with a stick, a rather swish carved hardwood affair, though I don't detect a limp.

And a second person slowly follows him out – a young man. Who the hell is this? Strong-bodied, clean shaven, with long curly black hair?

Hmm, there's something odd about him. His sweat-shirt and jeans seem too big for him, but it's not that. Oh – he's not looking around, not admiring the yacht or the view, sort of staring into space. There's a sudden hiss of breath from next to me. Cal. 'Puta! Nando!' he says, in a fierce near-whisper. I elbow him gently to shut him up. The Captain will be maximally pissed off by a scene at this point.

I try to control my own face. It looks like Mr Ross has got his hands on one of his targets already.

Mr Ross leads them up the gangplank, Nando behind him and Rial last. I notice Rial's hand sits lightly on Nando's back.

The Captain does the formal intros, and we each nod as he names us. Mr Ross' eyes rest on me a little too long, or am I imagining that?

'Good to meet you all at last,' says Mr Ross smoothly. 'You all know who I am I think; this is my nephew, Nando. I'm afraid he isn't feeling all that well today, so I'd like to get him settled in his cabin quickly, please.' Elena is on my other side, and she nudges me at the name. She must remember yesterday's mealtime chat. Oops.

And Nando is his nephew! As well as his daughter's would-be boyfriend – well, I can see that might not go down well.

While this is happening, several large bags are being unloaded back on the quay. I guess all those fancy jackets take up some luggage space. Rial gestures at Cal, who glares, but troops back down onto the quay and starts lugging bags back up. As if having Mr Ross on board wasn't enough fun, we now have Cal and Nando too. Light blue touchpaper...

The protocol dictates that guests eat their meal and then the crew eat theirs. But Mr Ross decides both he and Nando will eat in his cabin, and Elena rushes off to set that up. The rest of us grab hurried plates from the usual buffet; off to Barra as soon as we can manage, the Captain says. The weather forecast has squalls.

'You met Nando already?' Velho inevitably asks when we are starting up the turbines a little later on.

'No, man,' I say. 'But when I was in Glasgow I went to a quick meeting with Mr Ross, and the name came up then.' Mebbe I'm getting better at lying.

Today's sailing is straightforward, back down the islands to Barra at the bottom. Tomorrow will be less so as we cross the Minch southeast and then dodge between various islands closer to the mainland to reach Jura.

About halfway down we do hit a squall and have to cut our speed for a while, but we still arrive well before 5 and anchor in Castlebay. And there is indeed a cool castle in it, not very far from the shore, on a tiny rocky island. No summons from Boris about navigation issues enroute. Rial must have found a way to keep their profile down.

I've knocked off and am on the way back to my cabin when my mobile goes. It's cousin Malcolm. Better answer that then.

'Hi Malcolm. Hang on while I get into my cabin.' Likely to be something I don't want publicly aired. I shut the door behind me. 'OK!'

'Helen, thank goodness you're there.' He sounds quite fraught. 'You're in danger. Watch your back. They want the memory stick.'

'Hold on, man. What memory stick? Who are "they"?'

'The one I gave you yesterday. The conference proceedings. Only it's not.'

That memory stick is still in my fleece pocket.

'But if it's not the conference proceedings, what is it?' I ask Malcom.

'I really don't know,' Malcolm says. 'But I was attacked. They were in a big black SUV. I think the Americans are behind it. Dean and Martha. They want the memory stick. So how's Lucy Lopez involved?'

Lucy Lopez? Memory stick?

'Slow down, man. Tell me what happened from the start.'

He tells me a scary story about being driven off the road, doesn't know who by, they put a bag over his head. A couple of men. American accents. He was sitting next to Lucy Lopez at the conference and picked up the wrong bag. So the memory stick he gave me is hers.

'Helen, I'm really very sorry. They asked me where it was, and I didn't think. I said I'd given it to you. I know I should never have said that.'

Oh dear. Typical Malcolm. But no point in tearing strips off him. If those prophecies work out, I'm going to need him on my side later.

'OK, man. Not the best news, but done is done. And tell you what, Martha and Dean nabbed me yesterday afternoon when I was waiting for my taxi and they were asking about Lucy Lopez. I think it's industrial espionage again, like before the Incident.'

'Bloody hell, Helen!' says Malcolm. 'You really had better watch your back. It didn't go well for you last time round. I am so sorry!'

'Forewarned is forearmed. Anyway, nobody is going to get an SUV to Barra tonight, and we're off to Jura tomorrow. But yes, for sure I will watch my back. And see what is on the memory stick.'

'You could just throw it over the side of your ship,' Malcolm says.

'Not sure that's a canny move, man. Better to know what we're dealing with. You could report the attack to the police?'

'The police round here is my neighbour Dougie. What can he do about it? And I can't stand the hassle. Do you want them on your back as well?'

'Good point, well made.' Attracting yet more police attention? No, not a good idea. 'Well, no gowk is going to put a bag over my head, don't worry. Take care now, man. You'll feel out of sorts after all that, have a quiet evening and recover.'

We end the call. I didn't remind him that the Americans know about the ship and can probably locate us quite easily. Hmm, when the slimy Ms Lopez met Boris in Stornoway, it probably wasn't about the drugs after all.

I need to see what's on the memory stick because the odds are that Boris will start looking for it. But I don't have the time now.

I whip out my laptop, insert it and copy the whole thing. There's only a few hundred meg so it doesn't take long. I turn it into a zip file called 'Holiday Snaps' and drag it into my Photos directory. I also create a directory called Holiday Snaps and drag some random pics into it. Then I upload the zip file to three different cloud locations. After which I close down the laptop and stow it. I leave the memory stick in full view on my bedside table.

I sit down with my e-reader and the latest Sword and Sorcery. Ten minutes later there's a tap on the door. It's Elena.

'Hi Hulkie. Velho says he wants to run some extra diagnostics before we eat, and can you come and give him a hand.'

Off I go. As I expect, it's trivial stuff that takes about ten minutes. That was a bit transparent. After that, me and Velho both go straight to the lounge for our scran.

Mr Ross and Nando are still eating in their cabins, so we can sit down right away. Elena has a trolley for their servings and Cal is there to push it along to the cabins. Out he goes and then there is a tremendous crash. What a surprise.

Elena rushes out and I can hear her raised voice.

'Is disaster that walks, Cal,' says Boris.

Elena is a while and Boris puts a cover over her food. She comes back without Cal.

'How does he do it?' she says, sitting down and taking the lid off her food. 'Bounced the trolley off the passage wall, broke a glass and half the water jug slopped everywhere.'

'Not sure he enjoys working for Mr Ross,' I say. 'I think he's on some kind of restrictive local contract.'

'Won't enjoy Mr Ross when angry,' Boris comments. I wonder how he knows?

'I helped him in with the trolley, to avoid any other accidents,' says Elena. 'That young nephew seems a bit odd. What they call 'a learning difficulty' perhaps? In a world of his own.'

I could believe this if I hadn't heard very differently from Malcolm, but I don't comment. Boris won't remember what Rial did to him, but Nando has the same blankness. Though I haven't heard any weird Rial music, so I bet it's down to Mr Ross. Poor Nando.

I agree to a backgammon session with Velho but I have my Friday WhatsApp with Wilf to do first. Back in my cabin, I note that the memory stick is still there but not quite in the same place. Oh, at a closer look, not the same memory stick. Well, that's more intelligent of Boris than I expected. I plan to look at the files much later on.

I have a twenty-minute chat with Wilf, and it goes better than last week. He tells me his work gossip and I give him a very edited version of mine, including my short Glasgow trip and a version of meeting Mr Ross. I leave out drugs and the Calanais stones, and don't tell him how events seem to be closing in on me and Malcolm both. If my ghostly ancestor is on the money, some big thing will happen soon, at the solstice. So probably on Jura.

I do tell him that the Captain says the reason we are going to Jura is that Mr Ross has a stake in some historical adventure film. He wants to inspect the cast and some location filming. Wilf is as much a sucker for film glamour as I am and so I promise I'll nose around if I can and take some pics, check out if there are any big stars. No news on how long we'll be there, I tell him, but every likelihood my gig will finish in not too many days.

156

'So mebbe I'll be ganning hyem soon,' I tell him.

'Really hope so, Hulkie,' he says, 'Love you.'

He always says that. I know I ought to say the same, but is it really true?

'Looking forward to being back,' is all I manage. It will have to do.

Journal June 17 - 18.

In fact it's now some god-awful hour of the next day. I started on the memory stick files when I knocked off the backgammon at 10, after losing every game. Velho looked happy.

A few hundred meg isn't much for copying but it's a lot in textual material, even though quite a bit is pictures and diagrams. It's clearly a dump of a sizeable part of *Quantum Solutions* private archives. Wow!

I wonder how the slippery Ms Lopez got hold of all this? She must have an accomplice working in the plant. I've spent hours so far going through it all and I can see that it probably has enough detailed technical material on the design and construction of the *QS* quantum computer to reproduce their work. Industrial espionage in action! Boris is not just into drugs then, though this seems more likely to be the ship owner's ballgame.

Here's the thing though. I kept going through all the specification and implementation material until I got to test suites and test results, with performance graphs. Seems like quantum computers can be a bit uncertain about which world their results relate to – if I get one of the technical position papers right. Oh yes, I remember the Americans talking about this back on South Uist. *QS* claiming 95% accuracy on 'quantum collapse', I think they said.

The Americans. I wonder whether she's been playing both ends against the middle and trying to sell this stuff to two opposing groups? All that designer kit she has must cost a bit.

Anyway, there is a table labelled 'quantum collapse accuracy' for different runs. It starts two summers ago and rises all the way until nearly the end of September that year. And then it drops from 95% to 69% and stays there! That's very odd timing too, almost as if the Incident is involved somehow.

And right on the end of the archive, there's a set of emails between various *QS* people. That graph is what they are talking about, or rather arguing about. One of them says the current prototype machine and the design behind it must be ditched, it's no good. They've tried everything they can think of to get it back to 95%. And 69% is useless for all the practical applications they have been targeting.

And there is a very heavy email from a guy called Gustav Heinz – like the beans – who is the site director. Recent as well, only a couple of weeks back. They are to keep totally schtum about the results and the discussion because the conference is coming up and they have a patent application in as well. Well, high-tech overselling and hyping is what they all do. But not often do you get hard evidence of it.

I wonder whether Lucy Lopez knows all this then? It wouldn't be in her interest to destroy the illusions of the wasps round the jampot. But my guess is she hasn't gone through it like I just did. And she's no more a quantum person than I am.

The question is what do about it now.

I could carry on pretending I haven't seen any of it. Though another possibility is inventing an anonymous whistle blower and dumping it all into public spaces, like Wikileaks. That's a better plan. Because when it's not secret anymore that gets everyone off my back. As long as they can't prove I made it public, anyway.

And those items at the end would probably stop that big road project across the moor Malcolm says *QS* are pushing. Oh yes, he said there was a campaign group, what was it? *Rannoch Against Quanta*, I think.

Google agrees, and they have a contact email.

I just need to check anonymisation and away we go – it's irresistible.

Chapter 23 - Malcolm

Saturday June18th - Rannoch Moor

I woke to the cat pawing at my face, claws barely retracted. I batted it away, and sleepily reached for my phone. Which wasn't there. Of course. It was still on the Moor. I really had to retrieve it.

I went through to the kitchen. The clock on the microwave said 10am. I hadn't slept so late in years. I opened a tin of fishy grey goop, spooned half into the cat's bowl, and filled the kettle. While the water boiled, I rootled in the cupboard for my old phone. The battery was long flat. I set it up to charge. Then I realised I was still naked, and I hadn't shut the curtains last night. So I fled to the shower, not that I needed one, in an attempt to wake myself up.

Standing under the warm spray, I pondered my phone call with Helen. Things were getting more and more entangled. She was heading for Jura. Maybe we could meet up there if I went with Polly. So much to try and resolve.

I couldn't believe how accepting Helen had been of my dobbing her in to Martha and Dean's thugs. But I still didn't get the connection with Lucy Lopez. Were they rivals, or working together? And why were we involved? I knew Helen could look after herself, but, still, she hadn't ripped into me, as well she might. I wondered what she wanted of me. Something to do with green stones, no doubt.

After I'd dried myself and dressed, I had a cup of tea and a big bowl of cornflakes. My old phone was now 50% charged. I vaguely recalled getting an unwanted SIM with £10 of credit, when I bought the new phone. More rootling turned it up in a dresser drawer. I installed the

SIM into the old phone, and, manfully resisting the urge to set it up, left the cottage.

'Nice all over tan you've got, Malco!' called Dougie, from their front yard. 'Must be that Highland sunbathing!'

I waved ruefully at him, and set off for the Moor. The road was very busy, but the traffic flowed smoothly. At the *Altnafeadh Hotel*, I turned off onto the track to the Menzies Stone. Not for the first time, I mused on how convenient tarmac would be, especially in the winter.

The travellers were still camped up beyond the *Black Corries Lodge*. Maybe I'd check in on them on the way back.

At the Menzies Stone, I parked up, phoned my longstanding number, and followed the ring tone. The phone was nestled in the gorse, not far from the fresh tracks left yesterday by the Land Rover. Luckily, the phone had gone to sleep. I woke it up and checked for messages. There was one from Polly, saying she should be with me mid-morning. I'd never quite got around to phoning her, so she'd no idea what had happened to me. If she arrived before I got home, she could always go and see Glenys.

I pocketed the phone and set off west. At the *Black Corries Lodge*, I followed the sheep track north to the travellers' encampment, nestled by Lochan Meall a' Phuill, at the foot of Meall nan Ruadhag. The track was now deeply rutted, and going was slow.

As I approached the encampment, I felt my green stone starting to vibrate. Who could be there? Rial, most likely. Certainly not Peyroux. I hoped it wasn't one of the witches. Their return would be bad news.

The travellers had formed a circle with their vehicles around half a dozen tipis. Dougie would have commented on western inversions. I walked round the motley selection of motorhomes and caravans, checking the stone. The vibrations grew stronger as I neared an ageing single decker bus, painted day-glo yellow.

There seemed to be no one around. I stopped beside the bus, and rang the wind chimes hanging from the wing mirror.

'Too much, magic bus,' I said as a tough looking woman emerged from the tipi next to the bus, sweeping her dreadlocks back over her shoulders.

'The old ones are the best,' said the woman. 'Maggie West. Who are you?'

'Malcolm Nicholson, *Rural Resources*,' I said.

'Have you come to check on us?' said Maggie. 'We've every right to be here, you know.'

'Of course you have,' I said. 'I just thought I'd drop by and introduce myself, in case you need any help with anything.'

'We're quite self-sufficient, thank you,' said Maggie. 'Anyway, isn't this your day off?'

'There's no rest for the Rural Rangers,' I drawled, channelling Dougie.

Maggie laughed.

'You're all right,' she said. 'What can we do you for?'

Green stone. Brain working overtime, I moused up the photo of Miran.

'Ah,' said Maggie. 'Miran. Yes, she's here.'

'That's a relief,' I said. 'How did you meet up with her?'

'She stumbled into our camp at Balloch, just before they moved us on,' said Maggie. 'How did you know she'd be here?'

'Ranger's intuition,' I said. 'Can I see her?'

'How do we know we can trust you?' said Maggie.

'Let me talk with her,' I said. 'She can decide.'

Maggie disappeared into the bus, and came out with Miran.

'Miran!' I said. 'Are you OK? Alison's really worried about you. And she says the boy's missing you.'

'They were very kind,' said Miran, 'but I couldn't stay. I have to find Nando.'

'Maybe there's a branch in Fort William,' said Maggie.

To my relief, Miran smiled. It was obvious this was now a standing joke for her.

'Maybe your stone can help?' said Miran.

Maggie looked puzzled.

'We don't need the stone,' I said. 'He's with your father.'

Miran's face fell.

'My father wishes him ill,' she said. 'I must go to him.'

'But maybe *I* can help,' I said. 'My cousin Helen works for your father. On his boat. But she's really suspicious of him.'

'Is that the large woman who was at the christening?' said Miran. 'She has a stone, as well, doesn't she.'

'What's with the stones?' said Maggie.

'The stones speak to us,' said Miran, 'for good or ill.'

'And people say I'm loopy,' said Maggie. 'Can I see this famous stone?'

I took out the stone and handed it to Maggie.

'It doesn't do anything for me,' said Maggie, handing it to Miran.

The stone came alive in Miran's hand, pulsing heartbeat green.

'Cosmic!' said Maggie. 'What's it saying to you?'

'It says I can trust him,' said Miran, passing me back the stone. 'Please help me find Nando.'

'Well,' I said. 'Helen told me that the boat's heading for Jura. Maybe Nando and your father will be onboard. I'm going there anyway, tomorrow. You can come with me, if you like.'

Miran looked a Maggie. Maggie nodded assent.

'Very well,' said Miran. 'I'll gather up my possessions.'

'It's good that she trusts you,' I said, as Miran returned to the bus.

'It's good that she trusts you!' said Maggie.

'Where are you off to next?' I asked.

'After the solstice,' said Maggie, 'we're slowly heading east, for the fruit picking on Tayside.'

I was filled with sudden devilment.

'There's a new road,' I said, 'running east from the Menzies Stone. If you head south the way I came, you'll meet the bigger track to the Stone. It'll keep you away from the main roads, and be a lot gentler on your vehicles.'

'Thanks!' said Maggie. 'That's really helpful!'

Miran came out of the bus carrying a backpack. I recognised it as one I'd bought for Alison, so many birthdays ago.

'Let's get going,' I said.

'How can I contact you,' said Maggie, 'to make sure Miran's all right?'

'Here,' I said, proffering Maggie my business card.

'Rural Ranger,' read Maggie. 'For real! Do you always get your man?'

'That's the Mounties,' I said, 'but I'll do my best.'

I retraced my route back to *Altnafeadh Hotel*, and parked next to Dougie's car.

'Why are we stopping?' said Miran, anxiously.

'It's lunchtime,' I said. 'And I'm hungry. Aren't you? It's all right. It's quite safe here.'

As we got out of the car, Dougie came through the hotel doors.

'Malco!' he called. 'You're late today. And who's this fine young lady?'

'Hey Dougie,' I said. "This is Miran, a friend of my daughter Alison.'

'Howdy Miran!' said Dougie. 'I'm the sheriff round these parts. Can't stop. Cattle to rustle.'

Dougie got into his car and drove away.

'What a strange man,' said Miran, as we made our way into the restaurant.

'Och, Dougie's very decent,' I said, sitting down at what I increasingly thought of as our table in the window. 'Come and join me.'

'You're late today,' said Jeannie, appearing from the kitchen. 'What'll it be?'

'I'll have the usual, thanks,' I said. 'What would you like, Miran?'

But Miran was entranced by the brown décor I'd long since ceased to notice. She flitted round the walls, inspecting the fading photos of hunting and skiing parties, and peering into the glass fronted cabinets of Victorian crockery.

'She'll have egg and chips,' said Jeannie, firmly. 'Everyone likes that.'

Miran joined me at the table.

'This place is wonderous!' she said. 'Frozen images of multitudes. Yet no notice of who they are.'

'They'll be long forgotten,' I said. 'As will we all, eventually, I suppose.'

'How can that be?' said Miran. 'I can clearly recall everyone I've ever met.'

'Goodness!' I said, not wishing to wrestle with the complexities of time and memory. 'I certainly can't.'

Jeannie arrived with the food. We ate in companionable silence, Miran with gusto, as if she were famished. I wondered how old she was, and whence she came. She speech was almost archaic, and everything seemed surprising or frightening to her. Yet she'd survived as a stranger in a strange land.

When we'd finished, I settled up with Jeannie, and drove us down the moor to Achallader.

Megan's car was parked outside Glenys and Dougie's cottage. There was no sign of Polly's car, yet her wheely luggage was just inside my front door. Perhaps she'd come by train, and Megan had picked her up. Why hadn't she asked me?

There was a strangely familiar smell in the kitchen. And a strangely unfamiliar stainless steel flask sat amongst freshly washed mugs on the draining board.

'Oh!' said Miran, eyes wide. 'Travellers!'

Before I could stop her, she poured herself a draught, and downed it in one.

'Here,' she said pushing past me into the living room.

On the floor sat Polly, Glenys and Megan, cross-legged, eyes closed, holding hands. Glenys and Polly smiled beatifically, as they moved sideways to make space for Miran.

'Join us!' mouthed Polly, without opening her eyes.

'I think not,' I whispered, backing out of the room, and closing the door.

Ayahuasca. From Helen's boat, no doubt. Glenys must have known all along. That must have been why she was keen to get to my Land Rover before Dougie. Come to think of it, Polly and Megan must have known all along as well.

I went outside to get some air. They'd be half an hour or so. I hoped they weren't too sick afterwards. I knew who'd have to clean up.

Eerie music crept up on me. I turned round to face Rial.

'You didn't go with them.'

An observation.

'No,' I said. 'Once was enough.'

'It lets you see, but it doesn't let you do,' said Rial, wistfully.

'I really can't be doing with any of this,' I said. 'Why are you here?'

'Why are *you* here?' said Rial. 'Why aren't you with Helen?'

'Why would I be with Helen?' I asked.

'The prophecies,' said Rial. 'The stone will take what the stone gave. When the two take the path of the whirling waters.'

'Do you mean Miran and Nando?' I asked. 'Or do you mean Helen and me?'

'Had you travelled with the others, all would have been clear,' Rial said. 'The solstice is the time when our worlds may be untangled. You and Helen must face the whirling waters and conjoin your stones. Together, they are stronger than my master.'

'Why should I believe anything you say?' I asked. 'As far as I can see, all you've done is cause us both grief.'

'For Miran,' said Rial. 'To free Nando.'

Before I could ask exactly what that meant, the music faded as Rial evanesced into nothingness.

I returned to the cottage. Retching sounds came from the bathroom. I poured the rest of the ayahuasca down the sink, and made a large pot of tea.

Polly emerged, beaming, and threw her arms around me.

'Oh Malcolm!' she said. 'It's really good to finally see you again.'

'Come on, kids,' said Glenys, encouraging Megan and Miran out of the cottage. 'Let's leave these love birds to it. Don't forget to close the curtains.'

We disentangled ourselves, and stood facing each other, holding hands. I raised an eyebrow.

'I'm so sorry, Malcolm,' said Polly. 'I'd love to, but I've got to get back.'

'But you only just got here,' I said. 'I thought we were spending the weekend together.'

'I've finally been summonsed,' said Polly, 'by the big boss, but it's all for the good. We can still meet on Jura. I've booked us into The *Blair Arms*, at Barnhill. Can you be there tomorrow evening?'

'Can't we go together?' I said.

'No,' said Polly. 'It's too complicated.'

'Did you only come for the drugs?' I said.

'Don't be like that,' said Polly. 'Of course I wanted to see you. And it's not as if you haven't tried it.'

'Certainly not by choice,' I said. 'Anyway, what's this all about? I thought Wiccans were into ritual and tradition.'

'We're way beyond that,' said Polly. 'The old ways are too haphazard, now we know it's all connected, the quantum many worlds and dreamtime travelling. And today was astonishing!'

'You've done this before,' I said. 'Is that why you're so tight with Glenys and Megan?'

Polly ignored this.

'We hadn't realised how much the participants affect the experience,' said Polly. 'When Miran joined our circle, everything shifted subtly into the space she shares with the three of us, which is far more substantial than we'd ever have thought.'

'Is this like some sort of Venn diagram of timelines?' I said, grasping at analogies.

'That's a good way of putting it,' said Polly, 'and you and Helen are at the intersection of this one. You're the link that binds it all together.'

Rial's prophecy.

'How do we resolve things?' I asked.

Of course I knew.

'You have to come to Jura,' said Polly, firmly. 'For the solstice.'

'And what are we supposed to do on Jura?' I said.

'I haven't a clue,' said Polly. 'But I'm sure we'll work it out.'

'That doesn't sound at all like you,' I said. 'You're usually the analytic one. Decisive.'

'Things change,' said Polly. 'People change. You know that. Look, I do need to go.'

'But I've made tea,' I said, pathetically. 'Can't I at least take you to the station?'

'Thanks,' said Polly, 'but I've arranged to go with Megan. We've a couple of things to do. I'll see you tomorrow night.'

'The *Blair Arms*,' I said.

'Yes,' said Polly, 'and if I'm not there, find the Tarbert standing stone.'

She gave me a lingering kiss, led me outside, and banged on Glenys' door.

The three women joined us.

'We'd best be off,' said Megan. 'Don't forget your bag.'

I watched helplessly as they drove away.

'Come on,' said Glenys, linking her arm in mine. 'How about that tea.'

Chapter 24 – Helen

Saturday June 18th – The Minch

Why do we always get an early start after a night when I haven't had enough kip? The captain is worrying about the weather again, a rising wind, and wants us across most of the Minch by midday. I help Velho get the turbines started for 8am once more, feeling way below full fettle.

Not only did I spend half the night on the *Quantum Solutions* memory key, when I finally turned in, I had another session of horrible dreams. More diving through whirling waters, pursued by Mr Ross this time, finishing with a glare of light. I woke up with a headache as well. Jura's going to be where things do or don't happen. Of course I'm not scared.

The wind is already rising by the time we are underway, and it's a bouncy ride. Though as so often in these parts, it's a westerly, which makes it partly behind us as we steer south-east. But there will be nothing between us and it until we're nearly there.

After half an hour I see Mr Ross and Rial on the main deck, looking wind-blown. Sensible decision if you lack good sea legs. I wonder if the hapless Nando is throwing up below. Mr Ross and Rial are having some kind of argument I'd say. Mr Ross gestures in the air and turns to Rial, who shakes their head. More than once. I'd love to know what that's about. I wonder whether Mr Ross wants Rial to do something they have agreed not to do for fear of fouling up our navigation again. Though goodness knows what.

After a while, they both retreat to the lounge. It may be midsummer, but that doesn't mean it's especially warm at this latitude. Elena brings

Mr Ross some coffee. I'm in and out of the lounge, as I have to keep an eye on the engine parameters. But by mid-morning I need a coffee myself to deal with my sleep deficit. I go to grab one from the machine behind the lounge bar. And I hear Mr Ross tearing strips off Cal. He keeps his voice down for sure, but my hearing is good.

'You think you can deceive me don't you? You think I don't know your black heart, that you'd like to do me harm? You will do what I say or you will pay for it.'

I watch from the corner of my eye as I operate the machine. He points his hand at Cal with the fingers spread and says something not in English. It makes me shiver, whatever it is. Faint green lines appear on Cal's body, and he cries out as if he's been struck. Mebbe he has. That man is a bully. I decide I'd like to do him down too if I ever get the chance. No wonder Cal has such an air of bitterness. I get myself out of there through the back of the bar.

The morning wears on and we pass Tiree on the port side. It's a low island, with nothing much to see, but it means we're halfway across. Our next island will be Colonsay, and then we'll start to be out of the wind. It seems we're taking the long way to Jura – all the way south round its neighbour, Islay, and back up the two east coasts.

Velho passed on what Boris said about the route: going across the north of Jura is risky as there are dreadful tides, and routing between the two islands involves synchronising with the inter-islands ferry crossings. We're heading for a tiny place called Lagg on Jura's east coast because that's where the film crew are based. No riotous nights on shore I assume.

By midday we're heading round Islay and conditions are much less choppy. There's a good view of the mainland and its mountains. Mr Ross and Rial sit down at a table in the dining area with the Captain and Elena serves them selections from Monsieur's buffet. I wait until that's done, then grab a plate for myself and a plate to take down to the engine room for Velho. Elena is collecting a plate to take to the Bridge for Boris, and I ask her very quietly as we leave the lounge how Nando is doing.

'The poor guy was pretty ill earlier,' she tells me, also with her voice right down. 'I left him a bowl and some cleaning cloths. Though I'm not sure he was together enough to sort himself out. When I've taken this up to Yuri Petrovitch, I'll have another look.'

If Mr Ross wants people to believe in his sick nephew story, he probably needs to show a bit more concern.

An hour or so later we reach Lagg. It's a small bay with an old landing stage and a new pier with a couple of pontoons, which probably has something to do with the *Lagg Sea Sports* installation I can see on the shore. This has a large sign 'Sea kayaking, Sailing School, Blue Space Eco-therapy'.

It's hard to connect 'Blue Space Eco-therapy' with bouncing across the Minch in a half-gale, but mebbe it brings in the punters. Something has to, given how empty this coast looked as we sailed up it. But there was a great view of the Paps, the Jura mountains. I'd love to tackle them but it looks like we're on the wrong side of the island for easy access. But how about some sea kayaking? That might work.

We drop anchor about a hundred metres out in the bay. Velho, who seems to know what is going on without any obvious effort, tells me Mr Ross wanted us to tie-up. The Captain vetoed it because according to the charts, there was a chance we'd end up aground at low tide. That means we'll have to shuttle to-and-fro in the tender again.

Naturally I'm dying to scope out the film people. Disappointingly, there's nothing very visible from where we are moored. So when the Captain asks me if I could possibly take Rial over on the tender I jump at the opportunity.

'We plan to host the film director and a few others this evening,' the Captain tells me. Excellente! I suppose Rial is the messenger. I'd like to think Mr Ross is cleaning the vomit off Nando but somehow, I don't think so.

Velho brings the tender round to the yacht's rear platform for me. Cal appears unexpectedly alongside Rial.

'I'll come too,' he says grumpily. Then: 'Please.' Looking at Rial, not at me.

I don't have him down as impressed by film glamour but after seeing him on the receiving end of Mr Ross, I can see why he might prefer to be off the ship for a while.

Rial shrugs and we all three get ourselves into the tender.

Once we're ashore, Rial heads past the *Lagg Sea Sports Centre*, looking as if they know where they are going. Then suddenly stops, freezes, turning their head as if they are listening to a radio broadcast I can't hear.

'I'm sorry, there is something I must do. Wait for me here. There's a café in the Sports Centre,' Rial says, gesturing at the white-painted stone house behind the boat sheds. Before my astonished eyes, they fade out of sight.

'Whoa! What happened there, man?' I say. 'Where's Rial?'

'El burro sabe más que tú,' says Cal in a tone of insult. Then, before I can work out quite how rude he was: 'You know Rial can spirit-walk whenever they like. Across anything, times and places. Rial told me you know this!'

'Oh, sort of, man,' I say. He's right, I guess. 'Bit different from watching them doing it though.' Deep breath. 'OK, let's find the sports centre café.' I can ask about sea kayaking too.

Inside the white house two downstairs rooms have been knocked into one large one. There's a reception desk at one end and a counter with a flashy expresso machine and a small display of tray bakes at the other. There are a couple of small tables.

The man at reception looks up from his computer screen with a welcoming smile. Very tanned face, lots of unkempt fair hair with a bit of grey in it, and extremely white even teeth.

'Hey guys, come on in! How can I help?' An American from his voice. Hence the teeth.

'Thanks, man,' I say. 'Can we get a couple of coffees and some of those delicious tray bakes you have?' Something about American enthusiasm is catching.

I install us at the further of the tables with our coffees and tray bakes. I assure the man, who says he's called Emerson, that we are just fine, are off the ship out in the bay, are waiting for a friend, and just have a few business things to chat about together while we are waiting. Which does send him back to his computer, luckily.

In the lowest voice I can manage, I ask Cal: 'Look man, I saw Mr Ross having a go at you earlier. Why do you put up with it? Why didn't you just desert the ship before we got here?'

Cal gives me a contemptuous look. 'You still don't get it do you? We can't leave. If he calls for us, we have to come. Or it hurts more and more.' He keeps his voice down to a near whisper.

'OK, man. Then how did this happen? When?'

Cal sighs deeply. 'He stole my mother's island. My mother was an obeah-woman, a woman of respect. Driven away from her people after a gringo attacked her and she conceived me. She fled to an island where nobody was. She found Rial there and bound them to her aid.'

'Sounds like she was into enslaving as well then?'

He glares at me and makes a hissing sound.

'What could she do? She could only survive and defend her child like that. Rial was like a parent to me when I was small. They filled the island with music. We were happy.'

'OK, then what?'

'When I was ten, Mr Ross came to the island with Miran. He said he was driven out by his own brother. Miran was only three. My mother was sorry for him. She welcomed him and showed him the island and how to live. In return el hijo de puta had her arrested for using ayahuasca like all obeah-women do for spirit-walking. They said it was drugs and took her away. I never saw her again. She went to the spirits.'

Ouf, heavy stuff. Explains a lot about the way Cal behaves.'He made documents to say he owned the island. He bound Rial to himself and then me as well so I couldn't stop him.'

Well, Cal could be making it up, but what I've seen of Mr Ross makes it pretty believable. What a shit that man is. I'm about to ask some more questions when quite predictably, Rial walks in. Cal shuts up right away.

Rial nods at Emerson, who gives him the same routine as us.

'Just here to collect my friends,' Rial tells him. 'We are visiting the film crew up at *Sealladh Bàgh House*.'

'Gee,' says Emerson. 'That's my little sister Zelda directing it! Tell her to bring them all down for tray bakes when they have a moment.'

'Sure, man, we will,' I say, paying for what we had. Hmm, mebbe a bit of nepotism is why they are filming here?

'What was that, man?' I ask Rial as we walk uphill towards a large stone house on the road. 'Yet another anomaly?'

'Your cousin must come to Jura,' Rial says.

Oh, did Rial somehow go off to see Malcolm when he vanished just then? I don't ask. I know Rial needs Malcolm. But whether Malcolm will perform the way Rial wants him to is a different question. How about I tell him Cal's story? Surely he'll see that if we can free them both then that's what we should do.

There's chaos up at the house when we get there. A good dozen people milling around, one of them apparently flying a drone. A couple of Highland ponies tethered to the fence. Equipment being unloaded from two minibuses. Rial tells us to wait outside, and I watch it all with great interest and take a few sneaky pics. No stars that I recognise but why would I? I don't have the time to watch a lot of films or TV. But Wilf is into streaming and all that.

Rial emerges and back down the hill we go. There are four people coming to dinner on the ship, Rial says. Zelda, the author of the book the film is based on – a man called Henry something – and two male actors. Neither of the actors have names I know. Disappointing. But it will give Monsieur the sort of challenge he enjoys. I pop into *Lagg*

Sea Sports enroute to get some sea kayaking gen off Emerson and then it's back to the ship.

Journal June 18

I sent Wilf a long and gossipy email with my pics from this afternoon and an account of the meal. Such as I managed, given of course I wasn't at it. But I did earwig a certain amount of their chat from the other end of the lounge. Well – it can't have been confidential. And I took another quick pic for Wilf.

We did the full dress-uniforms-on-deck reception again for them and they looked suitably impressed. Zelda isn't that young a kid sister, must be a bit older than me, though a lot smaller. She doesn't look much like Emerson, her hair is bright pink, but I suppose she could be fair, like he is. She has that air of command I bet she needs to boss a film crew and actors, and she didn't let all those men talk over her at dinner, though of course they tried.

The writer, Henry, had lots to say, a real full-of-himself gowk. The film's about a church minister called Preacher Man, who's more into derring-do and romance than saving souls by the sound of it. Sort of a Hebridean *Thornbirds*. They are going to film, of all things a 'horse chase' where the baddie is after the Preacher Man, which is why they have the two ponies I saw. This sounds more like comedy than drama to me. And when Mr Ross – schmoozing away – asked the two actors how good they were on ponies, they sounded very cagey.

Still, Zelda seemed right on top of things. She even said some of us could join the extras if we liked! I'd love to but I just know at my size I'd stand out far too much. Literally.

All that distracted me from fuming about Cal's story. After hearing that, if there's any way of shafting Mr Ross, then I'm in.

And talking of shafting Mr Ross, I've been looking out for news on *Quantum Solutions*. Nothing as yet. Could be I should have sent stuff to some actual journalists, not that I know any. I'll leave things for a few days and then mebbe have another go. At least, if the solstice doesn't change things. That's only a few days now. Of course I'm not scared.

Chapter 25 – Malcolm

Sunday June 19th – Rannoch Moor

I awoke to the sound of running water. Mindful of Miran, I pulled on my dressing gown, and went into the corridor. The floor was awash, water pouring from under the bathroom door. I banged on the door and opened it. Entranced, Miran, fully clothed, was perched on the edge of the bath. Both taps were running and, even though the plug was out, the bath was overflowing. I must get the drain cleared.

'Turn it off!' I called.

Instead of complying, Miran smiled and made a pass with her hands. The water reversed direction, back into the bath and then up the taps. Within 30 seconds, the bathroom and corridor were dry.

'Astonishing!' I said. 'How did you learn to do that?'

'My father taught me,' said Miran.

'Was your father a wizard?' I said.

'Cal said father was a sorcerer,' said Miran, 'but I think he's a mage. He studied ancient lore from a book he called his grimoire. I wasn't allowed to read it.'

'Why did he teach you how to control water?' I asked.

'Father said that, on an island, water is our biggest fear,' said Miran. 'When do we leave?'

'After breakfast,' I said. 'After my shower. After I've bought the ferry tickets. And I better let Helen know we're coming.'

'These are my pearls,' said Miran, picking up the soap dish.

'Yes,' I said. 'I'm afraid that your waistcoat fell to bits when I washed it.'

'Thank you for rescuing them,' said Miran, scooping up the pearls. 'They remind me of my home, so far away, so close.'

The ferry departure was in the late afternoon, from Kennacraig on the Kintyre peninsula, a couple of hours to the southwest. Under normal circumstances, it's a straight run, so I was relaxed about leaving mid-morning.

But, 20 minutes out, just beyond Dalmally, we were flagged down by Dougie, whose Battenburg was blocking the road. I pulled over into the layby, and got out.

'Hey Dougie,' I said. 'What's happening?'

'Oh man,' said Dougie. 'There's a big demo at Cruachan. The road's been clogged up at the junction by a lorry load of logs. It's crazy. Some of the protestors are dressed as beavers. They claim they're building a dam. I'm sure it's Henry's mob, but there's no sign of him.'

'What are they protesting about?' I asked.

'The new road,' said Dougie, looking me straight in the eye. 'I wonder how they found out about it.'

'I wonder,' I said, avoiding his gaze.

'They must know it's linked to *Quantum Solutions*,' said Dougie. 'They're calling themselves *Rannoch Against Quanta*. They've got some cracking placards though. "We're all entangled!" and "If you're part of the Solution, You're Part of the Problem!"'

'Is there press interest?' I said, hopefully.

'Oh yes,' said Dougie. 'There's even a TV team. It'll be all over the news. Anyway, where are you bound for?'

'We're heading to Kennacraig,' I said, 'for the afternoon ferry to Islay.'

'What takes you to Islay?' said Dougie. 'It's a fine place for whisky.'

'I'm meeting up with Polly on Jura,' I said.

'That's Orwell country, isn't it,' said Dougie. 'Didn't he say a dram's better than a dam?'

'Boom, boom,' I said. 'But that was Huxley's *Brave New World*, not *1984*. Is there really no way through?'

'It'll take three or four hours to clear the road,' said Dougie. 'You'd do best to turn tail and go down Lomondside.'

'Aye well,' I said. 'That'll add a good hour. We'll be on our way then. Have fun!'

I re-joined Miran in the Land Rover, made a U turn, and headed back east.

Miran was very quiet. Once we'd taken the road south at Crianlarich, I asked her what was eating her.

'I know that place,' she said.

'Cruachan?' I said. 'How do you know it?'

Of course I knew.

'That's where the whirling waters brought us,' said Miran. 'Nando and I. But we lost each other.'

'How exactly did you wind up there?' I said. 'And where are you from, really?'

'We're from the island,' said Miran. 'I've always lived there, with father.'

'Is that an island with palm trees and sandy beaches?' I asked, remembering the ayahuasca trip.

'That's right!' said Miran, excitedly. 'Have you been there?'

'Not exactly,' I said. 'I've seen it. How did you come to live there?'

Miran's tale sounded like the plot for a Mafia film. She was an only child, and her mother had died when she was very young. Her father and uncle had a longstanding feud over who controlled the family business, which sounded pretty dodgy, not that Miran knew any details. When her uncle gained the upper hand, he forced her father to flee the city. They'd moved to the island, where they'd lived quietly ever since. Quite recently, her father and uncle had begun to patch things up, and her cousin, Nando, came to visit.

Her voice lit up as she said his name.

They had fallen in love more or less on sight, but her father had forbidden the tryst. So, not really knowing what they were doing, they'd stolen away in what she called a jollyboat, and set off for the next island. They didn't make it very far, though, at least not by boat. A huge storm blew up, and they were driven back onto the cliffs. Miran tried to use her skills to calm the waves, and they were swept into a cave. The next thing she remembered was coming out of the waters at Cruachan.

'I waited for dear Nando as long as I could,' said Miran. 'But he must have arrived before me. I pray that we can find him.'

A curious turn of phrase.

'Who do you pray to?' I said.

'Cal prayed to the old gods,' said Miran. 'The words were beautiful. That's where I learnt of travelling, of seeing other worlds that are almost like ours.'

They must use ayahuasca for their rituals on the island.

'Who's Cal?' I asked.

Miran wasn't sure. Cal had always been there. From how she talked about him, he seemed to be some sort of servant. He claimed the island had belonged to his mother, and that Miran's father had stolen it. I couldn't really see how that would work, and decided to let it drop.

'Was anyone else there?' I asked.

'Just Rial,' said Miran. 'Rial did father's bidding.'

'As a servant, like Cal?' I said.

'Not exactly,' said Miran. 'They were more of a free spirit.'

'Not very free, by the sound of it,' I said.

At Tarbet, halfway down Loch Lomond, the road turned west over the spur towards Loch Long. There was a standing stone just after the junction, but I was sure that wasn't the one that Polly meant. It was midday. I tried the radio for the news bulletin, in case there was any word of the demo, but reception was poor as always.

I stopped for lunch at Arrochar, at the head of the loch. Miran picked at her food, clearly anxious to get going. I agreed. The steep and winding Rest and be Thankful was notoriously beset with long tailbacks. Luckily, the road was clear, and we continued to make good time, down to Inverary on Loch Fyne.

As we left Inverary, Miran, who had been snoozing on and off, suddenly said: 'What is your story, Malcolm? Tell me about the green stone. Where did it come from? Why do you have it?'

I did my best to summarise the strange events of the Equinox that wasn't, what Helen calls The Incident. When I'd finished, Miran said:

'Your stones came from the witches' familiars. We do not have green stones on the island, yet your stone speaks to me, and I can sense Helen's.'

'But you have other things,' I said, slowly twigging on, 'with the same effect?'

'Yes,' said Miran. 'My father has a crystal orb and a wand.'

'Did Cal have anything like that?' I asked.

'Not that I knew of,' said Miran.

'Who was Cal's mother?' I said.

'Father said she was a witch,' said Miran.

Oh, right.

'Do you like Cal?' I said.

'Not as much as he says he likes me,' said Miran. 'He behaves as if we have some mutual obligation, because we grew up together. But, at best, I feel sorry for him. After dear Nando came, he became troublesome. I hope he will leave me alone, once Nando and I are united.'

That doesn't sound good.

We followed the east bank of Loch Fyne south as far as Tarbert – yes, another one, and another standing stone. Just as we turned west across the peninsula, I thought I spotted someone emerging from round the back of the stone, but we were moving too fast to see clearly.

It was a short distance to the Kennacraig terminal. The ferry was just boarding but there was a long queue. I was glad I'd booked ahead that morning, as cars without tickets were being turned away.

The weather was squally as we crossed, and the waves were choppy. I feared that I might lose my lunch, but Miran was really in her element, standing in the bows facing the wind, hair streaming behind her. After two hours, we berthed at Port Askaig, and joined the queue for the five-minute crossing to Jura.

I hadn't reckoned with the diversion on the way, and the Land Rover was running low on diesel. Jura's pretty desolate even by Western Island standards, and I was relieved when we finally arrived at Lagg, about halfway to Barnhill. Just offshore, I spotted a sleek super-yacht. That had to be where Helen was moored.

'I think that's your father's ship,' I said to Miran.

Miran said nothing.

The *Lagg Coop*, next door to the *Sea Sports Centre*, had pumps, so I stopped to fill up the tank. I wasn't sure how far I could trust Miran to stick with me. I put my mobile number, and The *Blair Arms* details, into my spare phone, and showed her how to turn it on and make a call.

As I was paying for the fuel, I asked the storekeeper where the film crew was based.

'You'll be wanting *Sealladh Bàgh House*,' said the storekeeper. 'It's just through town. You can't miss it.'

Of course, when I got back to the Land Rover, Miran had gone. I was worn out. And she'd shown she could well look after herself. There was no way she'd get onto Helen's ship, but if she needed help she could always call me.

I drove on north to Barnhill, passing the sign for the Tarbert standing stone a wee way out of Lagg. I slowed down, but there was no sign of Polly.

At Barnhill, The *Blair Arms* was opposite Orwell's last home, where he wrote *1984*. But the hotel sign sported a caricature of Tony Blair, someone I was sure Orwell would have loathed. My heart sank when I saw a minibus in the carpark labelled *Official Orwell Tours*.

The hotel itself was a solid sandstone building, which seemed almost rooted into the island bedrock. Inside, it was bright and warm. Opposite the reception desk was a glass case full of Orwell memorabilia. The famous black and white photo of Orwell at his typewriter, cigarette dangling, hung over the desk.

I pinged the brass bell, and the hotelier came out of the office to greet me. I said I was with Polly, but they said she still hadn't arrived. Would I be wanting dinner?

'I would,' I said. 'I would.'

Then I remembered Miran, and asked if there was a spare single room. The hotelier said that the place was quite busy, but there'd been a cancellation, if I wanted to take it. And would that person be wanting dinner as well?

'I suppose so,' I said, proffering my credit card.

I went up to our room, and checked my mobile. Still nothing from Polly. I wondered what had happened to her. I wasn't actually very sure when she was supposed to get to Jura, other than before me. I went downstairs for dinner.

At one end of the dining room, at a large circular table, a party of Orwell enthusiasts was being lectured at by a man full of opinions passing as facts. His assertions about how the older Orwell felt about his youthful dreams being dashed seemed entirely specious, but his audience lapped it up.

Dinner was perfectly decent British catering, as befitted Orwell: soup, meat and two veg, and fruit pie with custard. All that was missing was a litre of bitter. Replete, I returned to our room. Perhaps that was now my room.

I tried to call Miran, but she didn't pick up. I had forgotten to show her how. Anxious about Polly as much as Miran, I undressed, got into bed, and read myself to sleep.

Around 2am, Polly crept into bed beside me. Luckily, I woke up.

Chapter 26 - Helen

Sunday June 19th – Lagg, Jura

The Captain gave his approval for my kayak expedition, yesterday's wind dropped last evening and the forecast is good, at least until much later today. After I did my journal last night I checked out the local coast. And here's the thing: those 'dreadful tides' that made us avoid routing round the north end of Jura are actually the Corryvreckan whirlpool! The third largest whirlpool in the world!

I really have to get Rial on their own and ask them if this is what my ghostly ancestor might have been talking about. It's certainly a lot easier to access from here than Cruachan. On top of that, I've just had a ping from Malcolm and steps-back-in – he found Miran! And they are coming to Jura! Though it makes me feel like we are pieces on a board that Rial is moving about. But no idea whether Nando could be got away from Mr Ross.

Assuming that is, that Miran and Nando are 'the two' she was talking about. Given the number of dreams I've had about dropping through whirlpools, she could have meant me and someone else – probably Malcolm?

But I can't grab Rial this morning, because they are off with Mr Ross to visit the film-makers. And Boris is going as well, because he fancies himself as a film extra. Mebbe they need some extra baddies, who knows?

I manage to get myself included in the shore party and Velho ships us across in the tender. I feel like a minor servant on a royal visit. Mr Ross doesn't so much as glance at me, which is just as unnerving as if he did. But Rial gives me one of their intimidating blue stares. No way am I going to respond unless they are on their own. I stare out to sea instead.

Boris, on the other hand, makes snarky remarks in a low voice.

'Don't drown yourself McIver,' he says with a nasty smile.

Once ashore, they start off uphill to the film-makers house while I go into *Lagg Sea Sports*.

Emerson is delighted to see me – I hadn't promised him when I was in there yesterday that I'd be able to go out.

Emerson may look laid-back but he's very professional. We talk over my route, and how long I'll be out. I'd love to visit Corryvreckan of course, but he points out that it's more than 17 sea miles to the nearest landing point, a good five or six hours paddling, after which I still have to get back. He really doesn't recommend kayaking right up to Corryvreckan anyway as we are coming up to a spring tide when it's at its roughest. I agree not to try it.

We look at the charts and I get a waterproof version for about 10 miles of coast northwards, to wear round my neck. Then I dry-suit up and fit the helmet and life jacket. Emerson sells me his kayaking supply pack of high-energy bars and water. I'm ready to go.

It turns out to be just what I needed. Could be there is something in the 'blue space eco therapy' after all. I've had no decent exercise since my South Uist walk a week ago, and a lot of stress. This is all sunshine, blue water, little coves. In one of them, I see a group of red deer on the beach, who raise their heads from nibbling seaweed to give me a careful look. Then there's a pair of sea eagles – must have been, as one plummets down for a catch less than fifty metres away. Several seals follow me for almost an hour. I see a furry creature sunbathing on a rock with its legs in the air, and it's a sea otter. Yes, I take some pics.

Isn't all this why I went to sea in the first place? I could change jobs, become a guide at a sea centre like this one but on the Northumberland coast. Wilf might be up for it too.

It's easy to daydream though. Two days to the solstice, and something is going to happen. Probably. And I don't know what. I refocus on paddling. The tide is with me, rising with the strong north flow it has on this coast, and I can go a lot faster than I expected.

I stop for lunch about three hours out, at one of the little offshore islands. But because the wind has dropped, the midges are out, and I retreat quickly into the kayak. After this I start back. And now the tide is very much against me, so it is really hard work.

By the time I arrive at Lagg my muscles know they've been working. But it's about the time I told Emerson to expect me. I certainly wouldn't want to give him cause to worry.

I give him what he does want, which is a lot of positive feedback about how good for the soul it was, and he glows. And I ask for a coffee and a tray-bake to restore some of my energy.

'Hey,' he says, when I'm changed back into my own clothes and drinking the coffee. 'Your boss is Ross Peyroux, right?'

'Yes, that's him.'

'Guess he's gotta be *Peyroux Holdings* then?'

I nod.

'I've been catching up online with Eco-news – it's a list I follow. Seems there was a big demo yesterday over on Rannoch Moor about a *Peyroux Holdings* scheme to drive a new road through. It's for their company, *Quantum Solutions*, I think they said?'

'That's right, man. I have a cousin who's a ranger over there and he was telling me about the road.'

'Eco-news says the demo was a big success. But get this,' – he leans over the counter looking excited – 'it also says it's just come out that *Quantum Solutions* are a big fraud!'

Ka-boom! At last!

'Really?' I say, playing it as cool as I can.

'Yeah, they've been hyping it up the way tech companies do, but there's a leak where they say they've known for a good year their tech ain't working! Your guy must be a bit pissed.'

I keep my face straight. 'Wow, yes, sounds like he might not be very happy.'

'Let's hope you're not looking for another job then. Guess the company will be losing some money on this.'

'I'll be fine, man, I'm only on a short contract anyway. I usually free-lance. But thanks for the heads up!'

I finish the coffee and tray bake, and am on the way out, when Emerson adds: 'Oh, nearly forgot, a couple of buddies of yours called in a while back. I told them you'd be back soon, they took a coffee and said they'd hang loose to catch you then.'

Oh.

'Thanks again! It's been great knowing you, Emerson.' I can do American.

'Likewise! Come again, bring your buddies.'

The tender wasn't at the pier when I came in on the kayak, and so, Houston, I have a problem. I can't scarper back quickly to the ship so as not to meet my two 'buddies'. Who in fact are all too likely to be buddies of Martha and Dean.

I decide to walk up to the film-makers house where there should be a big crowd. Then I can call the tender over and walk back down when it arrives.

Good plan, but it doesn't work. I've gone about fifty metres when my back itches. I turn round and two hefty guys with short haircuts are running after me. I drop into the standard self-defence posture, wishing I didn't feel so damn exhausted.

They know what they are doing. They split apart as they get close, to take me one from each side. I do a sudden swivel as they grab and then force my elbows out hard and low. One guy has less resistance than he expected and his momentum carries him past me. My elbow catches the other one hard in the belly and he goes down. All good but now they'll feel entitled to hit me back which isn't as good. And it's still a long way uphill to the house where I can hold them off.

The guy who's now behind me shouts 'Get your hands up!'. I turn fast – because it could be a bluff. But no, he really does have a gun. While shooting me is a bad move unless they can escape quickly by sea – I bet they can't – people with guns can be very stupid.

'OK, OK!' I shout and raise my arms.

But at that point an unlikely white knight arrives as Boris – of all people – charges down the hill shouting 'Hey! You stop!' and what sounds like Russian expletives. He must have been up at the film-makers house.

I hope for a second they'll flee, but they hold their ground. Yes, professionals for sure. I remember how the physicists talked about 'the Company'.

Boris arrives, out of breath.

'What you do with my electronics officer?' he gasps.

'She has something that belongs to us,' the guy with the gun says. His marra is still wheezing. I'm happy to see that I winded him good and proper.

'I've got nothing that belongs to you,' I tell them in my best indignant tone. 'I don't know who the hell you are for a start.'

'You sure have,' says guy-with-a-gun. 'The memory stick you got from your cousin. He gave us all the gen.'

'The memory stick?' I say, in a now bewildered tone. 'He said that was a spare copy of the conference proceedings for the event we were both at. But it was a dud when I got round to looking at it – nothing on it at all.' Which is true of the one Boris switched it for, as he will well know. 'And anyway, it's back on the ship.' I gesture towards the *Midsummer Queen* out in the bay. And notice the tender has just left and is coming towards the shore. Boris must have called them up.

'You piss off now,' says Boris, with his phone out, 'or I call police.' Oh, good luck with that one, let's see if they know how far away the nearest police are likely to be. Calling the film-makers would be more sensible.

Guy-with-a-gun hesitates. He's had time to think about this and probably realises that shooting two people really would be stupid. Especially if the memory stick isn't on me. He puts the gun away.

'Don't think this is it,' he says, coldly. 'Return the memory stick or we'll be back.' Hasta La Vista, I finish for him – in my head. And I'm pretty sure they won't be back, now the *QS* stuff is public. But of course I don't say that either.

'Tender arrives McIver,' Boris tells me. 'Leave these - ' he says something that sounds like 'gloopy oobliokei' which doesn't sound complimentary.

We walk away and they don't follow.

'Thanks for your help there, Yuri Petrovitch,' I tell Boris. 'That was beginning to look a bit grim.'

'So you try to stay out of trouble, McIver,' Boris says as we move smartly back downhill. 'Cannot always be there to bail out.'

Then: 'Say, McIver, what is this 'memory stick'?' He's clearly fishing, I bet he wants to know whether I know about the switch.

'Search me, man. Like I said, I thought it was going to be conference proceedings but it was empty when I checked it out. I had a look when my cousin got in touch. He told me what sounded like the same goons attacked him.'

Boris gives me a sharp look and I try to take no notice. If he's looked at it himself then he knows I'm lying.

'By the way,' I say, in a change-the-subject tone. 'Emerson down there at *Sea Sports* tells me there's a big scandal about Mr Ross' *Quantum Solutions* company just breaking. Sounds like it could be financial trouble for him. I was wondering whether he'll end the charter early.'

'Scandal? They have fingers in till maybe?' I'm guessing he hasn't heard the news then.

'No. Emerson says there was a leak from some whistle-blower and their tech is all hype, doesn't actually work. These tech cos, eh?' I watch him as I say this.

He jolts slightly as if he is going to stop walking, but doesn't.

'Not my problem, McIver,' he says quickly. 'Owner and Mr Ross will talk if so.' I bet they will.

Journal June 19

It's taken me all evening to calm down again after the set-to with those goons – too much adrenaline. I still have that sicky-headachy feeling you get. The Captain was shocked when Boris told him about the attack. And he did report it to the police, who of course said they'd get round to it. Yes, the nearest station is on Islay. Their equivalent of 'whatever' I think. Anyway, I bet the goons will be away by now, especially if someone has told them *QS* are a busted flush.

I've only got one day before the solstice to get hold of Rial and find out what they think is going to happen. Is Rial sort-of seeing into the future like the *QS* computer was supposed to do? I've read enough sci-fi to know you get horrible paradoxes if you do that since then your knowledge means you change it. And what is 'the future' when there are loads of timelines?

Anyway, let's be practical. Rial needs Malcolm. And Malcolm is coming to Jura, and he's bringing Miran. But Rial has to convince him to help with the Ross green spiderweb, and realistically that means a deal where Malcolm gets something he wants. I will tell Malcolm about Cal but I don't think that'll be enough – he doesn't know Cal at all. I have to collar Rial on their own. And what about poor Nando? Let's hope Rial has some ideas.

In one way I'm very chuffed about the *QS* stuff coming out, but Mr Ross better not catch on to my part in it. You don't want to be on his wrong side. As long as I stay schtum I think I'm fire-proof. I hope so anyway.

Here's a late addition. I'd finished this entry and was turning in when my phone pinged.

It's a message from cousin Steven. 'Watch out tomorrow. Please delete.' Ooh dear, that sounds very ominous. And I did delete it.

Chapter 27 - Helen

Monday June 20th - Lagg, Jura

I catch an early breakfast before my shipmates, though Velho comes in just as I am finishing my coffee. Whatever Steven was warning me about, I want to have had breakfast at least. Also, if Mr Ross does appear, after the break of the QS scandal I'd rather not be present.

Then I'm up on the main deck staring soulfully into the distance. Well, I hope it looks like that and not a panicky scan for trouble on the horizon. When I look towards the shore, to my surprise I see a dinghy being rowed out. Surely that cannot be what Steven meant? It's being rowed by a woman. She knows her stuff too, and she's soon quite close, apparently aiming for us.

Then I recognise her. Miran. You'd think cousin Malcolm would have had more sense than to let her do this because if Mr Ross spots her, she's had it. I check nobody on board can see me and wave her away with a big scowl. She takes no notice and starts a circuit round us. I wave her away some more and then do a phone-call sign to suggest I'll contact her later.

She stops rowing suddenly at one point and I worry she'll drift into us, which will be game over, but she recovers and to my relief makes for the shore again. As she gets there, I see Emerson emerge. He doesn't look happy. I bet she's nabbed his dinghy without asking. Still, that isn't my problem.

Oh – that looks like Malcom as well, with his antique Land Rover. I need to talk to him. But I need to talk to Rial first. And I've still no idea how to corner them.

I decide to do some stretching exercises in the sunshine, because what with the kayaking and the goons, my shoulders and arms are pretty stiff and achy. And it gives me a reason to be standing here. I'm well into this when the Captain comes out on deck.

'I do hope you are not feeling too many effects from the attack, Helen?' he says, giving me a concerned look.

'Nothing serious, Sir,' I say, straightening up. 'Just a bit of stiffness.'

'I'm afraid I may have some bad news for you,' he says, with even greater concern.

I do wish he wouldn't lay the 'caring' bit on with a shovel like this.

'It seems Mr Ross has some sudden business issues. He will be making a quick trip to Glasgow, but it seems possible after that he may end the charter.'

'No problem, Sir,' I say. 'I'm used to this kind of thing, goes with the territory when you free-lance.'

His eyes suddenly leave me to look at something behind me, out to sea. His expression changes sharply. I turn round. There's what looks like a coast-guard patrol boat coming in. Heading for us I'd say. Oh dear.

The Captain's off at speed, presumably to warn the crew, or mebbe to get things dropped over the side, who knows? I send Malcolm a quick text warning him we're being raided and telling him we need to meet, but later. Assuming they don't drag me away of course. Then I get myself off the deck too. Best to be with my shipmates at this point.

When I join the crew in the lounge, Mr Ross and Rial are there, but not, I notice, Nando. Nobody is saying much but Boris glares at me, and even Elena, Monsieur and Velho are looking at me coldly. The Captain gives me a look of such sorrow and reproach I feel like I must have killed his cat. If he has one. Only Cal seems his usual grumpy self.

Oh, now I see! There are three officers on the police side of the operation sat at the other end of the lounge. One of them is Steven. By now the crew all know he's my cousin. I bet they think I dobbed them in after all.

Surprising that he's there, conflict of interest and all that. There again, Steven's been on the drugs trail on Lewis, interviewed Boris' marras, and met Boris and Elena. They probably want him in at the kill. If there is a kill. The customs officers will be searching the ship but surely these chuffs have managed to get the drugs offboard by now? And I didn't see a forensics team.

186

It's at least an hour, a very boring one, before the four customs officers reappear. They have a black holdall, which they hand over to the police with a muttered explanation. I look to see which shipmates react, and it's Boris, who else? His mouth is moving in what I bet are Russian curses.

Steven's older colleague – the third of their team is a uniform – stands up.

'We'll be interviewing everybody next. Mr Lisov first please, then Mr Peyroux. We'll get back to the rest of you after we have talked to them. Please remain here until you are called. If you need to use the facilities, one of my colleagues will accompany you.' He has a middle-class Glasgow voice, a bit like Bernie's. Not a local.

Ouf, this is going to be a tedious morning.

The police decamp to the Purser's office. Boris reappears after some time, in handcuffs, with a face like thunder, and is shipped out of the lounge, onto the coast guard boat I assume. Mr Ross is also in there for a while and is also escorted out, though not in handcuffs. He gives Rial an elaborate shrug and a tight smile.

The rest of us are quicker in and out, starting with the Captain, and are all sat back in the lounge after their session. But I am last in – which isn't going to help my rep with the crew. Most of the morning has gone by the time they get to me.

'I am Detective Superintendent John Robertson, and this is my uniform colleague PC Simpson, who will be taking notes. My other colleague, DI Steven McIver, will recuse himself at this point, as I gather he is a relative of yours.' Robertson sounds tired, as well he might after doing eight people already. Steven nods at me with a neutral face, gets up, and leaves.

It turns out to be no big deal as interviews go. I tell them how I came to take the job, that I am a newbie in the crew, that Boris is a bit of a misogynist and the other crew members are all fine. Well, Cal can be a bit grumpy. I detect a supressed sigh from Robertson when I say that – Cal was in just before me. No, I saw nothing out of the ordinary, but as I didn't take shore leave until Lewis I have no idea what the crew did in their free time. I read a lot and play backgammon with Mr Koskinen – that's Velho's actual family name. Didn't hear any gossip and nobody mentioned any large sums of money being on the ship.

That last question was useful. I bet that hold-all had all the drug sale money in it. Boris the gowk. There again, we haven't been anywhere he could have laundered it.

I am sent back to the lounge and Steven rejoins his colleagues. Another twenty long minutes and the three of them emerge.

'Thank you all for your assistance this morning,' Robertson says. 'Captain Tucker, you and your crew are now free to return to your duties. But we require you to stay in this port until we have finished more formal interviews with Mr Lisov and Mr Peyroux at our Islay base. We will be in touch.'

'Heard and understood,' says the Captain, and shakes their hands. That's carrying customer service a bit far, if you ask me, but still.

We all wait until we're sure the patrol boat has cast off, but before we can start the inevitable post-mortem, the Captain decides he should address us. According to him it's all a bit of a misunderstanding and he's sure the Owner and Mr Ross will clear it up quickly with the police. Then Yuri Petrovich will be back with us, and Mr Ross too, once he's made his delayed visit to Glasgow.

My own bet is the Owner will be donating to the Police Beneficence Fund.

Then the Captain reminds us that we are shorthanded without a First Mate, and in fact below regs for sailing anywhere even if we were allowed to. He asks us all to 'pull together' and avoid recriminations about this episode.

As the one who's in line for the recriminations I give him a grateful smile.

It's a bit of a scratch lunch given Monsieur was stuck in the lounge all morning, and I take my plate to my cabin. Nobody wants to talk to me just now anyway. While I'm eating, I have an idea. Now Mr Ross is off the boat, how about I nose round his cabin? 'Know your enemy' as they say.

I see nobody as I nip down the corridor to Mr Ross' cabin. As I hoped, the door is unlocked.

Inside it is much like the Captain's – large, with its own desk. Unlike the Captain's it has an odd scent. Has he been burning incense? Though that would risk setting off the sprinkler system for sure. The desk looks like the one in his office. A computer, a big black book lying open, and a glass paperweight flickering colours. There's a framed photo too, which turns out to be Miran, though much younger than she is now, against some sort of tropical background.

I check the computer first to see if it was left logged in. Yes, but the screen is locked.

Next I look at the book, which is very weird indeed. The print on its open pages is in red for a start, and it looks nothing like the print in the books I read. Blurry, with peculiar letters. In some language I don't know. I turn over the left-hand side, keeping the place with my fingers, to see the title on the front. 'Archidoxis magica'. Not English, but clearly about magic. Then I turn over a few pages in each direction. Some of it isn't even in our alphabet but in squiggly print that looks Arabic. This must be where he gets the enchantment stuff I've seen him using twice now.

Finally I check out the paper weight, with that eye-catching flicker. Only it's certainly not a paper weight! When I pick it up and look closely, I can see small moving images inside, people even, like a cut-up video. Hey, isn't that Mr Ross himself…now it's gone.

I'm so intent on trying to decode the images that I get the most terrible shock and nearly drop the thing when Rial – of course Rial – says: 'You might call that a crystal ball.' Rial is standing just inside the door. I didn't see it opening and I'm stood like a gowk at a total loss for words as I struggle for some explanation for being here. I put the globe down as if it had burnt my fingers.

'It shows what I see,' Rial continues in a calm tone.

'Really?' I get out. Then take a deep breath, with my heart still going far too fast. 'What exactly are you seeing?'

'Across the timelines,' Rial says. 'You know this. What may happen, is likely to happen. Or may not happen.'

Oh, quantum collapse, my brain supplies.

'Like a quantum computer?' I ask.

'My Master told me that when the quantum computer was working, he would not need me to see, and he would free me.' Rial's tone is still calm, as always, but their face suggests some anger.

'But the computer doesn't work, does it? Has only ever worked for a short time more than a year ago, and not since.'

'I told him this, but he didn't want to believe me. The Cailleach is not mocked.'

I wonder what that means? Margaret MacAskill said the very same thing. I suppose those witchy women are really in charge of the timelines – they certainly were at the Incident.

'And now you need me and Malcolm to free you?' Rial nods slowly.

'If we free you, then you said you could help me. Can you make my memory whole? How?'

'Through your stone. When I am free, I have the power, if you allow me, to destroy it. With it go all the memories tied to it.'

'I don't change timelines then?'

'No. That is for the Cailleach, though my Master has usurped her power more than once as we searched for Miran. Your memory will become whole. But some memories will also be lost. Be aware of what you wish for.'

Ah, nothing is for nothing then. But I just cannot carry on not knowing which memories are mine and which belong to the Hulkie of this timeline.

'I will. But you should worry much more about whether Malcolm will help you at all. Can't you offer him something he wants? He says you helped him when he had a panic attack in Cruachan? I know that's not the first one he's had. Can't you stop those?'

'When I am free I can. I will if he asks me to.'

'Why leave it until now to tell me this stuff?'

Mebbe desperation? Because Rial could have mentioned all of this way earlier.

Rial sighs. 'You must know that to share the knowledge of the timelines also changes them. Telling you now makes the timeline where I become free more likely.'

OK, that sounds convincing. But it would, wouldn't it? Rial is trying to convince me after all.

'What about Nando? Doesn't he have to be freed too?'

'He does. But not yet. My Master's charm is still heavy upon him. It will fade in my Master's absence.'

'Tomorrow? The solstice? Like Margaret MacAskill told us?'

Rial doesn't reply.

'Look, I need to meet up with Malcolm and tell him what you said. But that means going over in the tender and I need a reason.'

'There is a reason. My Master asks me to tell the film-makers to suspend their filming until after his meeting in Glasgow tomorrow morning. You can take me to the shore. Later, when I am certain they will be at the film house.' Rial pauses.

Then: 'I think you should leave this cabin now.'

Phew, so do I. My head hurts.

Back in my cabin I text Malcolm to meet in the Sea Sports café at four. And soon before four I ferry Rial ashore in the tender. Here we go. Let's see whether I can be convincing too.

Chapter 28 - Malcolm

Monday June 20th – Barnhill, Jura

After a pleasingly sleep-short night, we were finally roused by urgent buzzing from Polly's muted phone.

'Zelda,' said Polly, checking the pop up. 'I bet she's really pissed off with me.'

'Who's Zelda?' I asked.

'The director,' said Polly. 'I missed yesterday's meeting with Peyroux.'

'Where did you get to?' I said.

'I got lost,' said Polly.

'How can you get lost?' I said. 'There's only one road.'

'I'll explain over breakfast,' said Polly, thumbing up the message. 'Oh wow!'

'What's happened?' I said.

'Looks like *Peyroux Holdings* is going down the Suwannee,' said Polly. 'Their investment arm has collapsed. I wonder if that'll kill the film. I'd better head over there.'

Polly got up and made for the shower.

I found my phone, and checked the news feed. The top Business headline was:

Peyroux Holdings shares collapse after Investment Fund fraud allegations

I quickly skimmed the report. There'd been a leak of internal document from *Quantum Solutions*, whose system powered Peyroux's unrivalled investment strategy. The scientists had been bigging up the performance to attract investors. It looked like the system was no better than any other, and Peyroux's success was actually based on insider trading.

Astonishing! All that hype! All that bluster! How did they get away with it for so long? How did that get out?

Ah, Lucy Lopez's memory stick. That's why those thugs were so keen to retrieve it. Helen must have leaked the contents. But why would she do that? And why would Lopez have a memory stick full of confidential documents?

Polly, pink, emerged from the ensuite, barely dry.

'You next,' she said, pulling on her underwear. 'I'll see you downstairs. Is it all right if I order for both of us.'

'Surely,' I said. 'But what's the hurry?'

'I need you to drive me,' said Polly.

'Don't you have a car?' I said.

'No,' said Polly. 'Look, we need to get going. I'll explain over breakfast. Honest!'

I showered and dressed as quickly as I could. Down in the dining room, Polly was already tucking into a full Scottish.

'You'd better eat yours before it coagulates,' she said, wiping egg yolk off the plate with a morning roll.

'What's been happening with you?' I asked, slicing into a sausage. 'You seem unusually hungry.'

'Do you have any idea how many Tarberts there are?' said Polly. 'And how many have standing stones?'

'As it happens, I do,' I said. 'And Megan did say something about travelling between them, but I assumed that was all metaphorical.'

'Oh no,' said Polly. 'It really does work.'

'Was that you I saw yesterday?' I said, 'near the stone at the Tarbert just north of here?'

'Oh dear,' said Polly. 'That seems likely. I was trying to be discreet.'

'It doesn't sound like it's an exact science,' I said.

'Well no,' said Polly. 'It's not as if there's a route map. You have to learn to feel where you're going.'

'What do you mean?' I said.

'OK,' said Polly. 'Suppose you go to hear a symphony orchestra. Can you tell all the instruments apart?'

I thought about this.

'Just the distinctive ones,' I said, finally. 'Like the timpani. Or the harpsichord. But not the mass instruments, like the violins.'

'Travelling between stones is like trying to tell the violins apart,' said Polly. 'You really have to get your ear in. The single stones all have a

192

distinct resonance, so there's no way you could confuse them with multiple stones, like at Callanish or Nether Largie. But telling individual stones apart is hard.'

'Thanks,' I said. 'That makes some sort of sense. Do the drugs help?'

'*The drugs*,' said Polly. 'You sound like a preacher man. Yes, the ayahuasca helps a lot. It acts like a filter. Gives you a focus. Just don't try this at home.'

'I suppose you thought you'd come here by stone,' I said, ignoring her sally, 'instead of driving?'

'Well yes,' said Polly. 'To the Tarbert just north of Lagg. I got there eventually, but it's a longer walk to Barnhill than I'd bargained for.'

'You should have phoned,' I said. 'I'd have been happy to collect you.'

'I know,' said Polly. 'I really appreciate that. I will next time, I promise.'

The single-track road back south to Lagg was quiet. On the way, I gave Polly a quick overview of the ongoing saga of Miran and Nando. Polly listened attentively, and asked good questions.

'Sounds more engaging than Henry's film,' she said, when I'd finished.

'I've not actually read the book,' I said.

'I wouldn't bother,' said Polly. 'Still, the job's quite interesting.'

'What's your role exactly?' I asked.

'I'm supposed to be in charge of communications for *Great Alien Plum*,' said Polly, 'so I spend most of my time at the Cambuslang studios, grinding out press releases, and trying to plant articles.'

'What are they doing out here' I asked, 'if the production's studio-based?'

'The climax of Henry's book is a race, which turns into a chase, here on Jura,' said Polly. 'And Zelda wants authenticity. I thought they could shoot somewhere local, like the Campsie Fells, but I got my head bitten off for suggesting it. The Paps do make a great backdrop. The cameraman claims it'd be hard to greenscreen that.'

'What'll you do if the funding's cut?' I said.

'I don't know,' said Polly. 'Maybe go back to teaching. Maybe take a holiday first. Might that interest you?'

'Oh yes,' I said.

We came over the hill, and down into Lagg. Peyroux's yacht was still offshore.

'Looks swanky,' said Polly. 'Sorry I missed the dinner. Zelda told me yesterday I was expected. Could we take a closer look?'

As I drove onto the quayside, I saw a man waving at a woman in a rowing boat. As we came closer, I saw that the woman was Miran. I parked, got out of the car and joined the man.

'Miran!' I called. 'Are you all right?'

'Do you know her?' said the man, in an American accent. 'She stole my boat!'

'I'm sure it's a misunderstanding.' I said. 'Let me pay.'

'It's not about the money!' said the man.

Miran sculled the boat against a pontoon, tied it to a stanchion, and leapt lightly up onto the boardwalk. It was clear she knew her way around small craft.

'What the hell do you think you're doing?' cried the man.

'Trying to find Nando,' said Miran, without guile.

'Who the hell's Nando?' said the man. 'Is he out there?'

'Not now,' I said, quickly to Miran.

Miran looked askance at me, but said nothing.

'No,' I said to Emerson, 'he's not out there.'

'You could have been drowned!' continued the man. 'You don't know the currents. On a rising tide, you could have been swept way up the coast. Though not as far as the whirlpool, thankfully.'

'A whirlpool?' said Miran, agog. 'Where is that?'

'At the very north of the island.' said the man. 'Correyvreckan.'

'Malcolm!' called Polly, from the Land Rover. 'I really need to get going.'

'We'll be back,' I said to the irate man. 'Come on.' And steered Miran to the car.

'You must be Miran,' said Polly, as we got in. 'I hope we can catch up later.'

Polly directed me through the village, and round to *Sealladh Bàgh House*. The forecourt was milling with people loading equipment into two minibuses.

'See you!' said Polly, blowing me a kiss, as she got out of the Land Rover.

She weaved through the film crew, towards a commanding woman with pink hair, who was waving a clipboard, while talking intently to Henry. That must be Zelda. Henry glanced round and saw me.

'Hello Malcolm!' he called, looking glad to escape, and came across as Zelda turned on Polly.

'Hello Henry,' I said. 'How's it going?'

'I don't really have a clue,' said Henry. 'It's all a bit chaotic. Nothing looks anything like I envisaged. And everything takes forever to happen.'

'Why are you here at all?' I said.

'To meet the moneybags,' said Henry.

'What's he like?' I asked. 'Oh, before you answer, that's his daughter, Miran, in the Land Rover.'

'Ah,' said Henry. 'Family friend?'

'Not exactly,' I said. 'It's complicated. Look, do you want to go and get a coffee? I feel like I'm in the way here.'

'Sure!' said Henry. 'I'll grab my stuff.'

Henry went back into the house.

'I hear you've been up to no good,' I said to Miran, smiling at her. 'What did you find out?'

'I saw dear Nando,' said Miran. 'He was at a cabin window. He looked so pale. I was going to try to board the yacht, but your cousin saw me. She looked cross, and made this sign at me.'

Miran clenched her fist, and held her pinkie and thumb to her mouth and ear.

'She wants us to contact her,' I said. 'Maybe we can meet her later on. Did anyone else see you?'

'I don't think so,' said Miran.

'That's good,' I said. 'I'd better sort things out with the boat owner. Are you coming.'

'No,' said Miran. 'I'll stay here. These are kindly people. They found me a bed last night. But we must help Nando.'

Goodness me! Miran was far more resourceful, if far more reckless, than I'd ever have guessed from our first meeting.

As Miran got out of the back of the Land Rover, Henry climbed into the front.

'I don't have very long,' said Henry. 'There's supposed to be a hire car arriving to take me to the ferry.'

'Blimey!' I said, firing up the engine, and heading away from the film crew. 'Who's paying for that?'

'*Great Alien Plum*, I suppose,' said Henry. 'They wanted me to come, and they said they'd cover all my expenses. It's not as if they can't afford it. Peyroux has deep pockets.'

'Maybe not for much longer,' I said. 'Oh, and well done for notifying *RAQ*. They've caused quite a stir.'

'Good!' said Henry. 'Good! I had to do something. I felt a bit of a sell-out. But a man has to feed his family.'

I didn't mention his trust fund.

'We might as well try here,' I said, stopping outside the *Sea Sports Centre*.

The American came out to greet us.

'I'm sorry I was pissed with you,' he said, 'but I was seriously worried for your friend.'

'I think she knows what she's doing,' I said.

'I realise that now,' said the man. 'No damage done.'

'Can we get some coffee, please?' I said.

'Come in and help yourself,' said the man. 'You can call me Emerson.'

'Malcolm,' I said. 'And this is Henry.'

Emerson opened the door, and gestured us over to the coffee machine. I buttoned up hot water for tea, soaked a tea bag, and joined Emerson at the table, where he was flattening out a nautical map.

'Lookee here,' he said, pointing at Lagg. 'The bay's quite sheltered, but once you're into the Sound you need sails or a motor if you're to stay abreast of the tides.'

'Good advice,' I said. 'Do you have motorboats?'

'Mostly kayaks,' said Emerson. 'There's an outboard for the dinghy your friend took, but that's kept in the locker outside.'

Henry's phone rang three times.

'That's the hire car,' said Henry. 'I'd better be off. See you on the other side.'

'See you,' I said.

My phone bleeped. A text from Helen.

Police raid! We must meet later!

Bloody hell! I hurried outside, and saw a Coast Guard patrol ship bearing down on the yacht. I hoped Helen was all right. Still, if anyone could look after themselves, Helen could.

Then my phone rang. Polly. I answered it immediately.

'Can you come now, please?' said Polly.

'Of course!' I said. 'What's happened?'

'We need the Land Rover,' said Polly. 'You'll see.'

'That sounds bad,' I said. 'Where are you?'

'About three miles south,' said Polly. 'You can't miss us.'

'On my way,' I said, ending the call.

Emerson came out to join me.

'It's all go!' he said.

'Certainly is!' I said. 'What do I owe you?'

'The coffee's free,' said Emerson. 'Don't worry about the dinghy.'

'Thank you!' I said. 'I'm sure we'll meet again.'

The film crew was assembled in a layby, just across a small bridge. To the west, a muddy track led along the burn up into the Paps. Piles of equipment lay everywhere.

'Talk about stupid,' said Polly, sotto voce. 'I wonder who chose this location.'

One of the minibuses was bogged down. The other's radiator had boiled over trying to pull it out. Sighing, I took charge. I separated the minivans, hitched the Land Rover to the steaming one, and towed it clear. Then I backed up to the other minivan and winched it free from the mud.

'What now?' I said to Zelda, who close up, looked curiously like Emerson.

'Oh thank you Malcolm,' said Zelda. 'You're a life saver. I couldn't ask you to ferry the equipment up onto the moor, could I? We've time while we're waiting for the ponies.'

I spent the next hour driving up and down the track. We'd moved all the key equipment, and the cameraman had set up the tripod, when the ponies arrived.

'Right!' bellowed Zelda, through the obligatory megaphone. 'Let's get cracking! Drone up! Actors on ponies!'

The two male actors, replete in 18th century costume, looked downcast.

'I thought there were stand-ins,' said one.

'Body doubles,' said the other.

'Come on guys!' bellowed Zelda. 'You're both supposed to be seasoned horsemen. You're not afraid of a horse, are you?'

Gingerly, the actors mounted their steeds, with considerable help from the handler.

'Action!' bellowed Zelda.

The two riders set off at a walking pace.

'Cut!' bellowed Zelda. 'Come on guys! This is supposed to be a chase. It doesn't involve any acting. Just stay on the horse. Action!'

After too many tumbles, and even more bad words, Zelda was finely satisfied.

'That's a wrap!' she bellowed. 'Well done guys!'

We spent another hour ferrying equipment back down to the road, where a tow truck was waiting.

197

'I could do with a drink,' I said to Polly.

'Me too,' said Polly. 'Shall we head back to the hotel?'

My phone bleeped. Another text from Helen.

4pm at the Sea Sports Centre.

'That's Helen,' I said. 'I really do need to meet her, and try and sort things out.'

'Fair enough,' said Polly. 'You could drop me at the House, and pick me up when you're done.'

'Might you look out for Miran?' I said.

'Of course,' said Polly. 'Of course.'

Chapter 29 - Malcolm and Helen

Monday June 20th – Lagg, Jura

Malcolm

I didn't have to wait very long before Helen joined me in the *Sea Sports Centre* café.

'Hello Helen,' I said. 'What the hell's going on with the boat?'

'I think you mean *ship*, man' Helen replied. 'Oh, just the little matter of a police raid. That drugs thing coming home to roost. Luckily the gowks did manage to offload the stuff but forgot about a big bag of money. The police were not amused.'

'Sounds fraught,' I said. 'Where does that leave you?'

'Not sure if cousin Steven put in a good word for me with his lot - yes, he was there,' said Helen 'But the whole crew think it's all my doing. I'm not shipmate of the month right now. Still, they carted off the first mate and also Mr Ross. Which is probably a win.'

'What's going on with the Peyroux empire?' I asked. 'It looks like Polly could be out of a job. Was that the memory stick? Did you share it?'

'Nothing to do with me,' Helen said, a little hastily I thought. 'That memory stick was a dud, nothing on it at all.'

'Maybe it was Lucy Lopez then,' I said. 'She seems to be playing loads of folk off against each other. Still, it's good news if it means the end of *Quantum Solutions* and the road they want to build.'

'Yes, man, silver linings,' said Helen, rather smugly. 'But I wouldn't be in the slippery Ms Lopez' shoes right now. Mr Ross is due in Glasgow - assuming he manages to schmooze the police. He doesn't seem a very forgiving man.'

'Is that it?' I asked. 'Can't say I won't be happy to see the last of Peyroux and that weird Rial. But Nando's still stuck on your ship, isn't he. I'd really like it if we, well you, can free him.'

'Look man. This is a very long way from 'that's it'. You've forgotten our ghostly ancestor's prophecies. You've forgotten the whirling waters and, most of all, you've forgotten Rial's problem.'

'Why do I care about Rial?' I said. 'Can they help free Nando?'

'Oh, people being enslaved is not your problem then, man? I thought better of you than that.'

'Why isn't cousin Steven sorting that out?' I said. 'Didn't you tell him? He is police after all.'

'Let me count to ten slowly,' said Helen, sounding quite angry. 'You want to try telling the police about that green spider web stuff? Or Mr Ross being a sorcerer who put a sort of zombie charm on Nando? They'll for sure believe all that, won't they man? Look, let me tell you what he did to Cal, who you also saw in that druggie vision.'

Helen quickly recounted Cal's story. But from what Miran had told me, I really wasn't that sympathetic.

'That sounds shitty,' I said. 'But I still don't see why that's my problem.'

'Well you haven't seen Mr Ross torturing Cal through that spider web stuff, have you? Do you have any feelings at all?' Helen said indignantly. 'Don't answer that question, I'll cut to the chase. Do you want Miran and Nando free?'

'Obviously!' I said. 'Why do you think I'm here in the first place?'

'Well, man, that's why you need Rial. Look - Mr Ross can take both of them while he has Rial under his control. Rial is like a one-person quantum computer. Like I told you, when I had bother with the first mate on South Uist, Rial just knocked him out with that eerie music. Right now Rial has to do what Mr Ross says. But freed, they don't. And then they will help all of us.'

'What do we have to do?' I said. 'Is this green stone stuff?'

'Of course it is,' said Helen. 'That's what Margaret MacAskill told me. Two green stones can free Rial. And Rial says they will repay each of us. They will sort out my memory. And if you want, they will sort out your panic attacks, for good.'

I had to think about the implications of this.

'When you say 'sort out my memory', do you mean another timeline shift?' I asked. 'I'm more than happy in this one, thank you. For once it feels like things are going well. Well, it did until all this Peyroux stuff blew up.'

'In fact, no, man,' said Helen. 'What I remember from before the Incident is tied up with my green stone Rial reckons. They can destroy it and those memories will go too. I'll just be the Hulkie of this timeline.'

'You're saying that Rial can change you without changing anything else?' I said. 'What about all the folk that know you as you are right now?'

'It's only the fifteen months since the Incident that makes any odds at all. All the people I care about knew me way before that in *this* timeline. Even you did.'

'And you really trust Rial?' I continued. 'They seem pretty dodgy to me.'

'Trust Rial or you don't get Miran and Nando free either,' said Helen. 'Rial says that Mr Ross' zombie spell on Nando will fade while he's away. By tomorrow Nando will have come to, and with Rial's help I think I could get him off the ship.'

I couldn't really see any options, unless we tried to break Nando out, and that could end really badly.

'All right,' I said, reluctantly. 'Let's give that a try. When and where?'

'Can Nando swim?' said Helen. 'It might come to that. Using the tender is much too obvious.'

As if out of a hat, Miran and Polly entered the cafe.

'Are you two still gossiping?' said Polly.

'I think we're almost done,' I said. 'Miran, we've been talking about how to free Nando. Can he swim?'

'Dear Nando swims like a spirit of the sea,' said Miran, admiringly.

'That's handy,' I said. 'Over to you, Helen.'

'Then later in the day, man. Tide's ebbing all morning and you don't want *dear Nando* swept out to sea,' said Helen.

'All right,' I said. 'Could you text me when Nando's free?'

'For sure, man,' said Helen. 'Howay, I'm guessing none of you want to meet Rial? They're just up the hill telling the film people to suspend after Mr Ross' little business problem, but they'll be back soon. Time to make a move.'

We got up and left the café. On the quayside, Miran stopped and looked down at the tender.

'How does that work?' asked Miran. 'There are no sails or oars.'

'It has a motor, what else, man?' said Helen. 'Much faster than sails or oars.'

'Like in a car,' I said hastily. 'Could you show us how it works, please, Helen?'

We walked down to the pontoon and Helen climbed into the boat.

'The motor's called an outboard,' said Helen. 'You can see it's mounted on a hinge. Right now it's out of the water. You free it here.'

Helen loosened a catch, and the outboard swung down.

'Then you start the outboard with the key,' said Helen.

She turned the key and the motor fired.

'And you accelerate by twisting this handle,' said Helen, pointing. 'But I can't do that while we're moored.'

Helen turned off the motor and rejoined us on the pontoon.

'How do you steer it?' asked Miran.

'You use the motor like a tiller,' said Helen. Then she glanced towards the hill behind us. 'Look, man. That's Rial coming to join us. You'd best be off.'

Helen

Meetings with cousin Malcolm are such fun. Bad for my blood pressure for sure. Still, I think he's come round at last.

Rial arrives and jumps lightly down onto the pontoon where I'm waiting for them.

'A good outcome is more likely,' they say.

I feel more pleased than mebbe I should, as if I've proved I'm no gowk.

'I need your help to free Nando tomorrow,' is all I say. And we sort that out as we cross back to the ship.

Nobody talks to me at our evening meal, not even Velho. And I wonder if Monsieur hockled in my pheasant tagine. After we've eaten, I get myself out onto the deck and stare at the sea for a bit. I always find that calming. Tomorrow's when it all happens, I'm sure. Of course I'm not scared.

'Now you know what it's like when people hate you.' That's Cal, who's come to join me.

'Now I know what it's like when people hate you for something you didn't do,' I tell him. 'Luckily this gig is going to end soon.'

'Did you tell people Mr Ross' business was fake, then?' Cal asks.

'Certainly not, man,' I say. 'How would I have known that? Did you know? Did Rial?'

'Rial always knows things,' Cal says. 'Rial says tomorrow is going to be an important day.'

'Let's hope they're right then,' I say. 'I'm for my cabin.'

And not up to chatting with people right now.

But as I go back inside, I meet Elena.

'How could you, Hulkie?' she says in a low voice. 'You told us you'd keep quiet.'

'And I did!' I say, trying not to raise my own voice. 'Believe it or not, you probably did more damage than I did. When you met Steven back on Lewis, at the Calanais, he got you to tell him you'd probably met Yuri Petrovich's friends. Remember he asked you if you'd been to the Ness? There's only one road! Don't assume policemen are stupid. He's not, that's for sure.'

I lower my voice again with an effort of will. 'After that I guess those 'friends' were rounded up and interviewed. *That* is probably why we got raided.'

'Oh', says Elena.

Then: 'I'm sorry. We're just upset about Yuri Petrovich being arrested.'

'Yes, I know you are. And I'm guessing that money was going to be shared out. But look: the Owner will more than likely get Yuri Petrovich off the hook. All they have to do is say they gave Yuri Petrovich the cash for running expenses during the trip or some such story. I bet that would work. Especially if a chunk ends up with the police, as it might.'

That makes an impression, and Elena visibly cheers up.

'And changing the subject,' I add, 'how's Nando? I hope he isn't being left to fester with Mr Ross being away?'

'Oh no,' Elena says. 'I wouldn't do that! In fact he seems better tonight than any time since he came on board. Maybe he has been ill. Tonight he was asking me about some woman, Miran, I think he said. His girlfriend. He seemed to think she was on Jura.'

'That's encouraging,' I say. 'OK, I'm turning in. Too much excitement of the wrong kind today.'

'I'll tell the others,' Elena says.

Let's hope it convinces them. I don't want to end up in the water. Though with Boris missing, they do really need me.

Journal June 20

What am I going to do about this journal now? I've got to quite like it, as if I'm chatting to myself. But it has the Incident in it and everything important that happened since. If I don't remember any of this after tomorrow, what will I make of it? Ouf, makes my head hurt trying to think it through. Mebbe I should delete it all? But I can't quite make myself do that.

And will I be OK, the way I told cousin Malcolm? Well, Hulkie on this timeline still has parents and friends and Wilf. Could be Hulkie on this timeline was getting on better with Wilf than I was just before the Incident, and for sure better than things have been since. And I won't be freaked out by his cat anymore.

You can know that there are goodness knows how many versions of you, and yet the one you actually are seems like the only one, if that makes sense. I do just want to be that one. Of course I'm not scared. 'Face the storm' – that's what Dad says when things are tricky. And I will.

Oh, right on cue the laptop has one of those operating system upgrades coming in. That will take all night. I better plug it in. And read some Sword and Sorcery, and then turn in.

Chapter 30 – Helen

Tuesday June 21st – Lagg, Jura

The frostiness level has gone down at breakfast, which should mean Elena passed on what I told her. Just as well, because I'm also below full fettle after yet another bad night. This time stressing rather than sleeping for what felt like a good half of it. Rial told me some memories will be lost, just not which ones. That sounds pretty scary, but what good are these memories doing me right now? Nothing ventured, nothing gained.

After she's taken Nando his breakfast, Elena says to me: 'Nando really seems like a different person this morning. Chatty, and with it.'

'Well, man, that's good news.'

'But he wants to know why we have him locked into the cabin and when he can go ashore to look for that girlfriend of his,' she says.

'What did you say?' I ask.

'I told him we have to wait for his uncle to come back. Then he came out with some wild-sounding stuff about Mr Ross drugging him to keep him away from his Miran. That all seemed rather worrying. Maybe the Captain can take it up with Mr Ross when he gets back?'

'Sounds a good idea,' I say, non-committedly.

It seems like Nando will be up for his swim. But we have to wait until after the tide turns. That's at 14.07, according to the tide tables.

Mid-morning, I find Rial on the main deck.

'Meet here at two-thirty?' I say. 'You won't forget I need the key?'

'How would I forget?' Rial says, with that intimidating blue stare.

The day drags, the way it does when you are waiting. The weather looks a little changeable, and the wind goes round to the north-west, but with Jura between us and the Minch it's no big deal. It's not blowing enough to raise the sort of white caps that could make Nando's swim tricky.

I collect a plateful from Monsieur's buffet at midday and decide to eat in the lounge for a change. Cal comes and sits next to me to eat his. Just my luck.

'Rial says Mr Ross is coming back today,' he grumbles. 'Hijo de Puta. I hoped the police would put him in jail. But he never gets caught.'

Yes, and there's a reason for that, I think to myself.

'Could be that his business crashing will put a dent in him though,' I say. 'Look, man!'

I call up the BBC Scotland news page on my phone and hand it to Cal.

'Scottish entrepreneur in business crisis meeting,' is the headline.

'That's this morning in Glasgow, so if he is coming back today it won't be until late afternoon at best,' I tell Cal.

'You think that's good?' Cal asks bitterly. 'When he's angry, he always takes it out on me.'

Poor Cal, I'm sure he's right. But I'm not dropping any hints about what might happen today, because who knows who he might tell? Mr Ross probably, as soon as he gets back, just to piss him off.

Next I go off to help Velho with his endless turbine-tuning project. He treats me just as if yesterday's drama hadn't happened, which is a relief.

Finally it's nearly two-thirty. There's that very slight bobble on our mooring that says the tide has turned. I go onto the main deck, and yes, Rial is there, staring outwards as they do so often. I get the feeling that they're not looking at the sea.

'Here', says Rial, handing me the bunch of cabin keys Elena keeps in the Purser's office.

'You will need to touch Nando with your green stone or his mind will join the others elsewhere.' The eerie music starts up. 'And the crew will remain elsewhere until you hand me back the keys.'

Them I'm off to Nando's cabin. Sure enough when I unlock the door he is standing looking at nothing in particular, the way Boris did on South Uist.

When I take my stone out, it is glowing, as it has done before when Rial's music is playing. I touch it against Nando's arm, and he suddenly focuses.

'Who are you? Why are you here?'

'You want to find Miran,' I say. 'I'm here to help you do that.'

He grabs both my hands. 'Yes, yes, I must find Miran, my beloved! She is not far away! I saw her in a boat yesterday. Unless that was a dream?' He looks uncertain.

'No dream, man. She's on the island. But you are going to have to swim there from the ship, OK?'

'I will do anything! Swim through water, walk through fire if I must.'

'Right, man. Now listen. I'm going to tell you what to do.'

He looks so excited that I'm not convinced he really takes it in when I explain that he must find the road behind Lagg and then the film house. But I can't give him a map. I did extract two large freezer bags and some cooking twine last night from Monsieur's supplies, and now I get him to remove his shoes and his jeans and put them in the bags, which I tie to his waist. They'll probably get wet but he'll swim better like that.

I escort him from the cabin and grab his arm when he looks as if he's about to dash off in the wrong direction.

'Look Nando, keep calm will you? Don't foul this up, man,' I growl at him.

Keeping hold of his arm, I move him to the ship's rear launch platform. The ship has swung round a bit in the tide and there's a good view of Lagg.

'Look, see that pier?' I point to the landing stage in the centre. 'Make for that. Keep going. The water's cold but it's not that far.' Good thing it's summer or he might go down with hyperthermia. I'm not giving him a life jacket either, that would just slow him.

'In you go then, gently please, no big splash.'

'My deepest and most profound thanks! You have my undying gratitude.'

'Yes, yes, man. Just get going, will you?' He and Miran certainly match each other for chatter.

He slides off the platform and away he goes. No front crawl, but his breaststroke looks effective thank goodness, if not quite at water spirit level.

This is the worst bit. I need to make sure he gets to the shore before Rial wakes everyone up. If he gets into trouble, rescuing him will be a nasty problem.

I watch his bobbing head as it progresses. And of course the incoming tide is pushing him way over to the right and there is nothing I can do about that. A hundred metres, and around ten long minutes later, he reaches the shore. Just nowhere near the landing stage. And there's no road on that side of the bay, plus it is wooded. At least that will hide him I guess.

Well, I've done what I can. I pull out my phone and text Malcolm. Then I head for the deck and Rial.

Rial gives me that look and holds out their hand for the keys.

'It'd be handy if Elena couldn't remember whether she locked the door when she took his lunch dishes away, man,' I say hopefully.

'Maybe so,' is all Rial says. And I make myself scarce. In a few minutes the eerie music stops. With a bit of luck nobody will notice Nando has gone until he's due his evening meal.

Or when Mr Ross returns, if that's sooner. He won't be pleased. I do hope he won't just coerce Rial into telling him everything.

Chapter 31 - Malcolm

Tuesday June 21st – Barnhill, Jura

After another sleep-short night, Polly and I came down to breakfast around 10am. Miran looked as if she was on her third round of the buffet.

'Happy solstice!' she called to us.

I glanced at the calendar over the fireplace. Sure enough, today was the solstice.

'Happy solstice!' I said. 'Do you celebrate it on your island?'

'We rise at dawn to greet the sun,' said Miran. 'The longest day is joyous, yet bittersweet, for the days begin to shorten.'

Polly raised an eyebrow at me.

'I wonder what your Wiccan friends are up to,' I said to her, feeding wholemeal bread into the chain link toaster.

'No good, I trust,' said Polly, filling a teapot from the hot water urn. 'I hope some of that's for me. Now for the moment I've been dreading.'

Polly turned on her mobile, and was bombarded with message notifications.

'Zelda?' I said.

'Zelda,' said Polly. 'She's really panicking. The funding's died. She can't get everyone off Jura, let alone pay the locals. I'd better go and help sort things out.'

'You don't sound very bothered,' I said, loading up a plate with congealing fried eggs, bacon and Lorne sausage.

'Well no,' said Polly. 'I've had a belly full of *Great Alien Plum* and *Preacher Man*. I'm sure something will turn up.'

'Maybe a bit nearer the moor?' I hinted.

'Maybe,' said Polly. 'How are you, Miran?'

'I am well, thank you,' said Miran. 'What are we going to do today? When do we rescue dear Nando?'

'We have to wait for Helen to tell us he's free,' I said. 'That'll be mid-afternoon. Maybe we could go for a walk.'

'Oh yes!' said Miran. 'Might we see the whirlpool?'

'I suppose,' I said. 'Look, why don't you go to reception and borrow a map.'

No sooner said than done.

'Blimey, she's hard work,' I said. 'Like a puppy.'

'She's actually really tough,' said Polly. 'I saw that on our journey.'

'The drugs?' I said. 'What did you see?'

'Not now,' said Polly, as Miran rejoined us. She swept the breakfast things to the side, and unfolded the map.

'The whirlpool's here,' said Miran pointing at the top of the map, 'just off the cape.'

'It's a good hour's walk to a decent vantage point,' I said. 'This looks promising. An Cruachan.'

Cruachan again. There are no coincidences.

'Maybe you could take a picnic,' said Polly.

'That's a great suggestion,' I said. 'Are you sure you won't come?'

'I'd love to,' said Polly, 'but I really should go and service Zelda. Might I take the Land Rover, please? You could ping me when you're ready to leave.'

'Of course,' I said. 'You should still be on the insurance.'

After breakfast, we waved Polly off, and returned to reception, where I ordered a packed lunch for two. I also borrowed some walking boots for Miran.

What with one thing and another, it was well after eleven when we finally set off. The day was bright and warm, with clear views across the Sound of Jura to the mainland of Argyll. But the track along the cliff top was in poor repair, and our progress was further hindered by Miran stopping to examine every feature on the map, especially caves and waterfalls. It was well past one when we reached the top of An Cruachan.

The whirlpool was far bigger than I expected, roiling loudly in the centre of the gulf between Jura and Scarba to the north. Miran sat quietly, watching the waters whirl. I read the information board, wishing we could afford signage of equal quality on the moor.

Like all information boards, this one was full of facts. Most striking was the ancient legend of the Cailleach Bheur, the hag goddess of winter, who used the gulf like a vast public laundromat. I took this a lot more seriously than I would have done a couple of years ago. Thank goodness it was midsummer.

The packed lunch was boiled egg and luncheon meat, sandwiched between slices of well margarined white bread, washed down with child-size cartons of apple juice. Still, I was hungry after scrabbling up the gully to the summit, and Miran ate as if she hadn't seen food for a week.

As we were finishing up, the sound of the whirlpool died away. There was a brief moment of calm, and then the whirlpool, even vaster than before, roared with renewed strength. The tide must be on the turn. I wouldn't want to be anywhere near the whirlpool in a small boat. The information board said that Orwell himself had nearly drowned here.

I checked my watch. It was just after two. This was when Helen had suggested she might be able to free Nando. I gathered up our litter, and we set off back to Barnhill.

Miran was very quiet. I'd no idea how to read that.

'What did you make of the whirlpool?' I asked her.

'Corryvreckan is awe inspiring,' said Miran, thoughtfully.

Then she bounded on ahead.

I couldn't get her earlier question out of my head. What were we doing today?

Maybe Nando could be freed. What then? Well, with Peyroux away, there was nothing to stop them escaping from Jura. Perhaps to somewhere too distant for him to track them down? After all, his business problems should divert him for a while.

But why would Helen trust Rial so far as to let them mess with her brain? She was usually self-assured and resilient. She must be really desperate. Anyway, why would I trust Rial to mess with mine? After all, panic attacks in dark, wet, confined spaces aren't exactly irrational, unless you're a submariner, or a plumber.

As we neared the hotel, my mobile phone reconnected and a message from Helen came through.

The Eagle has landed. Over on the right of the bay. Your move.

I quickly messaged Polly to come and collect us. She replied immediately that she was just finishing up, and would be with us in 20 minutes or so.

I checked the time on Helen's message. 14.50. Assuming he'd got away successfully, Nando had a head start on us. But Polly hadn't mentioned seeing him at the filming base, as she surely would have done. Nando seemed pretty witless. I hoped he hadn't got lost.

We went into the hotel, up to our rooms, and gathered our things together. Downstairs, I settled the bill with the proprietor. The Land Rover proved more reliable than a standing stone; Polly arrived shortly thereafter. As we drove away from the hotel, I realised that Miran was still wearing the borrowed boots. I'd have to post them back.

When we got to *Sealladh Bàgh House*, there was no sign of Nando. I dropped Polly off, with a vague arrangement to synchronise for the trip back to Rannoch. Then, I checked the map, which, fortuitously, I also hadn't returned. I hoped the *Blair Arms* proprietor wasn't too annoyed with us.

Ideally, Nando would have come ashore in Lagg Bay, but, if he'd been caught by the current, he might well have been carried further north. He'd then have to make his way up the cliffs or, less risky, follow the shore to where a burn ran into the Sound.

Go for it.

I took the main road back a mile or so towards Barnhill, to a stretch running through a fir plantation, and parked up just over a burn. Then we followed the burn down through the trees to the water's edge, calling 'Nando! Nando!' the while.

Chapter 32 – Malcolm and Helen

Tuesday June 21st – Lagg, Jura

Malcolm

After the best part of an hour, we found Nando on the short stretch of strand between the cliffs, thoroughly soaked and utterly forlorn.

'Dearest Nando!' cried Miran, gathering him to her breast. 'At last we are together again!'

I gave them a few moments to become reacquainted with each other's mouths, and then coughed politely.

'Come on,' I said. 'Let's find Polly and head home.'

'No!' said Miran. 'No! I must confront father, and make him realise how deeply he has wounded me.'

'I don't think he'll be very sympathetic,' I said, 'from what little I know of him. Besides, he's not on the boat. We should go.'

'No!' said Miran. 'Father must accept my choice.'

I sighed deeply.

'All right,' I said. 'But it won't end well.'

We helped Nando up to the Land Rover, and returned to Lagg. As I parked outside the cafe, I saw the tender from Helen's boat making its way towards us. I hoped Helen was on board.

'Coffee?' said Emerson, as we went inside. 'Looks like someone could use a towel. Through here.'

Emerson encouraged Nando into the changing rooms. Miran hovered at the window.

'Look,' she said. 'The jollyboat's arrived.'

'Is Helen on board?' I asked, joining her.

'No,' said Miran. 'Just a man.'

The tender tied up at the pontoon and the sailor climbed out. But he headed away from the cafe, up the hill towards *Sealladh Bàgh House*.

Nando and Emerson rejoined us, Nando wrapped in a towel.

'You could do with some dry clothes,' I said. 'But I don't think I've anything that will fit you.'

'There is no time,' said Miran. 'We must leave. Now.'

'Where are you going?' I asked.

Of course I knew.

'To the whirlpool,' said Miran.

'I thought you wanted to see your father,' I said.

'No,' said Miran. 'You are right. There is no point. He will never accept Nando.'

'How are you going to get to the whirlpool?' I said. 'There's no way Emerson's going to let you take his boat again.'

Of course I knew.

'Come Nando!' said Miran, grabbing his hand and rushing for the door.

As I pursued them towards the pontoon, a large black saloon drew up outside the cafe. Peyroux got out of the driver's seat, and reached back in to pull out a carved walking stick.

'Miran!' he cried. 'I've found you at last!'

Miran took no notice, and ran with Nando along the boardwalk to the pontoon, where the tender was moored: Peyroux and I in hot pursuit. As Miran climbed into the tender, Nando turned to block Peyroux.

'Begone, you sorcerous old man!' shouted Nando. 'You will never again separate my beloved and me!'

Peyroux scowled, and raised his walking stick, pointing its end at Nando as if it were a sword.

'No more!' shouted Nando, and punched Peyroux foursquare on the jaw.

Peyroux fell backwards on top of me, and we both went over, hard onto the deck. I was temporarily winded. As I untangled myself from Peyroux, I heard the sound of the tender's motor starting. I struggled to my feet. Too late. The tender, bearing Nando and Miran, was already heading out into the bay.

I helped a stunned looking Peyroux to his feet.

'How dare he!' gasped Peyroux. 'How dare he! I'll make him pay. We must be after them!'

Helen

I spend most of the afternoon with Velho and his interminable turbine tuning project. I'm sure that Malcolm will get in touch if he needs me. We are both immersed in it, and a lot of time passes without us noticing, the way it does with techie jobs. Then the Captain calls Velho on the intercom.

'Viljami, I'd be grateful if you could take the tender over to meet Mr Ross. He tells me he is less than half an hour away now. And by the way, Yuri Petrovich got in touch this morning. You'll be glad to hear he expects to be back with us by tomorrow. But he also tells me he left his wallet with the film crew the other day when he was changing into costume and forgot to reclaim it. Please see whether they have it while you are onshore.'

We pack up, and I help Velho by hauling the tender round to the loading platform. Off he goes to the shore.

I have a bad feeling about Mr Ross coming back. I still worry he'll have found out it was me that dobbed in *Quantum Solutions*. And he will certainly not be happy when he finds Nando has gone.

I go up to the deck and watch the tender tie up at the pontoon. Velho moves off uphill to the film house.

Some minutes pass. Then people appear from the café. Well, two of them, at some speed. Miran and Nando! Heading for the pontoon I think. Malcolm shoots out behind them.

Everything happens rather fast. A flashy black car arrives, Mr Ross climbs out, arms are waved, there's some distant shouting. Oh, Christ-on-a-bike, Miran's in the tender, and I told her how it works!

Nando hits Mr Ross! Leaps into the tender! And it leaves at speed. Miran steers better than I fear, and manages to avoid crashing into anything, including us.

I look back to the pontoon and see Malcolm and Mr Ross picking themselves up from the ground. Where's Velho? Oh, rushing down the hill. With his phone out.

Next thing the Captain is out on the deck. Followed by Rial.

'Helen! Did you see what happened?'

'Yes Sir. Two people appear to have stolen our tender. Mr Ross was assaulted, though he's back on his feet, so hopefully not badly injured. What are your orders?'

'Viljami asks me to bring us to the pontoon to pick up himself and Mr Ross. As the tide's rising, I think we can manage this without grounding if we are careful. I need you to start the harbour motor.'

Phew, I wouldn't want to start the turbines on my own, but the harbour motor is a small diesel for manoeuvring. That I can do.

'Aye, aye, Sir.' He's too worried to wince.

And that's what we do, though of course it takes a while, and goodness knows where the tender has got to - last I saw, it was rounding the Lagg Bay point, heading north.

Ooh, that's the way to Corryvreckan! Whirling Waters! And will we follow? We'll see.

The Captain docks us carefully at the pontoon. I wait on the landing platform, and I leap off to tie us up. I avoid looking at Malcolm - there's nothing I can say right now that I want Mr Ross to hear.

Velho helps Mr Ross onto the ship.

Then I do look at Malcolm. 'You coming?' I ask quietly. 'It's likely we'll go after our tender. We could still catch them I think. Then goodness knows what Mr Ross will do. He seems pretty angry. And you did say you'd help me.'

Malcolm

I was frozen to the spot. I could just walk away. But what will happen to Miran? I could try to stop the boat. But how am I going to do that? Can they really survive Corryvreckan?

And, yes, Helen does need my help. The implications don't bear thinking about. But Helen reassured me that I wouldn't be affected by whatever Rial does to her. I guess I'll just have to trust her.

'All right,' I said. And climbed onto the ship.

On the main deck, Peyroux was arguing with a smartly dressed seaman, probably the Captain. Helen was very quiet. Quite unlike her.

'But it's not safe to go after them,' said the Captain. 'They're heading for dangerous waters. And, without my First Mate, I do not have a legal crew. I must call up the Coast Guard.'

'It'll take too long!' shouted Peyroux. 'We need to get after them now!'

'No!' I said, playing for time. 'We mustn't. You're risking all our lives. And the ship.'

'If they drown in the whirlpool,' shouted Peyroux, 'it'll be on your head, Captain! Manslaughter at least! You let them get away!'

Then Peyroux lifted his stick in the pointing gesture he'd tried with Nando.

'We will follow them!' he commanded.

'Very well,' said the Captain, after a pause, in a dazed tone. 'Viljami. Helen. Start the main engine.'

The four of them went inside the boat. I stayed on deck, agonising over whether I could have done anything else. Rial, who had taken no part in the argument, came over and joined me.

'You have made the correct choice,' they said. 'Now the prophecies will play themselves out.'

With a roar, the engines fired up. The boat moved away from the pontoon, and, gathering pace, headed out of the bay and north up the Sound.

Helen

I help Velho get the turbines started and then go out onto the main deck. Both Malcolm and Rial are there. The tender has mebbe a half-hour start, but our top speed is much higher than theirs. I've half-inched some binoculars from the lounge, where we keep them for guests, and I scan our forward path.

'Can you see anything?' Malcolm asks.

'Not yet,' I tell him.

'Not for a while yet,' says Rial, calmly.

'My Rial,' comes a familiar voice. My favourite person has just come onto the deck.

'Yes, master,' says Rial.

'Summon the wind against them,' says Mr Ross. 'Or we cannot catch them.'

'Master, I can summon the wind, but this will also blind our ship's navigation, as I told you.'

'Do it!'

Rial's pale figure turns a little hazy, as if they are not wholly present. In a couple of minutes the sky ahead of us darkens ominously and then the wind turns northerly from its current west and rises, blowing against our faces.

'Told you,' I mutter to Malcolm.

Even at our speed, seventeen sea miles takes a while. Time passes but it's a torment. Of course I'm not scared.

Then I see them through the binoculars. 'In sight,' I say, and point.

'How close are we to Corryvreckan now?' I ask out loud. I don't know this part of the coast at all. But, as we get nearer, the northerly current will pick up a great deal, and round the point on this rising tide it will sweep them - and us - very fast westwards. Can Mr Ross' zombie spell make the Captain wreck the ship?

'Just past Barnhill,' says Malcolm. 'Only about a mile to the whirlpool.'

217

Some minutes later, the engine noise drops and we slow. We are rounding the point. The tender is pretty close. I can see Nando looking back at us. The wind is blowing strongly against us, and the sky is so dark it feels like dusk. But the current carries them on.

'My Rial,' says Ross. 'We must stop them. Turn the tide! Reverse the current.'

'No, master,' says Rial, quietly. 'This tide is the Cailleach's to command.'

'No? You dare to disobey me! Turn the tide! It is within your power. Turn it!'

'I say again, no, master,' says Rial. 'The Cailleach will not be mocked.'

'You will pay for your disobedience!' says Ross.

He points his stick at Rial. Well, it's a wand really, I'm guessing. Then he mutters under his breath, in that same weird not-English I've heard before. Rial's pale body is suddenly cocooned with a web of glowing green lines, shining brighter and brighter. Rial cries out - Ross is hurting them.

The web gets even brighter, and Rial shrieks. 'Stop, master!'

This is the time, it must be.

'Malcolm!' I shout. 'Our stones! We must free Rial - look, Ross is torturing them. Rial will have to do as Ross says unless we free them.'

I grab my stone out of my pocket. It is also glowing. Malcolm hesitates, and I hold my breath. Then he takes his out too. 'Now!' I shout, pointing my stone at Rial. Green beams shine out from both stones and merge into one great light.

We direct our beams at the spider web and it suddenly dissolves.

'Look!' says Malcolm, pointing at the tender. 'Look!'

The tender, captured by the whirlpool, gyrates round and round, closer and closer to its vortex. As we watch, Miran stands up in the prow of the boat, smiles, and raises her arms. The waters become still, and the tender vanishes beneath them.

But there's no time to feel either triumph or terror. Ross is raising that wand above his head, his dark eyes furious. A blast of icy wind hits me.

'We'll see whether those stones protect you now,' he snarls, face horribly distorted by his rage. And there's a distant rumble of thunder from those black clouds. I hold my stone up, and brace myself. What else can I do?

Then, before Ross can bring his wand down on us, a startling blare of discordant music fills the air. It's Rial.

Their voice is a world away from its usual calm, and sings out at an unearthly pitch: 'The Cailleach will not be mocked! I call on the Cailleach!'

The world explodes with a blinding white light and what sounds like a bomb going off. I'm flung to the deck, and for a moment can't tell which way is up or down. I think the ship's been struck by lightning.

My sight clears, and I manage to scramble back onto my feet. Seems like it didn't strike me. I can see that Malcolm and Ross have also been flung down and are stumbling back up. I blink – Rial seems to have expanded into something like a pillar of mist.

And then I see, standing on the deck, a little old woman, who has appeared from nowhere.

I recognise her, and Malcolm does too. We exchange a look. Malcolm seems horrified. This is the oldest of the three witchy woman who caused the Incident. Her face is a weathered brown and seamed with age, she has small glittery eyes, a long coat and a battered hat. Ah, seems she is also the Cailleach. And she does not look pleased.

Everything around us seems to have frozen. The sea has stopped moving. So has the ship. There's no wind. No sound at all now, once my ears have stopped ringing.

'You were warned,' she says in a matter-of-fact voice, looking at Ross. 'Jumping timelines. We do not authorise this. Yet you persisted. Trying to control the future with your technology. We do not allow this.'

Ross seems to have shrunk. He's clearly scared – well, he should be. At the time of the Incident the witchy women told us they had charge of all timelines, which makes them – what? – something like gods.

'Enslaving the child of my daughter,' she continues. She extends her arm slightly and Cal appears from nowhere, also visibly tangled in green spiderweb. One more slight gesture, and it dissolves – she doesn't need green stones. Cal topples over, looking terrified.

'But I had to find my daughter,' Ross says, in a small and apologetic voice. 'Surely you understand that.'

The woman chuckles. 'Good excuse. But looks like she didn't want to be found, doesn't it.' Her tone changes. 'She is beyond your reach. You have done enough. Our patience is exhausted. You will return to where you belong, with your brother. And stay there.'

One more slight gesture and Ross's wand crumbles into a dusty scatter on the deck. 'Go now.' Ross vanishes, just like that.

She turns, but before she can – well, leave I suppose – Cal struggles to his feet.

'Please, por favor, send me too, back to my Mother's Island. She was one of your daughters, please help me.'

She smiles and makes another of those small gestures. 'Very well,' she says. Cal also vanishes.

She turns to Rial. 'Spirit of the air, you are free to go wherever your heart takes you. But do not forget the promises you have made – we expect you to honour them. We have done enough here, there are more important matters to attend to.'

And then she has gone, and the sea and the ship are moving again.

Rial shrinks and solidifies back into a familiar form. I hear more of that ghostly music, which means that nobody else on the ship is conscious except us two, with our stones.

Rial looks at me. 'I will honour my promise. If you ask me to. I have told you what it means. Do you wish me to change your memories?'

'Helen,' says Malcolm, anxiously. 'Are you quite sure? There's no going back.'

Of course I'm not scared. 'Yes,' I say. 'Yes.' I hold out my stone. And Rial touches it.

Malcolm

The weird music rose to a crescendo as Helen was enveloped in a green corona. Suddenly lifeless, she collapsed onto the deck. Terrified, I crouched beside her and felt her neck. I found a pulse but she wasn't breathing. As I gave CPR, I shouted:

'Get help! Get help!'

Helen started breathing but didn't stir. I put her in the recovery position, and dashed up to the Bridge.

'Helen's down!' I shouted at the Captain, who was staring into space. 'Get help!'

The Captain was unresponsive. Rial must have enchanted everyone. I ran back down to the deck.

'What have you done?' I screamed at Rial. 'Helen needs help. Stop your enchantment!'

'All will be well,' said Rial, too calmly. 'Shall I help you now?'

'Get away from me!' I shouted. 'Get away!'

Rial smiled, and the music faded, as they evaporated into nothingness. All that was left was the sound of the wind and the sea. I was suddenly aware the ship's engines were silent.

A young woman crew member came running onto the deck.

'Where's Helen?' she cried. 'The Captain needs her now, to help Velho restart the engines. We're drifting and the current's taking us towards the whirlpool!'

Then she saw Helen, prostrate beside me.

'Oh my god!' cried the young woman. 'Was she hit by the lightning? We must call out Search and Rescue.' She rushed back to the Bridge.

The ship drifted closer and closer to the whirlpool. Then I heard an engine starting. The ship slowed and hovered in the current.

The young woman re-joined me.

'How is she?'

'Breathing,' I said, 'but still out cold.'

'There's a helicopter on the way from Stornoway,' said the young woman. 'If you'll stay with her, I'll get her things.'

'You stay,' I said, well aware that there might be stuff Helen didn't want anyone to know about. 'Where's her quarters?'

'Lower deck,' said the young woman. '"Electronics Officer" on the door.'

As I made my way down the stairs in the companionway, the fire alarm grew more and more insistent. On the central corridor, the sprinkler system was playing, adding to the chaos.

Helen's room looked as if it had been hit by a tornado. The TV and minifridge were smouldering wrecks. Her laptop was plugged in on her bedside table, and looked fried beyond recovery.

I packed Helen's clothes and effects into her kitbag, and returned aloft. As we waited, I kept checking Helen, but there was no change in her heart rate or breathing. Was that a good or a bad thing?

'Here it comes,' said the young woman, as the helicopter approached.

The helicopter hung noisily above us, and a paramedic with a stretcher was winched down. He checked Helen over, and we helped him manoeuvre her onto the stretcher.

'Who are you?' said the paramedic, as Helen was slowly winched up into the helicopter. 'Are you her boyfriend?'

'I'm her cousin Malcolm,' I said.

'Do you want to come with her?' said the paramedic. 'We'll take her to Glasgow.'

I didn't need to think twice.

'Yes,' I said. 'Oh yes.'

Chapter 33 - Helen

Fri June 24th – Glasgow

I'm staring out of the window at a grey sky and digesting the last few days. Try waking up with no idea where you are or how you got there. My recent memory starts just under two days ago, that'll be late on Wednesday. I opened my eyes to find I was lying in a bed.

'Hulkie!' came a familiar voice. 'Howay, you're back! Thank goodness!' That was Wilf, who was sitting next to the bed. What was he doing here?

The room was nowhere I knew but turning my head cautiously I could see it was bare except for a cluster of small machines next to me, with a monitor beeping gently. Also a stand with a hanging bag of fluid and a tube going into my left arm. It had to be a hospital. I was on a drip.

'What happened? Was I in an accident?' My voice still worked.

'Your cousin said your ship was struck by lightning and you collapsed. Do you remember?'

I thought about that. No, I didn't.

A ship? What was the last ship I remembered being on? Didn't I do a gig with Marine Scotland? Though that felt as if it might have been a while back.

Well, I'm really glad Wilf was there. I didn't feel quite such a gowk asking him a series of questions to which I ought to have known the answers. Bottom line is that I don't remember any of the last eighteen months or so. Nothing. One big blank.

At least I'm still alive, and not everyone struck by lightning can say that. Let's hope I didn't do anything in the blank bit that's going to come back to bite me on the bum.

Wilf got a phone call about me Wednesday morning. He says he dropped everything and drove straight here. That gives me a warm feeling. He was very patient. And sounded very relieved as well. Mebbe he thought I'd been completely brain zapped.

He passed on what he knew. My gig was a private yacht, we were at the north end of Jura and we were struck by lightning. But I still don't actually remember any of it. Though I can't help trying to. It's like when I lost my first teeth as a kid and my tongue kept looking for a tooth that wasn't there.

Teeth grow back, but the doctor who examined me yesterday – a neurologist, she said – told me nobody knows whether this sort of memory loss will right itself. It's still one big nothing now.

But apart from a headache that soon faded, no other injuries. No burn marks. A bruised right elbow, probably from hitting the deck. I've got away lightly.

I still have no idea what my cousin Malcolm was doing on a ship I was working on. That seems very unlikely. But Wilf told me Malcolm was there when the lightning struck, and was airlifted with me. To Glasgow. Here. Wilf said they talked, and Malcolm decided that since Wilf was there, he could go and fetch his Land Rover back from Jura. He'll probably turn up over the weekend, if I'm still here.

At least I still know who I am and who Wilf is. And my parents too. The Marine Scotland gig did happen, Wilf told me, but it was autumn of the year before last! Everything since seems to have gone. Even the family wedding – my cousin Malcom's daughter – we both went to straight after. That's a long chunk of blankness.

Dad arrived yesterday morning, before I got shipped off for an MRI. Apparently he was down south with Mam and hard to contact. There was a new grandchild that I don't remember hearing about either. The bairn appeared too early and Donnie needed help with young Lily, while Louise and the little boy were in hospital. But they're both fine. Dad says I sent them a present.

He gave me a big hug and sounded almost tearful. Which was a bit upsetting. But he said he'd worried that I was damaged for good. I asked about the big blank but he said it was all normal stuff for me as far as he knew, though mebbe I'd been a bit stressed and mardy. Well, I guess I'll find out what that was about if it was important. He was back again yesterday evening after the MRI and I told him all about it. Very noisy but otherwise no big deal.

Then the neurologist appeared too and told me they found 'nothing unusual'. No evidence of stroke or epilepsy. Phew, that's good. They took the tube out and told me to drink lots as they'd stuck some dye into me that should be flushed out. 'So several rounds of single malts, man?' I said, and the neurologist did a comical frown.

They moved me into a shared ward after the MRI, and this morning I'm up and dressed. They could let me go, but Julie, the woman in the next bed, says she bets they won't because it's a Friday. They need to send a social worker to see me and check my home arrangements, she says, and by the time they do that it'll be too late today and they hate letting people out at weekends. It'll be Monday. Oh joy.

Still, Malcolm arranged for Wilf to stay with his daughter here in Glasgow, which was good of him. And Wilf is going to stop over until they let me go, he says. It's great to have him here. He got me a new e-reader yesterday. He found my old one in the bedside locker, but the lightning EM blast seems to have zapped it. My laptop is wrecked too. It got zapped and also soaked. I guess the lightning must have triggered the fire alarm.

Now it's mid-morning, and I'm reading a Sword-and-Sorcery on the new e-reader. I started one I don't remember having read, though the online library says I did. A nurse appears.

'Helen, you've a visitor. He says he's a cousin of yours, but he's also a police officer. From Stornoway he says. Are you up to meeting him? You don't have to, he says.'

'Sure, man,' I say. On principle. I'm not sure who he is, I have a bunch of cousins over there. But it's a way of finding out more of what I've been involved in recently. Something serious, it sounds like.

It turns out to be my cousin Steven, that I remember from way back and my Ganny McIver's funeral. But he tells me we did meet in the last few weeks. Twice. On Lewis, where it seems I had a meal with him and visited the Calanais stones. And then – no easy way of telling me this he says, if I don't remember - he and his colleagues raided my ship on suspicion of drug running! Arrested our first mate! But released him after the ship's owner was in touch and vouched for the bag of money he had. I detect an ironic look in his eyes as he tells me that.

Wow. Sounds like it was an exciting gig in all the wrong ways. Whyever did I take a gig on a private yacht anyway? None of what he says strikes a chord at all. Mebbe I'm better off not remembering it.

And it's a good thing they gave us a side-room for this chat – I don't want to become today's gossip on my ward.

'Well, Helen,' he says. 'It seems like the questions I wanted to ask you are going to be a little pointless if your memory of the whole trip has gone. But I'll ask them anyway if that's OK?'

'Sure, man, go ahead.'

'Three people seem to have been lost from your ship in that same storm in which you were injured. Mr Ross Peyroux, for whom you were working in fact, who had chartered the ship. And his two assistants, a Rial, and a Calvin Bane. Is there any light you can cast on this?'

'I wish I could help, man. I'm afraid right now I don't remember any of these people, never mind the storm.' Feeling a bit gob-smacked as I say this. Sounds as if I was in a major maritime disaster! What a thing not to be able to remember. God, I've been lucky.

'Have the bodies been recovered?'

'No sign of them, poor souls,' says Steven. 'But I'm told the currents are so fierce up there, they may never reappear. It's just that Mr Peyroux was also the subject of press speculation in the days leading up to this event.'

'What sort of speculation, man?' I ask.

'A company he was running was shown to have made deceptive claims about its technology and this caused him serious financial embarrassment. He'd just come from a very tough meeting in Glasgow, we've been told. So I'm afraid we have to try to establish whether his disappearance was really an accident. There's an insurance company involved who have to pay out if it was.'

Ooh dear. That sounds very heavy.

'Mebbe the rest of the crew could tell you more?' I suggest.

'The Captain was interviewed yesterday, here in Glasgow,' Steven says. 'But he seems to have been wholly occupied dealing with a difficult situation when the lightning strike knocked out the ship's electronic systems. So it goes.'

'Sorry to be so useless, man.'

'A Thighearna, it's good of you to speak to me at all, Helen, after what you've been through. Will you get back in touch if any of this comes back to you?'

'For sure.'

'And let me know if you are ever back in Stornoway and I'll make up for the meal you've forgotten with another.' He smiles, and I smile back. Certainly an easier cousin to get on with than I remember Malcolm being.

Well, that gave me plenty to think about.

I already know that hospital scran is not great. This time, the cottage pie is more onion and gravy than meat. And the jam roly-poly and custard is tepid, but only just. I decide not to go for the so-called coffee at all. Wilf says there is a chain coffee shop downstairs. Mebbe I'll gan away down there if the nurses are OK about it.

But before I can ask them, another visitor turns up. Who knew I was so popular? Though this is getting a bit tiring.

The visitor is an imposing man, tall, dark skinned, in a very elegant white dress uniform. He must be the Captain that Steven mentioned.

I get up to meet him, seems proper.

'Oh Helen,' he says, 'please don't get up for me. How are you?'

Ouf, this is like being caught in headlights. Some people have far too much charisma. I can see Julie clocking him, and I decide the coffee shop is a much better idea than talking on the ward.

Downstairs he insists on buying me my latte. We find a table.

'Do excuse me, man,' I say once we're sat down. 'I don't know if they told you, but it seems I collapsed when lightning hit the ship, and it seems to have zapped all my recent memory. I'm sure I should know who you are but...'

'Captain Tucker, *Midsummer Queen*,' he says at once. 'You were hired by Mr Ross, God rest his soul, and you've been in the crew – as a very valuable member – since we left the Caribbean last month.'

Am I mistaken, or was that a slight look of relief on his face? Mebbe they were drug-running? If so, I definitely don't want to know.

Like Steven, he asks what I remember of the lightning strike and whether I saw Ross Peyroux being washed overboard. 'Nothing at all' and 'no' seem to be good answers, judging from his reactions.

'I had to ask, Helen,' he explained, 'because I've been asked myself. But our electronics were all blown by the lightning strike. That meant we couldn't restart our turbines and I had to get Viljami to operate the harbour motor manually from the engine room to keep us out of the dangerous whirlpool we were drifting towards. So my hands were full.'

Whatever were we doing that close to a dangerous whirlpool, I wonder?

'Then Eirini rushed into the Bridge to say you'd been struck and called Search and Rescue. By the time we stabilised the situation it was clear we were missing Mr Ross and both his assistants, but nobody saw what happened to them.'

Of course I ask about the whirlpool, and he tells me that two people stole the ship's tender and we were trying to rescue them. But we failed. Christ-on-a-bike, that's FIVE fatalities then! A total shambles. Won't do his career much good really, though I suppose as it's a private yacht it'll depend on the Owner.

'But Helen,' he says, in a deeply sincere voice that makes me want to duck under a table, 'I didn't come to interrogate you, but to see how you were. I was in touch with your emergency contact early on Wednesday and he said he'd be here to support you. I hope that worked out?'

I assure him that it did.

'And there is one more thing. With the death of Mr Ross, God rest his soul, I fear that your final pay may be affected. I hear that his holding company has gone into receivership.'

Oh, I hadn't thought of that. Damn. Lucky I wasn't depending on it. I have a nice little stash, or I did, as far as I remember.

'In recognition of the valuable role you played in the crew, and in sympathy for the injury you sustained, act of God though it was, the Owner wishes to transfer a small sum in compensation to you. He has asked me to write you a ship's cheque. Here it is.' He hands me an envelope.

I thank him profusely and open it. Inside is a Get-Well card with five signatures, including his. That must be the crew. And a cheque, which isn't in fact all that small a sum. I ask him to pass my thanks onto the Owner and say how much I appreciate his thoughtfulness. Though if you ask me, it feels more like an inducement not to make a fuss. We shake hands and he leaves.

I'm about to leave the café myself when a young woman comes up. 'Helen McIver? What a surprise to meet you here.'

She speaks with a mid-Atlantic accent, has one of those expensive looking haircuts and far too much make-up, plus a designer handbag. Oh dear, yet another person it seems I should know. I need a badge, 'Memory damage alert: if it happened in the last 18 months then I won't remember.'

I explain all this yet again. Now I see her close-up she doesn't look all that well, there's a frightened look in her eyes. I hope I haven't behaved badly to her.

'We met at a meal, with your cousin Steven, in Stornoway. I'm Lucy Lopez.' Hmm, Steven didn't mention her.

'I heard you were on the ship where Mr Peyroux vanished. Do you know what happened to him? They say he was washed overboard.' Her voice is urgent.

Not another one. For the umpteenth time I explain that I remember nothing.

'Then you don't know for sure he's dead?' she asks, sounding very anxious.

'I don't. But you have to assume he went into the sea, and I'm told he hasn't been seen since. If he swam to shore, I'm sure we'd have heard by now.'

To my utter surprise, she starts shaking, bursts into tears and then begins to hyperventilate. Was she Peyroux's partner? Or fancy woman? Oh, could be she's a patient too.

Yes, it turns out she is a patient. Being treated in the psychiatric unit, I gather between her sobs and gasps. She's having a major panic attack. 'He said, he said,' she sobs, 'that I'd pay forever for what I did. Forever, he'd see to that. I want him to be dead...'

I'd rather not be hearing this. Sounds like my former employer was not a nice man at all. I wonder what she did? I decide not to ask.

I try and calm her, without much success, and take her back up to her ward. I wonder what Peyroux did exactly to put her into such a state.

I'm grateful the rest of the afternoon is quiet and I can just read. Wilf turns up as the evening meal appears. I'm so glad to see him. We hug each other. Mebbe after all this, the time's come to make a change in my life.

Chapter 34 - Malcolm

Saturday June 25th - Glasgow

The last three days are a bit of a blur. I seem to have spent a lot of time telling a lot of people the same things.

When the helicopter landed on the roof of the *Queen Elizabeth Hospital* in Glasgow I insisted on seeing Helen into the High Dependency Unit. It was now late evening. I phoned Alison, who sent Grant to pick me up.

After a poor night's sleep, I went straight back to the hospital. Helen still hadn't come round, but her family had been informed, and someone would be there soon. I sat by her bed, talking gently to her, as I'd read you were supposed to do, but to no avail.

At lunchtime, a nurse banished me to the cafeteria. Stoked full of bridie, beans and chips, I phoned the breakdown service. No, they couldn't rescue the Land Rover, as it wasn't broken down.

I phoned Polly, and recounted what have happened, this time missing nothing out. She was more than sympathetic, but couldn't get away to pick up the Land Rover; there weren't too many standing stones in Cambuslang. Besides, she didn't have the keys. I did. The good news was that the insurance company providing the film completion bond had stepped in. Because the film was so far advanced, they'd decided to cut their losses and let *Great Alien Plum* finish it.

I went back to Helen's bedside, and, using my mobile phone, tried to work out how to get to Jura by public transport. There was a bus from Buchanan Street that connected with the last ferry from the mainland, that was supposed to synchronise with another bus that would take me to Lagg. I phoned Emerson in the *Lagg Sea Sports Centre* who said, yes, he could find me a sleeping bag and a foam rubber mattress, if I needed them.

Mid-afternoon, I was in dire need of a cup of tea, when Wilf, Helen's boyfriend arrived. I barely knew him, and wondered what, if anything, Helen had said of me, but he was extremely friendly, praising me for looking after her. And once again, I recounted what had happened, again suitably edited.

Wilf told me he was a stranger to Glasgow. He could stay as long as it took. Maybe I could recommend somewhere to sleep. Helen is family. So I suppose Wilf's as good as. I phoned Alison, who said he was welcome to their spare room.

Wilf promised to get in touch as soon as Helen came round. We swapped contact details. But just as I was leaving for the bus station, my mobile rang, and I was instructed, albeit politely, to attend an urgent interview with the police.

At the City Centre Headquarters, I was ushered into a room with officers from Customs and Excise, the Fraud Squad, and Borders and Immigration, and asked to give my account of events. What could I do? Of course I told the truth, or as much of it as I thought was believable.

I was visiting my girlfriend, who was filming on Jura. My cousin Helen was engineer on the boat carrying Ross Peyroux, who was bankrolling the film. She had offered to show me round onboard. I'd met Miran and Nando entirely by chance. When they stole the tender, the boat gave chase. A storm blew up, and Helen was hit by lightning. By the time help arrived, Peyroux and two assistants, as well as Miran and Nando, had disappeared. I assumed that the tender had been swept into the whirlpool, and that the three others had been washed overboard.

This seemed to satisfy them. I was commended for my supposed heroism, and told that they'd be in touch.

Another night at Alison's. It's a good thing Bernie and I bought a decent sized house, or I'd have been on the sofa, what with Wilf coming.

On Thursday, after revising the travel timings, I executed my cunning plan. So, that evening, I was back home in Achallader, to be greeted by an inquisitive Dougie, a solicitous Glenys, and a most grumpy cat.

On Friday morning, I was awakened by Wilf's welcome text. Helen had come round. Might I come and see her, maybe on Saturday? She should be leaving on Monday. I'd spent more than enough time on the road of late, and a down day was long overdue.

Work was blessedly quiet. I phoned Fort William to say I was back, and was told that the *Midsummer Queen* disaster was all over the news, which was great publicity for *Rural Resources*. Perhaps I could write up how my staff training meant that I, like all of the RR team, always knew what to do in an emergency. Aye, right.

After the usual lunch with Dougie, recounting what had happened once again, an excited Henry phoned me. Had I heard the news? The road had been cancelled. No one wanted to take responsibility for the stretch that *Quantum Solution* had already built, so it would be left to return to nature. Such was the power of protest! And, despite *Peyroux Holdings* going down the tubes, his film was going to be completed! I bit my tongue, and congratulated him on both counts.

When I got back home, Glenys invited me in for dinner. Dougie had been called away to a robbery. Over a most welcome home-made steak and kidney pie, I recounted what had happened for the umpteenth time, this time omitting nothing.

'Well,' said Glenys, when I'd finished. 'Everything turned out as it was supposed to.'

'What do you mean "supposed to"?' I asked, wiping round my plate with the last potato.

'You've just described what we all saw,' said Glenys.

'You all knew what was going to happen?' I said, aghast. 'Polly and Miran knew?'

'Of course they knew,' said Glenys. 'Pudding?'

That was why Miran had been so confident. Why Polly was so laid back.

'Why didn't any of you tell me?' I said. 'Is this some sort of Wiccan omerta?'

'Don't be silly, Malcolm,' said Glenys, standing up and clearing the table. 'We didn't know how to interpret it, that's all. Anyway, what difference would it have made?'

I was too tired for metaphysics. The apple crumble was a delight.

This morning, I caught the main line train to Glasgow Queen Street, walked to Central, and got the local train to the Queen Elizabeth Hospital at Cardonald.

On the side ward, Helen was fully dressed, sitting in the bedside armchair. She had regained her determined look. Wilf got up from the chair beside her as I joined them.

'Howay Malcom,' he said. 'It's good to see you again. I rather fancy a coffee. Do either of you want anything?'

'Thanks Wilf,' I said. 'Tea please. Strong, with milk.'

'The usual,' said Helen.

I took Wilf's place.

'It's good to see you again,' I said to Helen. 'How do you feel?'

'I'm on the mend,' said Helen. 'Thanks, man. I really owe you.'

'I was just in the right place at the right time,' I said. 'And all that training kicked in. You'd have done the same.'

'I still don't get why you were there,' said Helen. 'That seems so unlikely. But my memory's just a blank.'

'Do you remember the christening?' I said.

'What christening?' said Helen.

'Christopher's,' I said. 'Alison's son. On South Uist.'

'Alison has a son?' said Helen. 'That's lovely. I was at the christening?'

'Yes,' I said. 'You told me you were going to Jura. I told you I was going there with Polly. You said you'd show me round your boat.'

'It's a ship,' said Helen. 'A private yacht they tell me. Who's Polly?'

'My girlfriend,' I said.

'You have a girlfriend?' said Helen. 'That's great. Does Bernie know?'

Wow. Helen's memory really has been wiped. Probably for the better, given her gaffe at the christening.

'It's none of her business,' I said, 'not that it's a secret. What do you remember?'

'Nothing at all, man, for about the last eighteen months. Let's hope I didn't rob any banks.'

I took the green stone out of my pocket.

'Oh man,' said Helen. 'You don't change, do you. What's the stone about?'

'It's just a nice stone,' I said. 'From Islay. Serpentine. Well marble really. I see you've still got your arrowhead.'

'Oh this,' said Helen, pulling out the thong from under her jersey. 'I'd wondered where it came from.'

'I gave it to you,' I said. 'I've got one too.'

I showed her my arrowhead.

'It's Neolithic,' I said. 'From an ancient quarry on the edge of Rannoch Moor. It's supposed to bring good fortune.'

'Sounds like something out of one of my Sword and Sorcery books,' said Helen. 'I didn't know you were into all that stuff, man. It feels right, though. And for sure I've been lucky! Not a lot of people survive being struck by lightning.'

'They're letting you leave?' I said. 'What will you do next?'

'Wilf says I can stop with him 'til I find my feet,' said Helen. 'Then mebbe we'll get a place together. We could settle down, like Mam keeps saying. Find something we can both do. Something outdoors.'

'That sounds grand,' I said, as Wilf returned, gingerly balancing three steaming cardboard cups.

We gently chatted, nursing our drinks. Wilf was really attentive to Helen. Helen was more relaxed than I could remember. This boded well.

Polly texted me.

'Where are you?'

'In Glasgow with Helen.'

'How is she?'

'Fine. Where are you?'

'Cambuslang. Lunch?'

We arranged to meet at midday at Central Station.

'Who was that?' said Helen.

'Polly,' I said.

'Must be serious, man,' said Helen.

'I think so,' I said.

We bantered amicably for half an hour or so, and I took my leave. We said we'd stay in touch. Maybe that was more likely, given recent history was less lumpy, for Helen at least. It was clear that, unlike me, she remembered nothing of *before*, or of the last little while. Clearly, Rial had been true to their word. I just hope there aren't unforeseen consequences.

Polly was waiting for me next to the Citizen Firefighter statue at the station entrance. Arm in arm, we sauntered across the city centre, to an Indian restaurant she knew near the Modern Art Gallery.

After we'd ordered, we sat holding hands across the table. This felt right.

'What now?' I said. 'I guess your filming will finish soon.'

'I've been offered a staff job,' said Polly. 'By *Great Alien Plum*.'

'Will you take it?' I said, feeling suddenly sad.

'I think so,' said Polly. 'It's what I'm good at. It is based here though.'

'I guess Rannoch's not for you,' I said, resignedly.

'No,' said Polly, 'but you are. I'm sure we can make this work.'

That felt much better.

The starters arrived.

'I wonder what became of Miran and Nando,' I said, dipping a popadom fragment into a bowl of coriander salsa.

'They're fine,' said Polly, definitively.

'How could you possibly know?' I said. 'I thought you did stones, not water.'

'The wild waves whist,' said Polly. 'It's all connected. Here, I've got something for you.'

She fossicked in her shoulder bag, and took out a small leather pouch. Inside the pouch were four silver coins. Each bore a king's head and the inscription *REX IOCABUS*. And, at the bottom of the pouch, were four pearls.

Acknowledgements

Many thanks to our beta-readers: Ian, Isa, Jon, Elinor, Catherine, Sue, Alistair, George and Nancy.

Other novels, novellas and short story collections available from
Stairwell Books

For further information please contact rose@stairwellbooks.com

www.stairwellbooks.co.uk
@stairwellbooks